# MY SECOND CHANCE

A RIDGEWATER HIGH NOVEL

CHERRY
BLOSSOM
ROMANCE

# MY
# second
# CHANCE

## JUDY CORRY

Also By Judy Corry

## Ridgewater High Series:

When We Began (Cassie and Liam)

Meet Me There (Ashlyn and Luke)

Don't Forget Me (Eliana and Jess)

It Was Always You (Lexi and Noah)

My Second Chance (Juliette and Easton)

My Mistletoe Mix-Up (Raven and Logan)

Forever Yours (Alyssa and Jace)

## Eden Falls Academy Series:

The Charade (Ava and Carter)

The Facade (Cambrielle and Mack)

The Ruse (Elyse and Asher)

The Confidant (Scarlett and Hunter)

The Confession (Kiara and Nash) — Coming 2023

## Standalone YA

Protect My Heart (Emma and Arie)

Kissing The Boy Next Door (Lauren and Wes)

## Rich and Famous Series:

Assisting My Brother's Best Friend (Kate and Drew)

Hollywood and Ivy (Ivy and Justin)

Her Football Star Ex (Emerson and Vincent)

Friend Zone to End Zone (Arianna and Cole)

Stolen Kisses from a Rock Star (Maya and Landon)

*For my daughter Jade*

# PLAYLIST

"Safest Place to Hide" - Backstreet Boys
"My Destiny" - Katharine McPhee
"Love" - Jana Kramer
"Gotta Be You" - One Direction

# CHAPTER ONE

I GRIPPED my carry-on as I walked into the waiting area of the Syracuse airport, hoping it would somehow give me the strength I needed to face everyone again after my semester abroad in Paris.

I scanned around for my best friend, knowing my mom wouldn't be there since she had to meet with a congressman this afternoon. It only took me a moment to find Lexi, with her short frame, long dark hair, and glasses, standing in the middle of the waiting crowd. And it only took a heart-pounding second for me to realize that she hadn't come alone. She was flanked by her new boyfriend, Noah, and her older brother, Easton.

Why had Easton come?

My heart was stupid enough to skip a beat when he met my gaze. He was still as gorgeous as he'd been months before. His light-brown hair was combed to the side in the trendy way he'd started wearing it last year. And even from twenty feet away, his blue eyes could still pierce me.

I forced my gaze back to his sister and corrected my body's stupid reaction to seeing Easton after all these months. He probably wasn't even here for me. Lexi had complained the last time

2

we'd spoken about how she and Noah were not allowed to be alone until they were deemed trustworthy by her father. Apparently, sneaking your brother's best friend into your closet to keep him from freezing in his car was not the selfless act Lexi thought it should be in her overprotective father's eyes. So, Easton was probably just their chaperone for the twenty-minute drive from Ridgewater.

"Juliette! I can't believe you're finally back." Lexi squealed as I reached her, attacking me with her hug.

"It's good to be home again," I said, returning her embrace. I had missed my best friend so much—had needed our video chats over the past few months more than she could ever know.

We pulled away, and I eyed her boyfriend. "Good to see you again, Noah. I hear congratulations are in order."

"Congratulations for what?" He narrowed his brown eyes at me.

I smiled. "Congratulations on finally seeing your best friend's little sister for the rockstar that she is."

He gave me a half smile and pulled Lexi close to his side. She was practically a midget next to his tall frame. "I hear you played a role in getting Lexi to make me see what I should have noticed all along."

I grinned. "Oh yeah. She had to—how do you put it? Make you want what you couldn't have."

He laughed. "Well, it most definitely worked."

I knew Easton was next in line for me to greet. He was also last, which meant I couldn't just quickly say hi and move on to the next person. So I put off what was sure to be an uncomfortable greeting a moment longer by asking Lexi, "Did Noah drive you here, or did your dad make Easton chaperone you guys?"

Lexi smiled. "Well, since I finished my babysitting punishment for the Vincenzo twins yesterday, Dad figured I was trustworthy—at least for another month or two."

Her dad was funny like that. But I'd probably be the same way if I'd become a grandpa at thirty-seven, thanks to Lexi's older sister. Everyone at school knew all about his rules for his children, and they knew better than to do anything to cross his path.

Which was exactly why I didn't know whether I'd be welcomed at his house anymore. I had no idea if Easton had told anyone yet.

"And of course we made Easton come along," Lexi said, breaking me away from my thoughts. "Since it wouldn't be the same without the four of us together."

I couldn't put off facing Easton any longer, so I turned toward him and smiled awkwardly. His hands were stuffed in his front pockets and he looked as uncomfortable as I felt.

Had he told anyone? Or was our secret summer fling still in fact a secret?

Easton cleared his throat. "Hi, Juliette."

"Hi," I barely managed to say, my mouth having gone dry.

"Come on, Easton," Lexi prodded. "You can give her a hug. I doubt Mercedes will freak out about that."

My heart plummeted into my stomach at the reminder that he had found a new girlfriend while I'd been away. What I'd seen on social media was true; he and Mercedes really were a thing.

Easton and I met each other's gaze for a second before he stepped forward and opened his arms. I leaned in for a quick hug, forcing myself not think about how perfectly I fit into his arms. My body felt warm, like it was finally home now that I'd hugged him.

But my body had been having a lot of strange things going on with it since the last time I saw him, so I decided to ignore the pull I had for him and stepped back before he could notice what was different about me. Tucking some of my grayish-blonde dyed hair behind my ear, I said, "It's good to see you again, Easton."

He nodded, his gaze briefly seeming to take me in. "Good to see you, too." The way he said those five little words made my heart thump harder than it had in months. Because he actually sounded sincere.

Could he have changed his mind about what he'd said to me the last time we were together?

I wanted to search his eyes, to try to figure out what he meant, but Lexi's voice cut through the air.

"How about we grab your luggage and get back on the road? I'm sure you're jet-lagged."

I *was* exhausted after the long flight. "Yeah, let's get going."

The boys led the way to the luggage carousel while Lexi walked beside me. "If you're not too tired, maybe we can stop by Emrie's for hot chocolate and take advantage of Easton's employee discount before taking you home."

I had to work hard to keep my eyes from glancing to Easton's back at the mention of Emrie's. Lexi had been busy babysitting her nephew over the summer, so she had no idea just how much time I had spent with Easton at his work. What had started off as innocent—me going there to beat the summer heat, requesting samples of every single flavor of ice cream on the menu just to annoy Easton before inevitably choosing my favorite, Rocky Road—had turned into a chance to get some of his undivided attention and flirt with him as he worked.

I swallowed the lump in my throat as the memories and everything that had happened because of them rushed to my mind. I needed to get a grip on myself, or there was no way I'd make it through the next few months with my secret still intact. I forced a smile on my lips. "Yeah, I'd love to go there."

WE ORDERED OUR HOT CHOCOLATE, which was the perfect thing to have on such a cold December day. Noah, Lexi, and I went to sit in a booth while Easton made us our drinks. He wasn't on duty, which made me think he was using it as an excuse to keep some distance between us for a little longer.

Easton stepped up to our booth a minute later with our drinks on a tray. He handed us our cups, and I noticed he was extra careful not to brush fingers with me in the exchange. He returned the tray behind the counter, and when he came back, he hesitated at the end of the table, like he wasn't sure if he should take the seat beside me.

So different from last summer when we'd talked and laughed and sat close in this very booth. He'd reach for my hand under the table, and we'd just sit and smile bashfully at each other, so giddy with our secret forbidden romance. Then when he finally got off work, I'd meet him at the back of the building and we'd make out against the wall for thirty minutes before going back to his house and pretending like nothing was going on.

It had been a great summer. I thought I'd found my person.

Until I made the stupidest decision I'd ever made and snuck into his tent at his family's end-of-summer camp-out.

I knew what happened after was wrong, and I regretted it almost as soon as it was over—when my brain wasn't so foggy— but I'd been delusional enough to hope that at least some part of him had cared about me like I'd cared about him. I'd given him something I'd never given anyone else before, and it had been agonizing to have him tell me that there was no "fixing things" and going back. That being with me was the biggest mistake of his life.

I should have seen it coming, especially with his family and their purity rings. But I'd been delusional enough to think he might say I was worth it.

I was so stupid.

"Take a seat," Lexi said to Easton after taking a sip from her hot chocolate. "Juliette was telling us about how pretty the lights are on the Eiffel Tower at night."

Easton met my gaze with an unsure expression. I scooted closer to the wall and pasted on a smile. We'd kept our relationship a secret from everyone last summer; there was no sense in letting anyone in on the truth now.

"Go ahead and sit, Easton." I forced as much cheeriness into my voice as I could muster. "I promise I won't bite."

He only hesitated for a second longer before lowering himself into the booth. I was immediately met with the scent that I'd come to know as his. He had always smelled so good, and I had to force away the memories his scent evoked.

"So how was Paris?" Easton asked, his Adam's apple bobbing with the question.

I wiped my sweaty palms along my black leggings. "It was fabulous. Just what I needed and I'm going to miss it." I had needed to escape from this town, this country, after the way things had ended between us. An ocean separating me from my humiliation was just what the doctor ordered.

"What was your favorite part about Paris?" Lexi asked, her eyes bright with excitement.

As I thought over my answer, I took a quick sip of my hot chocolate. It was delicious. Creamy-chocolatey with just the right amount of raspberry flavor. Easton was actually really good at his job...but that was a given since he was good at everything: Looking way too cute in his dorky work hat. Kissing me until I couldn't catch my breath. Breaking my heart.

I pushed those thoughts away. "My favorite part was probably the food. I could eat crêpes every day and never tire of them."

Lexi's expression brightened. "Well, that's good, because my dad talked about making them for Sunday brunch tomorrow. Do you think your mom would be okay letting you come?"

"What time?" I hedged.

Lexi looked at Easton. "Do you remember what time Dad said Maddie and Grant would be over?"

Maddie was their older sister. Grant was Maddie's cute little boy who had just turned two.

Easton glanced at me. "I think brunch is at eleven."

"Will that work?" Lexi asked.

I watched Easton cautiously, wondering how he felt about me coming over to his house.

Then an even scarier thought occurred to me. How would his dad feel?

Had Easton told him?

I eyed his hands on the table. He wasn't wearing his purity ring.

My heart pounded. Was this some sort of trap? Was his dad's invitation to come over for crêpes just a ploy to get me into his house, so he could lecture me about how I'd seduced his son into losing his purity ring?

"I don't know..." I said.

*Think of a good excuse, Juliette. Come on, you used to be so good at lying.*

"My dad has been practicing making crêpes all week," Easton said, noticing my hesitation. He'd always been so good at picking up on my mood—which was exactly why I had to be super careful around him now.

I looked at him. I wanted to ask him if his dad knew, just to make sure I wasn't about to walk into Drill Sergeant Stevens's disciplinary action meeting.

He gave me a slight nod. I sighed and turned back to Lexi with a smile. "I'm sure my mom will be busy, so yeah, I'd love to come."

"Yay!" Lexi bounced in her seat.

And Easton seemed to visibly relax at my response. Was it

possible he wanted me to come, too?

———

WHEN I GOT HOME, I took off my coat for the first time since landing and hung it in the closet by the front door. I caught a glimpse of myself in the mirror. How was I still standing? I looked like a zombie right now.

I inspected my reflection a little longer, smoothing down the fabric of my shirt. My belly hadn't popped out yet, but I was definitely looking pudgy around the middle. And if what I'd read online was true, I wouldn't be able to blame my thickening midsection on France's endless pastries much longer. The truth would become too obvious to ignore.

"Welcome home, sweetie." My mom stepped into the room and gave me a hug. "I'm so sorry I couldn't be at the airport to pick you up myself. I would have much rather been with you instead of talking to that stuffy congressman."

But of course, as Ridgewater's first female mayor, my mom had to bend over backwards to do her job. Which meant, sacrifices always needed to be made.

I knew she was doing her best, so instead of being annoyed at her job like I used to do, I wrapped my arms around her waist. I'd missed her so much over the past few months.

She held me for a few seconds before stepping back, her gaze taking me in and resting on my midsection briefly.

"You look really good," she said with a soft smile on her lips.

I nodded. "Thanks."

Then I just stood there uncomfortably, hoping she'd be the one to broach the awkward topic first.

She glanced at my stomach again. "I ordered takeout from the Chinese place on Elm. How about we catch up while we eat?"

I nodded and followed her into the kitchen. The house hadn't changed a bit in three and a half months. The kitchen was as bright and immaculately kept as ever—probably not such a hard thing to do since Mom had been alone at home and she barely cooked as it was. Cooking took time, and my mom never had enough of that.

I sat at the rectangular kitchen table in front of the bay window while my mom grabbed our takeout containers from the counter. She filled two glasses with water from the fridge then sat down across from me.

"I made you an appointment with Dr. Gunthrie for Monday morning at ten." She opened her box of stir-fry.

I nodded. "Okay."

"I figured you'd want to go in the morning when it was less likely for kids from school to see you at the hospital. She's a great OB-GYN and has promised that her staff will be extra discreet in your case."

Of course my mom would be worried about people being discreet about my pregnancy. It was an election year, and the last thing she wanted was a big scandal.

Mom continued, "And then I arranged with Grandma Irene for you to go live with her after Christmas. She's more than happy to have your company for the next few months."

I nodded as I twirled my fork in my food container, not feeling hungry after all.

"And I also have everything set up for you to start online school as soon as you'd like. You aren't showing yet, so you could still go to school for the next week before Christmas break and I doubt anyone will know you're pregnant. But if you want to just start it now, I think that's okay, too." She twisted some chow mein noodles onto her fork and looked me in the eye for the first time since sitting down. "Which would you prefer?"

I cleared my throat. "I guess I might as well just start with the online school thing. Doesn't make much sense to start here when I'll be gone again after Christmas break."

She blew on her hot noodles. "Sounds like a great idea. You can relax, spend time with your friends for the next couple of weeks, and then be gone before things become too obvious."

My cheeks heated up as she scrutinized me again.

"How far along did you say you were?"

"I think I'm eighteen weeks."

I had debated on whether I should lie to my mom, telling her that I'd gotten pregnant after I'd been in Paris for a few weeks. But since she'd be present at my doctor's appointments and would therefore hear the correct date while there, I decided to just make myself look even worse by telling her that I'd gotten pregnant right off the bat in a foreign country.

I hadn't dared tell her who the real father was, because then she'd make me tell him about the baby.

And I most definitely couldn't do that.

"Eighteen weeks," she said thoughtfully. "I think that's about the time I started wearing maternity clothes when I was pregnant with you."

"Yeah?"

She nodded and dug her fork into her takeout box again. "We'll have to buy maternity clothes before you go to Grandma's. If you can keep wearing your regular clothes a few weeks longer, I'm sure no one will suspect anything."

And there it was. Proof that I was a huge embarrassment to my mother.

"Sure."

I didn't know whether to be happy or sad that my mom was so determined to keep this baby a secret.

Mom eyed my untouched food. "You're not hungry?"

I pushed the container away and shook my head. "Not really. I'm pretty tired, actually."

"I bet you're jet-lagged. How about you go up and get some rest? We can talk about Paris tomorrow."

I nodded and gave her what was sure to be a tired smile. "Thanks." Then I stood and walked out of the kitchen and into the entryway.

My mom must have realized I was heading for my luggage because she called out, her voice drifting down the hall. "I can get those for you later. You shouldn't be doing a lot of heavy lifting right now."

I looked back toward the kitchen. "Thanks." Then I stepped closer to the staircase just off the entryway. I'd always imagined walking down these steps toward my prom date, wearing one of the super cute prom dresses they sold at the dress shop on main street. Or possibly one that I designed and sewed for myself.

I'd never pictured the dress being a maternity gown.

Why had I snuck into Easton's tent that night?

I gripped the railing and plodded up the gray-carpeted stairs to my room.

My room was just as I'd left it. My bed was neatly made with its white ruffled comforter. My sewing machine sat on my desk with the half-sewn red dress I'd started making last summer as my first attempt at designing my own clothes. And the photo of me and Easton at the lake was still safely hidden at the back of my sock drawer.

It was a sad reminder of how my life used to be. A life that was completely different from my new reality.

I got ready for bed quickly, and then lay down, pulling the covers tight around my shoulders. As I lay there, I felt the little fluttery kicks from inside me—different from the butterflies I had when I saw Easton today.

I ran a hand over my belly, but I still wasn't able to feel the kicks from the outside. Should I tell Easton about the baby?

I had no idea how to even begin that conversation. He'd

already freaked out on me about what we'd done. Losing his college money was a big deal. How could I tell him that I was carrying his baby?

Or *should* I tell him? I squeezed my eyes shut and tried to calm my breathing that went frantic every time I let myself think about my situation. The decision on whether to tell him or not had plagued me ever since I'd taken the pregnancy tests—well, after I'd decided not to throw myself in front of a train.

Telling him would only make him feel like I'd ruined his life even more. I knew his family. His sister had gotten pregnant in high school and had kept the baby. Would he feel obligated to do the same as his sister Maddie? He was a loyal guy. But that would totally derail his future. He had his whole life planned out. He was going to be a dentist, and that would take years of schooling. He couldn't have a baby to worry about while he did it all. That wasn't fair to him.

And I didn't need to give him another reason to hate me any more than he already did.

I just needed to stick with the plan my mom and I had come up with. Go away. Have the baby. Place the baby up for adoption with someone who could give him or her a stable environment— like two grownup parents who were ready for a kid.

Then I could come back home. Easton wouldn't ever have to know.

# CHAPTER TWO

TO SAY I slept badly would be an understatement, but I forced myself out of bed anyway, knowing I needed to put on a happy face. My plan was to go to the Stevens's house and pretend like Easton and I were never anything besides Lexi's best friend and Lexi's brother—two people who had known each other since we were kids but had never had a reason to care what the other was up to, or who they may or may not be dating.

If I could pretend, then maybe I'd have a chance at keeping my pregnancy a secret.

Mom was already gone when I came downstairs. She'd left a note on the counter.

*Went to the office for a few hours, be back in time for dinner. I promise we'll spend the night together and you can tell me all about Paris.*

I grabbed the house key from the hook by the garage, stuffing it in the front pocket of my jeans—which I had to leave unbuttoned at the top and fastened with a hair elastic—then grabbed my coat to walk to their house at the end of the street.

"Come on in. The crêpes are almost ready," Lexi said, beckoning me into her house a few minutes later. I looked around the living room. It was still the same as it had always been. Overstuffed furniture. Photos of Lexi and her family on the walls. It was a strange contrast from my house. You'd think that a home run by a man would have the less homey feeling out of the two, but my home was all straight clean lines with perfectly designed decor that matched—more like an extension of my mom's office instead of a home.

Lexi led me into the kitchen where her dad was flipping crêpes in a pan.

"Welcome back to the United States, Juliette," he said.

I swallowed and nodded. "Thanks. It's good to be back." I studied him for a moment longer just to see if he seemed tense at my presence. If he was, I couldn't tell. I sighed with relief. Hopefully, that meant Easton hadn't told him anything.

"Have a seat in the dining room. Breakfast will be ready in a couple of minutes," Mr. Stevens said over his shoulder as he cooked. "You'll have to tell us everything about Paris over breakfast."

"Sure," I said.

Lexi led me into their formal dining room, and I took my seat next to her at the already set table, grateful that Easton wasn't around yet.

"Now that we're alone, I want the real details on Paris," Lexi said, her eyes sparkling with excitement, like I had some sort of juicy gossip to tell.

Sadly for her and me, there wasn't anything really exciting that I could tell her that we hadn't already talked about over our video chats—aside from the fact that I'd taken a pregnancy test and it had come back positive.

But even though I was dying to confide in someone besides my mom, and have them assure me that everything would be okay, I couldn't tell Lexi. She was Easton's sister, and I couldn't risk him finding out.

Plus, she was asking about exciting events in Paris. The events that had caused my most life-altering news had happened here in New York and not there, anyway.

"What do you want to know?" I asked her.

"I don't know...everything. But mostly I want to know about all the boys who I'm sure were heartbroken when you left."

Of course Easton had to walk into the dining room with Grant's high chair just as Lexi mentioned boys.

But maybe this was good. It would help me plant some seeds in their minds if I was forced to use Plan B to explain why I was getting fat. If for some reason things fell through with me going to Grandma Irene's house, my plan was to tell everyone that a guy from Paris was the father of my baby. That way, Easton would be off the hook and he wouldn't have to hate me even more.

Easton set Grant's chair next to the spot where his dad usually sat for their family meals with Maddie. I eyed him as I formulated my next sentences in my head. I could tell he was listening for my answer, even if he pretended not to be.

"The boys there were just as amazing as we imagined. And their accents are to die for," I said.

Lexi's eyebrows lifted. "I knew there had to be more than just the one guy. Evan, right? The one you said—"

"The one that I said was super hot and had lips like an angel," I interrupted Lexi before she could finish. I had told her over video chat about how Evan was more like a stand-in to make someone jealous. Lexi just didn't know that it was Easton who I was trying to make jealous with that manufactured photo.

Easton's jaw tensed, and I didn't know whether to feel guilty or happy that my plan to make him jealous had possibly worked a little after all.

"So you kissed a lot of guys then?" Easton asked, his eyes tight as he took the seat across from mine.

I shrugged, hoping to come across that I wasn't nervous he was asking me about this. "When in France..." I gave my shoulder-length hair a flip with my hand for extra effect.

"I figured you'd have guys falling at your feet in Paris. Good for you."

That wasn't the reaction I'd expected at all. Based on the things he'd said the last time we were together, I'd almost expected him to call me a slut or something.

Except he didn't. He almost seemed sad that I was talking about kissing other guys.

But this shouldn't be happening, anyway. He was dating Mercedes Atkins, the town preacher's daughter. Easton was supposed to hate me for showing up at his tent that night.

Mr. Stevens set a plate of crêpes on the table at that moment, effectively bringing our conversation to a halt. He took his seat at the head of the table, unfolding his napkin and setting it on his lap.

"While we wait for Maddie and Grant to join us, why don't you tell us about all the wonderful places you went to visit?" Mr. Stevens said to me.

Easton eyed me from across the table, and I couldn't read what was in his expression, but he said, "Yes, I would love to hear what you've been up to."

What was he thinking about? I couldn't get a good read on him at all.

I sighed, giving up on analyzing his every facial expression for the moment, and finally said, "I'd love to hear what you've been up to as well."

---

"WHAT'S GOING on with you and Easton? Did something happen that I don't know about?" Lexi asked after breakfast. We were sitting on her bed in her room that didn't have any doors besides her the one to her en-suite bathroom. No bedroom door. No closet door.

"What's with the lack of doors?"

Lexi sighed. "My dad is teaching me a lesson about how privacy is a privilege." She waved her hand. "The whole Noah-sleeping-in-my-closet thing made him do it."

"Wow, did he catch you two making out in your room or something?"

She shook her head and leaned back against the pillows by her headboard. "No, I think it was because of me talking about how Noah had left his shirt there that morning. That really set him off."

I laughed. That would do it. I'd probably freak out on her if I saw and heard that, too.

And her dad would for sure never allow me in his house again if he found out about Easton and me. In fact, he'd probably ban Lexi from being my friend anymore.

Yikes. Why hadn't I been thinking more clearly months ago? He *really* couldn't find out.

"So you still didn't answer my question. Why are you and Easton acting so weird around each other?"

I shrugged. "Must be the awkwardness of not seeing each other for a few months. I'm always a little weird around people I haven't seen for a long time."

"Makes sense." She pursed her lips thoughtfully. "Wanna hear something weird?"

"Sure." I'd love to talk about anything that didn't involve Easton and me.

She grinned. "I had the craziest thought last week about how cool it would be if you and Easton got together."

"You did?" I asked cautiously.

"Yeah." She sat up straighter. "I mean, Easton and Noah are best friends. You and I are best friends. It would just be kind of perfect."

"Except for the fact that he's dating Mercedes Atkins right now." *Little Miss Perfect.*

She shrugged. "He was asking about you last week."

"He was?" I knew it was stupid to hope that he had missed me, but I still did.

"He even talked about going skateboarding at the indoor skate park in Syracuse. That's something we've only ever done with you."

"Yeah?" Not that it would be smart for me to get on a skateboard anytime soon. My balance was not the same as it used to be.

Lexi's grin was huge, like she'd just done some sort of matchmaking between me and her non-single brother. "We should totally arrange it. I mean, I wouldn't mind giving Noah some private lessons." She bit her lip at the thought.

I shook my head and jumped at the chance to talk about her and Noah instead of Easton and me. "This is so weird."

"You think Noah and me together is weird?"

I laughed. "No. I think you two are super adorable. It's just...when I left, you were the one who'd never kissed a guy, and I was the one who kissed too many. It's just so strange how the tables have turned."

"Well, I'm sure you'll have a new boyfriend in no time. You've never had trouble finding one before."

I forced a smile on my face. "You're probably right."

"So when do you need to be home?" Lexi asked.

"I can hang for a few hours."

"Wanna help me get my skateboard ready so we can go next week?"

"Sure."

Lexi jumped off her bed and grabbed her skateboard from her closet. She looked over her shoulder. "Just wait for me by the kitchen table, I think I have my skateboard tools in here somewhere." She proceeded to rummage through the mess in her closet, and I couldn't help but wonder how in the world tall Noah Taylor was ever able to fit in that clutter for two nights.

I left her room figuring it might be a while. I might as well grab a glass of water while I waited.

I turned the corner at the end of the hall and stumbled when I saw Easton sitting at the kitchen table with a math textbook open and his mechanical pencil scratching numbers onto a sheet of paper. Did he hear us talking about him? Lexi's room wasn't that far from the kitchen.

He looked up from his homework, and my face grew hot.

*Say something, Juliette. Don't just stand there and stare at his gorgeous face.*

I cleared my throat. "D-do you have work tonight?" Maybe if I started a normal conversation, things wouldn't be as awkward as they'd been during brunch.

He gave me a confused expression. "No. Why?"

I shrugged. "Oh, I just figured you must have work since you usually like to wait until the last minute to do all your weekend homework."

"Oh, no," Lexi said, coming up behind me and making me jump. She propped her skateboard against the wall. "This is the *new* Easton. Ever since he started dating Mercedes, he's on this whole overachiever kind of thing. I really think he's trying to impress her."

Oh, it was for Mercedes.

*Who names their daughter after a car, anyway?*

Easton set his pencil down. "Um, I'm actually just trying to get a scholarship. I still have a few more to apply for, and every grade counts."

"Don't you know dad's going to pay..." Lexi trailed off. And when I glanced at her, her eyes had gone wide like she'd said something she hadn't meant to say.

Did she know then? Did Mr. Stevens know too and, true to his word, had cut off Easton's tuition fund because he'd lost his purity ring?

I swallowed, feeling the air in the room change.

"Um, never mind." Lexi laughed awkwardly, and I didn't miss the frustrated look Easton gave her. "I, um, do you still have my skateboard tool kit? Juliette and I were thinking it might be fun to go boarding together next week."

Easton looked relieved that she had changed the subject. "I- it's just on my dresser. I can get it if you want."

"I can grab it real quick." Lexi left the kitchen, her footsteps thumping on the stairs.

Once we were alone, I stepped closer to Easton and lowered my voice to a whisper. "Does she know?"

"Shh." Easton glanced around, probably to make sure his dad wasn't within hearing range. "Of course I haven't told her."

"Okay."

There was a long pause as we both tried to think of something to say.

He closed his notebook and looked around again. "I said something last week about not misplacing my purity ring. But she doesn't know anything more."

"That's probably good." I released the breath I'd been holding. "Does your dad know, though? Is that why you need the scholarships?"

His eyes hardened. "I haven't told him yet, either. As far as he knows, I misplaced my ring while we were camping. I-it's not exactly a conversation I'm excited to have."

I cast my gaze down. "I know. I'm sorry."

"Are you?" He sounded like he didn't believe me.

I looked up to meet his eyes. "Of course I am. We both know it was wrong. If I could take it back I would." My life would be a heck of a lot simpler if I didn't have to read all those pregnancy articles online.

"Me too."

I knew those words shouldn't have hurt, since I'd just said the same thing, but I felt my heart shatter all over again.

"I found it." Lexi entered the kitchen, holding her tool kit in her hands. "Can you make room for us to work at the table, Easton?"

He closed his textbook and stacked his notebook on top. "I'm actually done for now. The kitchen is all yours."

Then he picked up his things and left the room.

# CHAPTER THREE

"DO you mind looking up the skate park in Syracuse to see if it's opened this weekend?" Lexi looked up at me briefly as she worked on her skateboard.

"Sure." I pulled up my phone and typed in the name of the skate park. A moment later, their website loaded with a bolded heading between asterisks at the top.

DUE TO A FAMILY EMERGENCY, SYRACUSE INDOOR SKATEPARK WILL BE CLOSED UNTIL JANUARY THIRD.

I frowned and turned to Lexi. "Looks like they'll be closed until the beginning of January."

"What?" Lexi asked. "Why?"

"It says there was some sort of family emergency."

Her face fell. "Oh no. I hope everything's okay with Kent."

Kent was the owner of the skatepark and pretty much lived there, or so it seemed since he was always there when we'd gone last summer.

"I hope he's okay too," I said. But at least it saved me from having to come up with an excuse for why I couldn't skateboard.

Lexi set her tool on the table. "Guess I don't really need to be fixing this now, do I?"

I sighed and pushed my phone back into my pocket.

"I'm sure we'll figure out something else to do for fun this weekend," I said.

Her eyes brightened. "I heard Ridgewater Peak has a new hill this year. Maybe we can go snowboarding instead."

*Oh, even better.* There's nothing like careening down a hill as fast as lightning to put a fetus in danger. I might not be ready to be a mother, but I didn't want to do anything that could hurt the baby.

I forced a smile on my face. "That sounds fun."

"I think Noah said something about his dad having a cabin up there. Maybe we could just make a whole day of it."

"You really don't need to invite me to everything you want to do with your boyfriend. I'm okay to spend time by myself," I said.

"We can invite Easton. Then the guys can have fun together and we can have fun together."

Yeah, way to make me want to go even less.

I was about to turn her down again when she pouted her lip and gave me her sad face.

"Please, Juliette. It'll be fun. Like old times."

I sighed. I was never great at saying no to my friend to her face. I'd just have to call her that morning to tell her I was sick.

"Okay, fine. I'll come."

She laughed. "Well, don't sound too excited about it."

I smiled again, wishing I could tell her what was really going on.

She knew how hard it was to have a baby in high school. She'd watched her sister go through the same thing and done her fair share of staying up with the crying baby.

I shook the thought away. She was Easton's sister. She could slip up so easily and tell Easton the truth.

"Well, I should probably jet. My mom's expecting me for dinner."

"Thanks for coming over. It's so great to have you back again. I missed you so much."

"I missed you, too."

"We'll have to plan our snowboarding trip with the guys tomorrow at school or something," she said.

"Oh, I didn't tell you," I said, feeling my cheeks heat up. "I'm not going back until after New Year's." It was a lie since I wasn't going back at all this year. But we were hoping to make my stay at Grandma Irene's house seem like a sudden thing, so lying was a necessary evil right now.

"What? You're not coming to school?" Her eyebrows shot up.

I rubbed at a spot on the table. "I already finished my first semester in Paris."

And the thought of anyone at school seeing how big I was getting and saying something about it gave me hives. At least with Lexi, she was nice enough not to say anything about it if she had noticed.

"You're so lucky." Lexi zipped her tools back into her kit. "Well, I guess we'll just have to make our plans after school then."

"Sure."

"Although I think I remember Easton saying something about hanging out with Mercedes. So it might be better to wait till he can be there."

"He'll be with Mercedes?" I knew they were dating, but it kind of felt like a knife was stabbed into my chest at the thought of him kissing another girl.

She smiled, like she understood the sullen look on my face. "I don't think they're that serious, though. So I'm sure we can still get my plan to work."

"What plan was this again?"

"Remember what I said earlier..." After quickly glancing around the room, she leaned closer and lowered her voice to just above a whisper. "My plan about you two dating."

My fingers went all tingly as a nervous flash of energy coursed through me. I swallowed. "I wouldn't put too much stock in that ever happening."

Her eyes widened. "But you think he's cute, right?"

Did humans need oxygen? Was Antarctica cold? Of course I thought he was cute! He was movie-star material. Greek-god material. Sneak-into-his-tent-and-forget-about-your-values-because-you-want-one-last-long-night-together material.

I cleared my throat. "I guess he's okay to look at."

"I saw the way you were looking at him during brunch. You think my brother is hot."

My cheeks got even hotter. "I don't want you to play matchmaker. I'm taking a break from guys right now."

She tilted her head to the side and gave me a look that told me she didn't believe me. "We'll see about that."

"No, Lexi. I really am."

She shrugged. "Okay, fine. Let's meet after school anyway, and if Easton can make it, then great. If not, then I won't try to play matchmaker."

"Okay."

"But remember, if he shows up, that'll just be even more proof that you and my brother are meant to be."

I rolled my eyes. "You're delusional, you know that?"

She laughed. "That's what I thought when I liked Noah. And just look at me now."

I WAS PUTTING on my polka-dotted coat and walking out the Stevens's front door when I noticed Easton enter the living room behind me.

"Hey, Juliette," he called.

My heart picked up speed as I panicked for something to do. Would it be so bad if I pretended I couldn't hear him? If Lexi saw us talking, she'd get even more ideas in that weird matchmaking brain of hers.

I kept my gaze focused on the sidewalk that led away from their house and continued down the front porch steps.

"Juliette!" His voice sounded closer.

I froze a moment too long because his hand was on my shoulder a second later.

I turned around slowly to look at him with my most surprised expression.

"H-hey, Easton."

He looked at me, and I couldn't be sure but there seemed to be nervousness in his eyes. "Can I talk to you real quick?"

I blinked, trying to come up with an excuse. "I'm kind of in a hurry right now. My mom wanted me home for dinner and I'm already late."

"It'll just take a second."

I looked around to see if anyone noticed we were together, a reflex from sneaking around this past summer.

Easton glanced around too, frustration evident on his face. "Can I walk you home? I really just want to say something real quick."

My stomach muscles tightened at the thought of being alone with him. How was it possible that I could want to be with him and want to run away from him at the same time?

"I really do need to hurry," I finally said, the logical part of my brain winning for once.

The hopefulness that had been in his eyes disappeared when I turned him down again.

What did he want to talk about so badly?

Before I could let my curiosity get the better of me, I remembered he had a girlfriend.

"I don't think Mercedes would really want us to talk, anyway."

"She won't mind. We aren't serious. We've only been on a few dates."

It wasn't serious? So there was a...

I shook my head. There was not a chance for Easton and me to get back together. Things had not ended well. I was trying to keep the fact that I was pregnant with his child a secret from him, for goodness' sake. I couldn't spend time with him. I needed to go away.

"Please." His blue eyes pleaded with me, and I couldn't help but think that whatever he had to say must be important.

"Okay, you can walk me home."

"Thank you." He darted back into his house and came back out a second later with his dark gray coat.

"What was it you needed to talk about?" I asked as he zipped up. I needed to get this conversation over with. My hands felt clammy, so I wiped them on the lining inside my coat pockets.

He ran a hand through his hair. "I—" He released a long sigh. "I just wanted to apologize to you." He eyed me cautiously. "I know that before you left for Paris, things kind of went differently than either of us had probably expected. And I kind of freaked out and said a lot of things I didn't really mean." He looked down. "Anyway, I just really want to try to forget about what happened. I was hoping that you can forgive me and that we can maybe move forward without any hard feelings."

I stared down at my boots and swallowed. "T-thanks for

saying that." I forced my gaze up to meet his blue eyes. "And I'm sorry, too. I know you didn't mean everything you said that night."

The *logical* side of my brain had known, anyway. My heart still didn't quite believe it. And my heart also knew that if I told him what the consequences were for that night, he would just probably freak out on me all over again.

He cleared his throat. "I'll probably tell my dad tonight."

I felt the blood drain from my face. "You're going to tell him about us?"

"I'm just going to say I broke his rules," he hurried to say. "I won't say who it was with. You don't have to worry about that."

I sighed, my chest loosening with relief. "Thanks." Then I had another thought. "Do you really have to tell him, though? I mean, you're almost eighteen. It doesn't seem like that should be his concern anymore?"

"But he'll go and pay for my college tuition if I don't tell him, and that would be like stealing from him. As tempting as it sounds, I can't take that money."

"I'm sorry." What else could I say to that? My mom had never put any kind of stipulation on her paying for my college tuition. Though, come to think of it, she was shipping me off to my grandma's house for the next six months.

I must've looked really distraught or something, because Easton reached over and touched my shoulder. And I was stupid enough to wish I could feel his hand through the thick fabric of my coat because I was still so unbelievably attracted to him.

"It's not your fault," he said. "It was a two-person decision. I was there, too. I chose to do what I did, and this is just a consequence of that choice."

I swallowed, and he removed his hand.

He was being so sweet right now. In all the scenarios I'd run through in my head, he'd always been just as upset as he'd been that night. He'd always looked at me with fear and anger in his eyes. Never like this.

A thought flashed through my mind—maybe it would be okay to tell him about the baby. Maybe he could handle it better than I thought.

But no. Having your college tuition taken away from you was one thing. Being told that you would become a daddy a month before high school graduation was a whole different thing. I couldn't take that from him, too.

"I appreciate you saying that," I said, pulling my coat tighter across my stomach. It wouldn't be long before I couldn't tie it shut anymore. "I'm sure you'll figure things out. You always do."

His gaze lingered down to my arms hugging my midsection for a moment too long. Did he just look at my stomach? Could he know?

I needed to cross the street and get inside my house now.

But he spoke before I could bolt. "Well, I just wanted to apologize. I know we'll be seeing a lot of each other since you're best friends with Lexi, and I didn't want things to keep being awkward between us."

I nodded and tried not to think about how I wished things could go back to the way they were before everything went down the drain.

"Well, I better get home now."

He touched my hand to stop me from stepping into the street. My skin burned at his touch. "It's good to have you back, Juliette." His gaze was more intense than it had been the second before, almost like he was trying to see into my soul.

I studied him, unable to form a coherent response. He really looked like he meant what he was saying—kind of like he was hopeful about something.

"It's good to be back," I finally managed to say, glancing at our hands. I wanted so badly to entwine my fingers with his and pretend like the past never happened.

When he noticed what he was doing, he let go before backing up on one foot. "I'll see you tomorrow at school."

I nodded and stepped off the curb to walk across the street, not having it in me to tell him I wouldn't be showing up for any of his senior year.

"See you later, Easton."

# CHAPTER FOUR

MY PHONE CHIMED as I sat in an exam room at Dr. Gunthrie's office.

Lexi: **You're so lucky you don't have to come to school this week. I'm so ready for Christmas break.**

The doctor knocked on the door a second later, so I quickly responded to Lexi, reminding her she only had four and a half days left until freedom. Then I tossed my phone to my mom who sat in the chair beside me, reading one of the many prenatal magazines in the room.

Dr. Gunthrie walked in with a big smile on her face. She looked to be in her fifties and had pink streaks in her brown hair. The nurse in purple scrubs who had helped me earlier followed behind her.

"Hello, Juliette," the doctor said, her voice much more upbeat than I'd expected. I'd always imagined doctors who were seeing pregnant teens to act a lot more solemn, or disapproving—like my mom had been when I told her the news. "I'm Dr. Gunthrie." She held a hand out for me to shake. "It's good to meet you."

"Nice to meet you, too." Though I wasn't nearly as excited as she was.

She looked down at the tablet in her hand. "It shows here that you think you're about eighteen weeks along. Is that correct?"

I swallowed the lump in my throat. "Yeah." That was what popped up in my notifications on Saturday, anyway.

"Great." She pulled a machine out of a drawer. "This is a fetal doppler. We'll see if we can get a good listen to the baby's heartbeat."

The nurse came to the side of the bed and helped me get all ready. My stomach muscles clenched when she squeezed some warm jelly-type stuff on my belly.

A moment later, the doctor put the doppler thing on my stomach.

I sighed as I looked up at the ceiling, not sure I was ready to hear the heartbeat. I shouldn't have a heartbeat in my stomach.

The machine made a weird screechy sound, kind of like I was a radio and the doctor was trying to find the right station. And then, a whooshing, beating sound that came through loud and clear.

I checked Dr. Gunthrie's face for any sign that things were not normal. What I found instead was a big smile. "Your baby has a good strong heartbeat. Clocking in at about 151 beats per minute."

I wanted to look at my mom, to see her reaction to all of this...but then I didn't know what I'd see in her expression—worry, disappointment, fear—so I just stared at the ceiling again.

With each beat of my baby's little heart, a thick wave of reality coursed over me.

There really was a baby inside there.

Up until this point I only had the little fluttery feeling inside me and the morning sickness. Those could have been passed off as gas bubbles and a really weird case of the flu. But this...this was real.

I drew in a deep breath, trying to get control over my emotions before a panic attack could hit. There was a real baby inside me. And it would only get bigger and bigger until I had to somehow push it out.

I blinked my eyes shut, trying to get the image of a baby ripping itself out of me from my mind.

I wasn't ready for this.

The doctor finished up our appointment and gave me a few forms—one for a lab order for a bunch of blood-work she said was typical for any pregnant woman, and the other for an ultrasound that would tell me whether the baby was a boy or girl.

"Just talk to the radiology department at the hospital and see if they can get you in within the next couple of weeks. I usually like to have the ultrasounds taken at twenty weeks."

I nodded and thanked her. That would be the week after Christmas. I could get the ultrasound done here, and then go to Grandma Irene's for the rest of my pregnancy.

I handed the papers to my mom as we walked out the door, feeling too overwhelmed with what was happening.

"I think I need to sit down," I told Mom once we made it to the main waiting area.

She gave me a look of understanding. "Take a seat. I'll schedule your next appointment while you rest."

I found a seat and pulled out my phone, hoping it could distract me for a few minutes.

"It can be a little overwhelming, can't it?" a woman said, startling me. She was a seat away from me, had blonde hair, and looked to be in her thirties. And from the size of her stomach, I guessed she was just a little further along in her pregnancy than I was.

"That's an understatement." I released a heavy sigh.

She gave me a warm smile that reached her eyes. "But it's a miracle. Every baby is a miracle."

I tried not to roll my eyes. Pretty sure a miracle would have been if I hadn't gotten pregnant the one time I had sex. "Yep."

"I'm guessing this is your first?"

Did I look like I had babies regularly? "Yeah. Can't say I have done anything like this before. I usually prefer to play basketball for my high school team this time of year."

She smiled and rubbed a hand over her stomach with such a loving look on her face. And it made me feel guilty that I wasn't like her. My baby deserved to have a mom like this woman. Someone who was so excited at the prospect of becoming a mother.

Not someone who was doing everything she could to hide it from everyone in her life.

"This is my first, too. Not for lack of trying." When I said nothing, she continued. "My husband and I have been trying for eight years. This baby is a true miracle. The doctor said I'd probably never be able to get pregnant, but here I am."

Women like her probably hated girls like me who got pregnant without thinking about it.

A door to the waiting area opened, and a nurse stepped through. "Nadia?" she called out the next patient's name.

The lady beside me picked up her purse from the floor and nodded to the nurse. "That's me." She stood to leave, but just before she walked past me, she said, "Have a great day. I'm proud of you for choosing the baby. I know it must have been a really hard choice."

And then she left, leaving me feeling a little better than I had a moment before. Maybe in the string of bad choices I'd made, I was actually making a good choice for once. Not an easy choice, of course, but maybe my bad choices could end up being a blessing to someone like Nadia who had a hard time having babies of their own.

---

"I THOUGHT Easton was supposed to be with Mercedes," I whispered to Lexi when Noah and Easton walked up from the basement at her house later that afternoon, laughing about something. I had just woken up from a nap twenty minutes ago, emotionally exhausted after my visit to the doctor. And since I didn't expect to see Easton this afternoon, I hadn't really taken the time to make myself look more presentable.

"I told him we were planning our snowboarding trip after school. I guess he canceled his plans with her."

I quickly ran a hand through my hair before he could look my way. But it probably wouldn't do much good, anyway. My roots were about two inches long now, and I really needed to dye my hair again. The grayish-blonde color had been fun when I was feeling rebellious or trying to catch my best friend's brother's eye, but now I was pregnant. I couldn't help but feel I should try to blend in as much as I could.

Lexi noticed my primping and gave me a knowing look. "I thought you weren't interested in guys."

"I'm not," I whispered back, hoping the guys were too distracted by their conversation to hear us.

Lexi leaned closer and whispered over my shoulder. "He canceled his plans with Mercedes. Pretty sure there's a chance."

I swatted her away and pushed as serene a look as I could muster onto my face as the boys joined us in the living room.

"So Lexi tells me you want to go snowboarding this weekend," Noah said, dropping down into the recliner beside Lexi's end of the couch.

"Yep." Though I was pretty sure I'd never said that, since I was planning to pretend to be sick once we got there.

"Did she tell you about my dad's cabin?" Noah asked. "I haven't been there in years, but from what I remember it's right off the main hill. He says we can hang there during the day if we want."

"Sounds great," I said. If I had no choice but to come up, then I'd have to pack a book or download shows in my tablet to keep me entertained—because I'd have to make a sudden excuse to stay off the slopes all day.

"Is Mercedes coming?" Lexi asked Easton who had sat on the loveseat across from us. I couldn't miss the way she not-so-discreetly eyed me as she did so.

He shifted in his seat and tugged on his jeans. "She can't make it. Her family's going to Vermont that morning."

Why did I suddenly feel lightheaded at the prospect of her being out of the state and off his mind for the next two weeks?

Lexi's smile got bigger. "That's too bad." Her words were in perfect contrast to the look on her face.

Noah leaned forward and rubbed his hands together. "Anyway, what time do you want to leave?"

I shrugged, since it didn't matter to me.

Lexi spoke up first. "How about eight? That way we can get there right as the lifts are opening."

"Works for me," Easton said. And my heart stuttered when I noticed his gaze wander to me for a moment.

What did he think of spending the day with me? He had to be thinking something. As much as Lexi said she would hang out with me and have the guys hang out together, I got the feeling she would actually try a little more matchmaking while we were gone.

"How long do you think your dad would be okay with you being gone that day?" Noah asked Lexi.

She shrugged. "I don't know. If Easton's coming with us, he'll probably be fine if we're there until dark."

"Yeah, I wouldn't be so sure about dad being super confident in my chaperoning skills right now," Easton said, his gaze flickering to me again.

Did that mean he followed through with what he'd said yesterday and had told his dad about us? What if he had changed his mind and decided to bring me down with him?

My stomach felt like it was filled up with bricks.

I checked the time on my phone. It was just barely after three. What time did his dad get home? How soon did I need to get out of here before he bit off my head for helping his son go over to the dark side?

"What time does your dad get home from work these days, anyway?" My voice cracked with anxiety.

Lexi gave me a confused expression. "Five or six. Why?"

I put my hand over my chest, hoping it would help to calm my racing heart. "Just wondering."

When she continued to give me a weird look, I cleared my throat. "I'm just...super thirsty. Mind if I go grab a glass of water?"

"Go ahead," Lexi said, still frowning, probably worried about me.

In the kitchen, I grabbed a glass from the cupboard and filled it a fourth of the way with ice before adding water. When Easton joined me a moment later, I startled and almost dropped my drink.

Working hard to keep my hand from shaking, I took a sip of my water, and tried not to watch Easton as he filled a glass of his own.

He took a drink and leaned against the counter across from me. Then he pressed his lips together and watched me for a minute.

"Worried about seeing my dad?" he said when I finally stopped gulping down my water.

I wiped the excess moisture from my lips with the sleeve of my sweater. "Um, yeah." I quickly looked behind me to make sure Lexi or Noah hadn't decided to come up, too. "I'm kind of freaking out about seeing your dad again after your comment on how he wouldn't trust you as a chaperone anymore. Just exactly how mad is he right now?"

Easton set his water on the counter behind him. "Well, I'd say he's somewhere between wanting to punch a hole in the wall and sending me off to an all-boy school."

I felt the blood drain from my face. I knew he would be upset, but it sounded like it had gone horribly wrong.

Then Easton's lip quirked up into a half smile. "I'm exaggerating, Juliette."

"You are?"

He took another long drink from his glass and set it on the side of the sink then stepped closer. He lowered his voice. "I won't pretend like he wasn't upset. He was really disappointed. But he didn't get mad or yell like I expected him to."

"He didn't yell?" Wasn't that what a drill sergeant did best?

Easton looked at me with sorrowful eyes. "No, he said he had actually been worried that this might be the case for some time. He figured this might be why I didn't try to replace my purity ring after *losing* it at the camp-out."

"But you didn't tell him it was with me, right?" I needed the reassurance even though he told me he wouldn't mention my name yesterday.

He shook his head. "No."

"But I'm guessing he's taking away your college tuition then?"

He cast his eyes down, and I couldn't help but cross my arms over my stomach as a reflex. I was wearing a baggy sweater today, but talking about this just made it seem so obvious that I should be pregnant. We hadn't used any sort of protection.

"He didn't say anything about it. But I think it was more so that he wouldn't be adding insult to injury, since he already knew how hard it was for me to tell him." He sighed and met my gaze again.

"Sorry," I said, his blue eyes making my knees feel hollowed out, weak. I gripped the counter to keep myself upright.

He nodded. "He was just relieved when I told him I hadn't gotten anyone pregnant or anything."

I swallowed the huge rock that had lodged itself in my throat. "That would have been bad."

He ran a hand through his hair. "That's an understatement."

I forced a smile on my lips, though all I wanted to do was run out of the room and hide before he could figure out the truth.

"I kind of feel bad for Lexi though," he said. "I think a huge part of why Dad's so paranoid about her is because he'd guessed this about me a while ago. Two out of his three kids have *fallen*. Those aren't great odds."

And he didn't even know the half of it.

"But Lexi is smart. She knows what she's doing," I said.

He nodded. "She is. And I'm sure Noah doesn't want to risk the wrath of my dad and attempt anything, either."

If only I'd been as smart.

An awkward silence hung in the air as neither of us seemed to know what to say.

"Anyway," he started. "It's kind of a relief not to have to worry about my dad finding out anymore."

"I'm glad you feel better. And thank you for not mentioning my name. I really appreciate it."

"Of course." He bit his lip. "And I know we—"

"*Are you guys coming back anytime soon, or did you turn into camels?*"

I jumped at the sound of Lexi's voice calling to us from the living room.

"Coming!" I yelled to her. Then I turned back to Easton, hoping he might finish his sentence. It sounded like it might be an important one.

But he was digging through the cupboard, probably thinking a snack or some candy would keep Noah and Lexi from asking us questions about why our drink break took so long.

"Sorry, guys. You caught us sneaking candy again," he said in a loud voice over his shoulder so that Lexi and Noah could hear him.

It was a trick he'd used a few times last summer when we'd snuck off to some corner of his house to make-out for a minute.

"Think chocolate-covered blueberries will make a good cover this time?" he asked in a quieter voice, coming out with a white zippered bag.

The sight of that particular candy, which I only ever saw at his house, instantly transported me back to the lazy afternoons of last summer.

He probably didn't even realize what he'd done until our eyes met. And my whole body burned when he looked at me. Was he remembering the same things I was? Him pushing me against the wall by the laundry room and kissing me until my mind went foggy. Me saying our secret code word, and then meeting in their back porch for a minute because sitting on the couch opposite from him as we hung out with Noah and Lexi had made me crazy, and I just needed a few minutes in his arms to satiate the hunger I had for him.

I tried to blink those memories away and urged the heat flashing across my face to cool.

We had been so dangerous—a wildfire that had been too hot to keep from burning out of control before inevitably, the only thing left for it to do was to burn out.

"I think the chocolate blueberries should work fine. She knows how I can't resist them," I said, holding out a shaky hand for the bag and scooping up a handful of the dark brown candy. "I remember that, too." He took the bag back, and unlike Saturday's hot chocolate exchange, he wasn't careful to keep our hands from brushing against each other.

When I looked at his face, his cheeks seemed pinker than they'd been a moment before. He pulled out a handful for himself.

"We better get back in there," I said, before I could do anything stupid. I needed to stop being so attracted to the guy I was keeping such a huge secret from. I needed to remember how badly he had hurt me before I left, and that he would just hurt me again if he ever found out the truth.

# CHAPTER FIVE

"YOU PROMISE you're not really going to go snowboarding today?" My mom walked into the front room Saturday morning with concern etched in her brown eyes. "Because I know you don't exactly want to have this baby, but you could also hurt yourself if something bad were to happen. You're not invincible, you know."

I sighed as I set my snowboard bag against the wall by the door. "I already told you I'm going to pretend I'm sick. I'm not stupid." Then after thinking about how that sounded, I added, "Okay, so I was stupid enough to get pregnant. But my brainless decisions do have a limit."

"I just want you to be safe."

"I will be."

Through the window, I saw Noah driving his dad's truck, so I shrugged into my coat just as he was parking at the end of our driveway.

"That's them," I said to my mom as I lifted my backpack and snowboard bag onto my shoulder.

"Let me help you with that," she said, taking the snowboard bag from me. "You shouldn't be lifting so much."

I resisted the urge to roll my eyes. It wasn't *that* heavy. "Pretty sure I saw a pregnant lady at the hospital on Monday pick up her screaming three-year-old and haul him outside without hurting herself."

"Yes. But it's good to be careful."

"Okay."

I walked outside, stepping as carefully as I could so I wouldn't slip on the ice. Noah jumped out of the truck and helped my mom put the snowboard in the back.

Lexi rolled down her window and pointed to the seat behind her. "You can sit there if you want."

I opened the back door and found a couple of blankets and pillows stacked in the middle of the bench seat.

Easton was on the other side of the pile, which was good. Having a barrier between us was smart. There would be no accidental brushing of fingers like what had happened at his house on Monday.

I climbed in and buckled my seatbelt, keeping the lap part of the belt low under my barely visible pooch—something I'd read about needing to do on a website somewhere.

"Have a great day, you guys. And drive safely," Mom called to us from the sidewalk.

"We will, Mrs. Cardini," Lexi said through her rolled-down window.

"Be back after dark." I waved to my mom.

Soon we were headed toward Ridgewater Peak. Twenty minutes later, we pulled onto the road that led to Noah's dad's cabin.

"Here it is," Noah said, putting the truck into park.

We all climbed out, grabbed our stuff, and headed inside.

"What's all that bedding for, anyway?" I asked Lexi when Noah set the stack of pillows and blankets on the couch.

"I guess someone broke into the cabin a while back and stole a bunch of stuff. Noah's step-mom asked him to bring up some new bedding, since apparently, the thieves needed all the quilts they had here." Lexi unzipped her snowboard bag and pulled out her helmet and boots.

"Oh, that sucks."

She nodded. "Yeah. I guess they've had a lot of break-ins in the cabins recently."

"That's too bad."

When she put sunscreen on her face, I realized she was planning to get on the hills soon. Which meant it was time for me to suddenly start acting sick.

But something like the flu couldn't just come on suddenly, could it? I should have started faking a stomachache on the ride up.

I grabbed my backpack and sifted through the contents, hoping to come up with a better excuse.

When I saw my sunglasses, I had an idea. I always had to wear sunglasses and a hat when I had to be outside for long—if I didn't want to get a headache. My migraines always came on suddenly. Maybe that could work.

"Noooo," I groaned as I riffled through my backpack.

Lexi's head popped up. "What's wrong?"

I blinked my eyes, like I was trying to focus them better. Whenever I got a migraine, the first sign was the visual aura where I had splotches of blind spots in my vision and couldn't see things clearly right in front of me.

"I think I'm getting a migraine," I said in my most annoyed voice. I looked up ahead of me at the staircase that led up to the loft and squinted as if I was trying to see around blurred spots. "So stupid!"

"Can you still snowboard?" Lexi asked.

I sighed heavily. "I don't know. I can't really see anything right now. And this part can last for up to an hour."

"Should we hang out around here for an hour, and then try?"

I shook my head. "That's just the vision problem. Once the pain hits, I'll need to be in a dark room, or it'll just get worse."

"Ah, dang it." Lexi pouted.

"Something wrong?" Easton's voice sounded behind me.

I whirled around to look at him before remembering I needed to look miserable. "I think I'm getting a headache."

"A migraine again?" he asked as he set his snowboard gear down on the wood floor.

"Yeah." I nodded, remembering the time I'd gotten one over the summer and how he'd driven me home and taken care of me while I threw up.

"Are you going to be okay?" He stepped closer, watching me closely.

I shrugged and tried to look depressed, hoping he wouldn't be able to read the deceit on my face. "I'll be okay, but I think I'll have to just stay back today."

"Do you want someone to stay with you?" He lowered his voice. "You know how you get with these."

"No!" I said too quickly. I pressed my lips together and forced a calmer expression on my face. "I mean, I'll be fine. You guys have fun."

Easton stepped back, probably surprised by my jumpiness. "I'm okay to stay so you're not alone," he offered.

Lexi came to stand by me. "I think that's a great idea."

*I bet she does.* I really needed to tell her I'd been there and done that, so she could stop trying to push us together.

I zipped my backpack up again before either of them could see all the things I'd packed in there to keep me busy for my day alone.

"No, I'll be fine, really. You guys go out and have fun. I'll probably just be sleeping the headache off, anyway."

"Are you sure?" Easton raised an eyebrow, still studying my face.

"I'm sure."

Lexi sighed heavily beside me like she couldn't believe I would turn down the opportunity to spend time alone with her brother. "Okay. I guess we'll just come back for lunch and hope you'll feel good enough to join us on the hills after that."

"Sounds good."

Noah came back in from one last trip to the truck and Lexi told him the news.

"I'm sure my step-mom keeps pain medicine in one of the cupboards in the kitchen, if you feel you need it," he said.

"Thanks," I said, feeling guiltier with each minute of lying to them. And I hated the thought that I'd just have to do even more when they got back for lunch.

But since the baby didn't deserve to take a tumble down the ski slope, I would keep on lying for him or her.

"You guys have fun. I'll see you when you get back."

---

I PULLED my tablet out of my backpack as soon as they left and settled in on the couch. It was a little chilly in the cabin, so I went in search of the thermostat to see if I could get the furnace kicked on.

I found it on the wall that led back to the bathroom and master bedroom area, turned it on, and moved the temperature up to seventy. But when it didn't kick on after a few minutes, I grabbed one of the quilts Noah had brought in. There was a wood-burning stove in the corner of the main living area, but since I didn't know the first thing about using one, I decided to wait and hope the guys could get a fire burning when they got back if the furnace was broken or something.

To pass the time, I decided to binge-watch a past season of my favorite reality TV dating show, *Finding Your Soulmate,* on my tablet.

"The Billionaire Bachelor," Drew Burrows, was just about to take a girl who didn't deserve him on a one-on-one date in London when I heard footsteps coming from outside.

I checked the time on my watch. My friends had only been gone for thirty minutes. Who could be coming in the cabin?

I turned off my show and listened, remembering what Lexi had told me about the recent break-ins. The footsteps were outside the window, but when I looked, all I saw was the back of someone's beanie as they walked past.

The footsteps got louder on the deck.

Who was it?

I froze and listened some more, my heart pounding.

I stood to get a better look out the window, and when I scanned the parking area, I only saw the truck we'd driven here in.

The footsteps stopped in front of the door, and I knew I needed to hide because I hadn't thought to lock the door behind my friends when they left. There could be a serial killer coming for me.

So I did what any sane person would do—I scrambled toward the master bedroom and hid in the closet, clicking the door shut as I squished myself in between the coats and snow pants hanging in there. Then I waited, only able to hear my breathing in the darkness.

The footsteps started again, but this time, they came from *inside* the cabin.

*Oh crap, oh crap, oh crap!* I was going to die.

The footsteps got closer until I heard them inside the room

with me. What were they looking for? It hadn't looked like Noah's family had replaced their stolen things with nice expensive stuff or anything.

If the thief wanted my tablet, they could take it and leave. I wasn't about to stop them and risk getting killed.

My face got sweaty despite the cold as I stood there, my hands and knees shaking.

I was going to pass out.

I drew in a deep breath, hoping against hope I wouldn't hyperventilate.

I needed to stay conscious.

Quiet breath in. Quiet breath out. In. Out. In and out.

And miraculously, the footsteps retreated from the room.

My heart rate calmed down enough for me to hear the intruder moving around the other areas of the cabin. For someone who was where they shouldn't be, they probably should have thought to remove their loud boots.

After what seemed like an eternity, I heard the door to the outside open and then mercifully shut again.

I breathed a sigh of relief but decided it would probably be smart to stay in the closet for a few more minutes just in case the person came back.

And then my ringtone sounded—a loud discordant sound that had me screaming.

I clamped one hand down over my mouth while the other pulled my phone out of my back pocket to silence it.

On the screen was Easton's face. Easton was calling me?

Did he somehow sense I was in trouble?

Not wanting to be one of those stupid people who answered the phone and gave away their hiding place when the intruder sneakily came back in the house, I declined his call and texted him instead.

Me: **Help! Can't talk now. Someone is at the cabin.**

I held my breath as I waited for him to respond.

*Please be close by. Please come and save me.*

His text came through a second later.

Easton: **Where are you? I looked everywhere.**

What?

Was *he* my intruder?

My knees buckled, and I sank to the ground as relief crashed over me. It had only been Easton.

I tried to stand, but apparently, my muscles had stopped working after such a huge surge of adrenaline.

Well, at least I figured out which kind of person I was in a fight-or-flight scenario. Definitely flight. Or more accurately, tremble-like-a-pansy-in-a-closet-and-almost-pee-my-pants-because-I-was-so-scared kind of person.

"Juliette?" Easton's voice came from the other room.

"I'm in here," I called. My legs may not work right now but at least my voice did.

"Juliette?" This time his voice sounded near.

"In the closet."

He opened the door, and I blinked my eyes from the brightness of the room.

"You know the closet is the first place a criminal would look, right?" He smiled, his tone teasing.

"Well, you didn't think to look in here, so turns out it was a pretty good spot." I held out my hand. "Can you help me out of here? My legs kind of gave out on me a minute ago."

He stepped closer and gripped my hand—thankfully, he wasn't laughing at me as he pulled me to my feet. "So I scared you that badly, huh?"

I let out a shaky laugh. "Um, yeah." And then I stumbled forward because my legs were still wobbly.

Easton caught me, and before I knew what was happening, I was hugging him.

"Sorry I scared you," he whispered, not resisting the hug at all. Instead, he pulled me more firmly against him.

"Why didn't you just call out my name?" I asked, resting my chin on his shoulder. I knew I should pull away because the feeling was coming back into my legs, but it felt too good to be so close to him again after so long. Plus, he was warm, and I was freezing without those blankets.

He rubbed his hand along my spine in a comforting gesture. "I didn't want to wake you if you were sleeping. I know how important quiet and sleep are when you have a migraine."

Oh yeah, my "migraine."

I pulled myself out of the hug and tucked some loose hair behind my ear. "Why did you come back early?"

He pressed his lips together and almost looked embarrassed. "I was worried about you. I didn't want you to be alone in an unfamiliar place if you needed something."

My limbs went weak all over again, and this time it wasn't because I was scared.

*Does Easton really care about me?*

*Even after everything?*

I kept myself upright and on my feet, but when I let myself look at him again and saw the depth of concern in his eyes, I just about melted.

And then I started shivering.

"You're freezing," he said, running a hand up and down my arm like he was trying to bring heat to it.

Freezing compounded with a little bit of shock had me shaking uncontrollably.

"Let's get you warmed up."

He took me back into the living room and had me sit on the

couch. Then he put one of the quilts on me, tucking it in all around me like my dad had done when I was little.

"Thanks," I said, watching him as he meticulously took care of me. The blanket was helping, but it had gotten cold on its own in the last ten minutes so I was still shaking under it.

"Is that any better?" he asked, his eyes traveling the length of my burrito-wrapped body.

"A little," I said through chattering teeth.

He unzipped his coat, tossing it to the floor, and before I knew what he was doing, he lifted one end of the quilt and scooted in beside me.

My breath caught in my throat as he pulled me against his chest, wrapping his warm arms around my torso and rubbing my back again.

"What are you doing?" I asked, completely surprised at our sudden closeness.

"I'm just warming you up."

I braced my hands against his chest, ready to push myself away. "No, I'm fine."

"I think you might be going into shock," he said, not letting me go. "I learned about it back when I was in scouts. Let me help you get warm, and then I'll move."

I sighed, not sure if I should stay so close to him or not. The memories of the last time we'd been wrapped up in a blanket together assaulted my mind. That night had not ended well.

I urged my body to stop shivering so he wouldn't feel like he had to keep being a good scout and keep trying to save me.

My shivering lasted for another minute, and once I figured I could convince him I was okay, I pushed myself away.

"Thanks," I said. "I'm all better now."

He narrowed his eyes and didn't look like he believed I could have such a quick recovery, but he let me move farther away from him without an argument.

"Why is it so cold in here, anyway?" He took one blanket and repositioned himself so his back was against the armrest and he was facing me.

I shrugged, pulling my blanket up higher. "I tried turning on the thermostat, but it wasn't working."

"Is it out of batteries?" he asked.

"I don't think so. It still showed the numbers."

He stood and walked over to the thermostat to check it himself. A moment later he turned back around with the blanket wrapped around his shoulders. "Maybe it's broken."

"Maybe. But there's a wood stove." I pointed to a corner of the room.

He walked over to inspect the stove, part of the quilt dragging on the floor behind him. "Did you see any wood?"

"I don't know the first thing about starting a fire in a wood stove, so I didn't even try to look."

"Lucky for us, I have one in my basement that my dad likes to use instead of the furnace, so I have plenty of experience."

"Good thing you've never once complained about keeping that thing lit then, huh?" I teased him. He had grumbled about the *stupid wood stove* in his basement and the *endless wood-chopping* it needed to maintain it many a time in the past.

"Yeah, yeah. Rub it in." He shot me a sassy look. "You didn't see any pre-chopped wood hiding in that closet, did you?"

"Ha ha, very funny."

"Well, if you're dishing it out, you gotta be able to take it, too." He winked, and this time the butterflies I felt in my stomach were not from the baby's movements.

Was Easton flirting with me?

I needed to put a stop to this before it could get started. I couldn't flirt with him. I couldn't toy with the fantasy of getting back together. I was going to my grandma's house in a few weeks. I was giving away his baby.

"Anyway, when I was in Paris, Lexi said something about you turning in your college applications pretty recently. Which schools did you apply to? Are Columbia and NYU still your top choices?" I asked, hoping he wouldn't notice the drastic topic change.

He ran a hand through his hair and walked back to sit on the couch, the wood stove conversation apparently forgotten for the moment. "Yeah, I applied to both. But I'm not sure I'll be able to afford them anymore. I'm pretty much just really hoping to get a scholarship."

I looked down and scratched at a spot on my cuticle. Why did I bring up college? My subconscious must be some sort of masochist.

Thankfully, he continued before I found myself apologizing to him again. "As a fallback, I applied to a few smaller schools in Central New York. I think I have a good chance of getting a scholarship to one of those, but since I didn't get a perfect score on the SAT, I'm not holding my breath for anything special to my top choices."

"I hope you get something good. You've worked hard and deserve it." What he didn't deserve was to have his whole future taken away because of one night of bad choices. I was keeping the baby a secret, so he wouldn't have to.

He pushed a smile onto his face. "But tell me about yourself. Were you able to go to any fashion shows while you were in Paris?"

I couldn't hide my grin. "Yes!"

His eyes brightened. "You did?"

"Yeah, one of my friends there took me to a few shows. Her parents have all sorts of connections in the fashion world, and so we had amazing seats. It was one of the coolest experiences in my life."

"I'm so happy for you. I know how much you were hoping to

do something like that while you were there." His smile got bigger, and it made my heart flutter at the sight of him being so happy for me even after all the things that had gone wrong between us.

"It was awesome."

"Did that make you want to study fashion design even more after high school?"

After high school? It was weird to think about life after high school right now. I'd been so focused on just getting through this year and everything with the baby, that I hadn't considered what would come next. But I still wanted to go after my dreams. It was one of my selfish reasons for placing the baby up for adoption. I wanted to have a regular life. Move past this mistake, and then just resume life as it was before.

"I'd love to get an internship with one of the fashion designers in New York after I graduate. That would be awesome. It would be so cool to be involved in something like that."

"You'd be great at it. You're fantastic with people. I remember the sketches you showed me over the summer. Those were really good."

My whole insides warmed at his compliment. I hadn't shown my sketches to very many people. I was normally an outgoing person, but when it came to my sketches, I didn't like to put them out there too often, always afraid that someone would tell me I sucked at it and totally ruin my dreams. "I appreciate you saying that."

"It's true. You're really good."

I looked down, suddenly feeling bashful at all this praise. But it was one reason I had fallen so hard for him before. My mom had always been so busy with work and everything else that I'd kind of felt like an afterthought. Him seeing me and believing in me had made me feel so special and *seen*.

I rubbed at a knot in my neck as I tried to think of something else to say. I liked talking to Easton about things like this.

"Is your neck out again?" he asked, watching me massage my neck. "Is that why you got a migraine?"

"I don't know. It could be. It's a little sore." I couldn't blame the headache on the sun this time around since I hadn't been outside today.

"Want me to massage it? That seemed to help last time."

I gulped. "Umm..."

A neck massage would feel amazing. I'd been sleeping horribly ever since I'd gotten back from Paris, having left behind my favorite pillow by accident...

But why would I want to continue dangling the carrot in front of myself? It was stupid to pretend I could just forget everything that happened in the past and move on like there wasn't a baby to hide.

I continued rubbing my shoulder. "I'm good. I'm sure I can get it on my own."

"It's not like I haven't touched you before, Juliette. Let me help."

"No, no, it's fine. I think I actually got it." I finished kneading my neck and held up my hands like it was all better.

He shook his head. "Yeah, right. It's not like anyone is here right now to find out about our past, if that's what you're worried about."

"I'm not worried about that," I lied.

I could tell he didn't believe me. "Just come on. I'll have your neck feeling better in no time."

He moved to the end of the sectional, so his back was against the armrest. Once he was situated comfortably, he motioned for me to come over. He was even thoughtful enough to grab a throw pillow and put it between us to prop me up better.

I sighed and moved to sit in front of him, hoping he wouldn't see how part of me wanted him to touch me again.

Sure he'd helped me get warmer just a few minutes ago, but a massage was a much more intimate thing. And I didn't know if I could handle it right now.

But I scooted close to him, anyway.

An instant later, his fingers brushed along the back of my neck, sending chills racing across my skin as he moved my hair out of the way. Then his nimble fingers pressed into my neck, kneading their way up and down the strained muscles.

"How's that?" he asked, his voice gentle and soothing.

I felt my eyes fighting to close. "Good." I breathed. I hadn't realized how sore my muscles had been until he took the pain out.

His fingers and thumbs worked all around my neck and shoulder area. I let my head fall backward as I relaxed, fighting the urge to moan because it felt so good.

His hands moved down to sort out the knots on my neck, his thumbs digging a little harder than usual.

"Mmm..." The sound was out before I could stop it. "This is...amazing." My eyes closed. I literally couldn't keep them open anymore.

"Is it helping?" he asked, continuing to massage my muscles in a rhythmic motion.

"Yeah..."

His fingers slowly grazed along the collar of my shirt, running across my shoulders and then up and down my arms—and I suddenly felt breathless. This felt way too good.

"You should probably..." I said, but I couldn't finish my sentence because I didn't want him to ever stop. This was the best I'd felt in a long time.

I drew in a deep breath, slowly, deeply. And I realized I had let the blanket drop, so it only rested on my lap now. I should be cold again.

But I wasn't.

"Juliette," he whispered.

"Hmm?" I asked.

"Do you think we—?"

And then the door to the outside opened, and Lexi and Noah appeared.

Panicking at being caught sitting so close to Easton, I flung myself two cushions over, hoping neither Noah nor Lexi had seen us.

When I looked at them—my face surely red as a beet—they were laughing about something and Noah was brushing snow out of Lexi's hair.

I dared a glance at Easton. Why did we both have to look like we'd been doing something illegal? We were totally going to get found out.

And we weren't even secretly dating this time.

# CHAPTER SIX

NOAH AND LEXI stomped the snow off their boots on the covered porch outside and then came in once they were done.

I cleared my throat. "You guys are back early. Were you worried about me, too?"

Did I sound guilty?

Of course I sounded guilty.

But luckily, Lexi seemed too preoccupied with whatever she and Noah had been laughing about to notice.

"Of course we were worried about you." Lexi was still laughing as she unzipped her coat and hung it on a hook by the door. "But that's not why we're back. We knew Easton was here with you."

She raised her eyebrows in a way that told me she'd been imagining all sorts of shenanigans happening between me and her brother while we were alone.

Or maybe she'd seen something and was just playing dumb for our sake.

Noah sat down on a chair at the table and removed his boots.

"I don't know if you've looked outside lately, but I think we have a blizzard on our hands."

I craned my neck to look out the window behind me, grateful for the distraction. Sure enough, snow was falling like crazy from the sky, making everything completely white. I couldn't even see the truck outside anymore—it was *that* bad.

"How's your head feeling, anyway?" Lexi took off her snow pants, revealing her black-and-white striped leggings beneath.

Would they try to make me go snowboarding in that kind of weather if I told them I was feeling better?

How long did I need to keep this going today?

"A little better. I can see now, so that's good," I said.

"How were the hills?" Easton asked as Noah and Lexi made their way to the other end of the sectional and plopped down. Noah placed his arm around Lexi's shoulders and pulled her close to his side.

"Great. Until the clouds decided to poop on us." Lexi frowned. "I mean, I know we live in New York, but it should be okay for Mother Nature to be on our side for once."

Easton leaned forward. "Did the ski patrol say anything about the weather?"

"Yeah." Noah shifted in his seat and stretched out his long legs. "They said the storm would probably only get worse as the afternoon goes on."

"Are we driving home then?" I asked, feeling alarmed. I hated driving in the snow.

Lexi gave me a soft, understanding look. "No, we won't risk it."

"I have my dad's truck. It should be able to make it," Noah said matter-of-factly, ignoring Lexi's answer. "It has four-wheel drive, if you're worried about getting stuck in the snow."

More like I was worried about going off the road like my dad did while coming home from work one day when I was eight.

He never made it home.

I did everything I could to avoid driving in the snow.

Lexi leaned closer to Noah and whispered something in his ear. I tried not to feel too awkward about what I knew she was telling him.

I wanted to turn invisible as everyone stared at me, the paranoid girl in the room. But I made the mistake of glancing at Easton who was giving me a look I didn't understand. I couldn't tell if he was feeling annoyed or fine with the prospect at waiting out the storm, trapped inside a cabin with me.

We decided to call our parents to let them know about the weather. I went into the master bedroom to make my call.

"Just stay safe inside and keep me updated on when you decide to come home. If you have to stay the night at the cabin, that's okay," my mom said. "I don't want you risking anything."

"Okay, thanks, Mom." I sighed as I hung up the phone.

When I walked into the other room, Lexi was the only one there.

"What did your mom say?" Lexi asked when I sat on the couch and pulled the quilt over my lap again.

"She said we can stay. What about your dad?" If any of our parents were the deciding factor on us staying or going home, it would be Lexi and Easton's dad.

Lexi shrugged. "He's not excited about me staying at the cabin with my boyfriend. But since you and Easton are here, he says we'll all just have to stay in the same room if we do end up sleeping tonight. He doesn't want any sneaking around going on while he's not close by."

"I'm surprised he didn't tell you he was driving up here this minute," I said. Especially with what he'd just found out from his son this week.

"Me too, actually." She shrugged.

I turned my gaze to the floor above us, so Lexi wouldn't notice how uncomfortable I was. There were two queen-sized beds up there along with a couch.

"Do you think the loft is Mr. Stevens-approved?" I cocked an eyebrow at Lexi.

"I think so." She rubbed her hands along her arms. "Man, it's cold in here."

I nodded. "Yeah, it's super cold. Easton and I had to use blankets the whole time you were gone." I lifted the blanket on my lap and gestured for her to join me.

She scooted closer on the couch, and soon we were huddling together. "Easton said the furnace wasn't working. Hopefully, the guys can start a fire for us," she said, sounding like she was trying to keep from shivering. "They're outside looking for firewood right now."

"Great." I huddled closer because it really was cold.

"So do you think having Easton come back helped you feel better?" Lexi asked with a smirk on her lips.

What did she know?

I was still trying to come up with a response to her question when the guys came back inside with their coats and hair dusted with snow. They stomped their feet on the porch steps and then shut the door before the wind could blow too much snow inside.

"Did you guys find wood?" Lexi asked.

From the expression on Noah's face, I guessed that they hadn't. "We found a stack covered in snow, so we moved what we could under the deck and brushed it off." He shrugged and held up his hands at his sides. "Hopefully it will be dry enough to light in a couple of hours."

"Well, we have two quilts over here. Are there any more?" Lexi asked.

Noah furrowed his brow as he walked around the main living area. "Is that all we brought?"

"I think so." Easton rubbed his hands together to warm them.

Noah's shoulders sagged, and he smacked his forehead with the palm of his hand. "I must have left a stack of blankets at the house in my rush to get you guys this morning."

Easton hung his coat on a hook by the door. "There are probably some upstairs, right?"

"No, they all got taken when the cabin was broken into. These are the replacements."

"We can share. I don't mind cuddling," Lexi said, a half-smile on her lips.

Of course *she* didn't mind cuddling. She had her hot boyfriend here to keep her warm.

I draped my arm across her shoulders, pretending like I thought she had meant she wanted to cuddle with me.

"There are two quilts. You and Easton could share one," I said to Noah jokingly, knowing they were way too macho to do that.

I watched the guys' faces as they went from surprised to disgusted. "Yeah, not happening," Noah said.

Lexi laughed. "You're best friends, guys. It's not like we're going to tell anyone at school."

They both shot us dirty looks before sizing each other up for a moment.

"No offense," Noah said to Easton. "But you're not my type."

Easton raised his hands up in the air. "Right back at ya, bro. I'd rather wear my coat and snowsuit all day instead of sharing a couch cushion with you."

Noah shrugged and smiled. "Fine with me." He grabbed the blanket off the corner where Easton had been, and once he was seated on the other end of the sectional, he draped it over himself and said, "There's room for two over here." He winked at Lexi.

Lexi craned her neck to face me. "You don't mind if I...?" She nodded over to her boyfriend.

"Go ahead."

Then she scooted back to the corner of the couch to snuggle with Noah.

I pulled the rest of the blanket closer to trap some heat inside. When I looked back at Lexi, I saw her eyes darting between me and her brother.

"You and Juliette could always just share the blanket," Lexi suggested to Easton.

My face burned, and I couldn't keep my jaw from dropping at Lexi's brazenness. Why was she so intent on matching me and Easton together?

When neither Easton or I said anything, she added, "We all know cooties aren't real anymore. It doesn't make sense for you to just freeze when there's a perfectly good blanket sitting right there."

"Umm..." I tried to say. But I had no other argument because even though I knew how stupid it was, part of me really wanted to cuddle with Easton again.

But Easton just stood where he was, hesitating and not saying anything. When our eyes locked, though, I couldn't be sure but it almost looked like he was hoping I would say it was okay.

Or was that just me wanting an excuse to be with him again?

"I doubt Mercedes would want to find out he cuddled with me while she was away. Most girlfriends don't like that."

I wouldn't mention the fact that we'd pretty much just done that very thing when we were alone.

Why hadn't I remembered his girlfriend then?

Easton's jaw flexed, and I couldn't help but think that maybe he'd forgotten about Mercedes for a while.

Lexi spoke up for us. "I think Mercedes would be okay with it if you tell her it saved you from freezing to death, Easton."

He rubbed his hands along his arms. He was cold. But now that he'd remembered his girlfriend, it was obvious that he didn't want to do anything that would seem like cheating.

But it's not like we would do anything. We could share a blanket without touching, right?

"Come on, Easton." I lifted a part of the blanket. "I'd feel bad if you got hypothermia and died because I was too selfish with my blanket."

That seemed to be all the encouragement he needed to join me on the couch.

He came to sit closely beside me, and I worked hard not to let my face show how relieved I was that he hadn't turned me down now that we had people watching us.

His arm brushed against mine as he situated himself more comfortably. "Sorry," he said.

I forced myself to meet his gaze. "It's okay."

But he was careful not to touch me too much after and maintained the couple of inches of space between us.

Was he embarrassed to be with me? Was that what this was all about?

He'd been giving me a massage earlier and hadn't seemed to mind, but now that Lexi and Noah were in the room it was like I was infected with some disease.

Was that the real reason we'd kept our relationship a secret last summer? Not because it was fun and exciting, but because he was ashamed that he had liked me? His little sister's best friend?

"Should we watch a movie?" Noah suggested.

"Yes, let's do," Lexi said loudly.

Did they notice how the air had shifted in the room when Easton sat by me?

Could they feel the awkwardness between us?

I pulled the quilt closer to my chin, tucking it more tightly around my shoulders as Noah and Lexi picked a movie. "Do you think it's really that much colder outside than it is in here?" I whispered to Easton, hoping by talking I could get rid of the weirdness between us.

He looked out the kitchen window that didn't have the curtains drawn. Snow was still falling briskly from the white sky. "Just a *little* warmer inside."

He moved his arm and it brushed against mine, causing me to shiver involuntarily.

"Are you still cold?"

"I'm okay," I said, not wanting to admit that such a brief skin contact could make my nerves stand on edge. "Are *you* cold?"

He shrugged. "A little."

A little? What did that mean? Did he want an excuse to cuddle with me?

What was going through his mind?

It was then that I noticed that the blanket didn't quite cover part of his arm. We would have to get closer to each other if he was going to be fully covered by the quilt.

He looked down at the blanket as well.

"I can always get my coat if you want more space." His gaze darted to Noah and Lexi.

Maybe he wasn't embarrassed by me. Maybe he was more worried about how I felt about it. Did he think that *I* was embarrassed to be caught next to him, because I had jumped away from him earlier when Lexi and Noah got back from the slopes?

"No, it's fine." I could do this. I could pretend like things weren't completely weird between us right now.

He adjusted himself on the couch until we were only a few inches apart, so close that our thighs were touching, our arms brushing against each other.

"Um..." He moved his arm forward then back, as if trying to find a comfortable place for it. "Is it okay if..." His voice drifted off as he held his arm up.

"Go ahead," I said.

He hesitantly draped his arm around my shoulder. I held my breath, telling myself not to try to inhale his deodorant. Yes, I was the weird girl who loved the smell of his deodorant and had discreetly sniffed his armpit more than a few times while we'd dated because he just smelled so amazing.

Then something occurred to me. What if the baby kicked? Would he be able to feel it if I was this close to him?

Had he felt it earlier when he was warming me up?

I hadn't even been thinking about that.

I put a hand on my stomach just to test it. As if on cue, I felt little gas bubbles moving around inside. But my hand still felt nothing.

I could do this. I could handle sitting like this for the movie.

By the time we had situated ourselves more comfortably, if not awkwardly, the movie had officially started. And when I peeked a glance at Noah and Lexi who were cuddled up to each other, her head resting on his chest, I noticed a sneaky grin on her face. She raised her eyebrows and winked at me, and I knew I would never live this down.

But I'd try not to think about it, because even though it probably meant nothing, this was the first time Easton and I had ever been able to cuddle in public.

# CHAPTER SEVEN

I WOKE up sometime later with my face pressed against something solid but warm. I blinked, feeling disoriented for a moment before I realized a hand was drawing lines down my back.

Who...?

It only took my foggy mind a minute to remember where I was and who I must have snuggled up to when I'd fallen asleep.

Easton.

I sat up quickly, worried he'd think I was taking advantage of the situation. I pushed away the hair that had fallen across my face. "Sorry I fell asleep on you. I had no idea I was so tired," I blurted.

Stupid pregnancy making me fall asleep anytime I tried to watch something boring.

"Don't worry about it. I didn't mind." He looked down at me through his lashes, and the low tone of his voice made my insides melt.

I glanced around the room before I could go complete-ly starry-eyed and mushy-brained. The TV screen was black, which told me the movie had ended. And Noah and Lexi were gone.

"Where'd they go?" I asked, my gaze trained on the empty spot where Noah and Lexi had been before I'd fallen asleep.

"Noah's giving Lexi a tour of the cabin since it looks like we'll be sleeping here tonight."

"We'll be sleeping *here*?" My voice was raised an octave higher than usual.

He nodded. "Yeah. My dad called to tell us that the roads are horrible and there have been a few accidents. We'll have to wait until tomorrow and hope the weather is better."

"Okay." I sighed, not sure how to feel. Should I be relieved that we wouldn't be risking the roads, or nervous about being here with Easton?

He was bound to find out my secrets if we spent so much time together. The secret that I was pregnant, and the secret that I might still have feelings for him.

"So how long have they been downstairs?" I asked, switching the conversation back to Noah and Lexi before I could say my worries out loud.

"About ten minutes."

"That's a long time to be in the basement," I said before realizing what a stupid thing that was to say.

Easton laughed awkwardly. "Are you trying to say that my best friend might be making out with my sister down there?"

Heat rushed up my neck, and I really hoped my cheeks weren't noticeably pinker. "It's a popular thing to do when you're dating."

"Yeah." He adjusted his position on the couch, and I kept my gaze straight ahead, not able to look at him.

This was so awkward.

We sat there in silence for a while, and I wondered if he was thinking of the same things I was—about all the times we had left a room together to sneak time alone.

"Think we should go break them up?" I asked, needing to fill the silence.

Easton gave me a wary look. "Yeah, I don't really want to see that."

"So you haven't caught them kissing yet?"

I tried to imagine the giant Noah with my tiny friend. He would probably have to bend over in half while she stood on her tiptoes to kiss. I still hadn't witnessed it myself, because Lexi had been nice enough not to do tons of PDA in front of me—yet another reason why Lexi was so cool—but it was an interesting dynamic to think about.

As if they had overheard us somehow, Lexi and Noah appeared at the basement door a moment later. And they had split logs in their arms.

"Look what we found downstairs," Lexi said with a smile.

"You found wood?" I asked.

Noah walked over to the wood stove and set his armload on the tray beside it. "Yeah, I guess my dad found a new spot to store wood. Something I would've known if I'd been here in the last five years, I guess."

"Need help getting the fire started?" Easton immediately stood from the couch. I couldn't help but notice how quickly he did it. Maybe my worries had been right before and sitting close had been more torturous than he'd let on. I tried to keep my chest from deflating with the thought.

Noah hunched over on one knee as he opened the stove to look inside. He scanned it for a second before looking up at Easton who was now standing beside him. "That would be great. I've never used one of these before."

Easton grabbed a few newspapers from a pile by the stove, crumpled them, and tossed them inside. Then he used the hatchet that was on a shelf on the wall to strip smaller chunks of wood off a split log, which he threw on top of the paper.

"Do you have a lighter or matches anywhere?" Easton stood and wiped his hands off on his jeans.

Noah grabbed one from the shelf where the hatchet had been. "Here you go."

Easton got the fire lit pretty quickly, and once the smaller pieces of wood were burning, he added a small log on top. About fifteen minutes later the room was nice and toasty, and I felt a little twinge of pride for Easton.

I knew from things he'd said in the past that he often felt overlooked next to his best friend Noah, who had the towering height, the outgoing personality, and muscles that came more naturally. But it wasn't those things we'd needed to stay warm throughout the night. We needed someone who knew how to use a wood stove without giving us carbon monoxide poisoning or burning the cabin down.

And Easton, with his often reserved personality and just under six-foot frame, had been the perfect man for the job.

---

WE FOUND cans of food to heat on the stove for dinner—thank goodness to Noah's dad and step-mom for knowing winter in New York could be unpredictable and you never knew when you'd need good food storage.

We played card games. Easton dominated at Slap Jack with his cat-like reflexes. Lexi won at Rummy. Noah was a master at Poker. And I lost at pretty much everything. But despite my horrible luck tonight, I had a great time with my friends. It was nice to forget about the stress I had in my life and just be a teenager for a while.

We finally headed up to the loft around eleven, taking the quilts and other bedding up with us for the queen beds.

"Now, I don't want to wake up and find you spooning me or anything," Noah said to Easton as they pulled the fitted sheet over the mattress.

Easton made a face before saying, "You think *you* need to be worried? I'm not the one dating the girl version of me. We all know you're just dating Lexi because you like my pretty face but knew I'd never be interested in you that way."

"You wish." Noah threw a pillow at Easton, smacking him right in the face.

"Hey!" Easton rubbed his eye where the corner of the pillow must have hit him. He threw the pillow back on the bed and sat down, still rubbing his eye.

"We're sleeping back to back, okay?" Noah said, plopping onto the bed and pulling the covers up to his chest as he turned to face the bed that Lexi and I would be using tonight.

"Would you like me to grab books off the shelf downstairs to create a barrier between us?" Easton asked. He'd stopped rubbing his eye by now, but it was red.

Noah waved his hand behind him. "No, I trust you not to spoon me and risk getting punched in the face."

"You guys are ridiculous," Lexi said, fluffing her pillow a little before climbing onto the left side of the bed, which was closest to Noah.

I pulled back the covers and climbed on the right side. "Yeah, me and Lexi are planning to sleep in the middle so we can stay warmer."

Noah propped himself up on his elbow. "Well, if I was lucky enough to share a bed with Lexi I'd sleep in the middle, too."

"Noah!" Lexi gasped. It was so sweet how much she blushed at her boyfriend's flirting.

He grinned and winked. "You know you were wishing for the same thing, babe."

Easton cleared his throat loudly. "Which is exactly why I'm here. Maybe I should switch sides with you so there isn't any forbidden hand-holding going on across the nightstand when my back is turned."

"Come on, I saw the look on your face when Juliette fell asleep cuddled next to you," Noah said. "You can't tell me you wouldn't mind switching things up."

I sat there stunned, having no idea how to respond to that. I allowed my gaze to dart over to Easton, though, my curiosity too much to resist.

His jaw hung open like he was as shocked as I was.

What did Noah mean about the look on Easton's face when I'd fallen asleep? He'd been running his fingers along my back when I'd awoken. I hadn't thought too much of it since I'd been so embarrassed about falling asleep in the first place, but could he have been doing it with affection?

Easton blinked and shook his head, coming out of a momentary daze. "There will be no bed swapping."

And that was all he said before turning his back to all of us and settling further under the covers.

Lexi removed her glasses and set them on the nightstand beside her.

"Well, goodnight, guys," she said, her voice sounding overly cheery.

Why did Noah have to make things so awkward for everyone?

But Noah had no idea what he was doing since he didn't know Easton's history with me.

"I guess I'll turn the light off then." Noah grunted like he didn't understand why we were acting so weird. He reached over to the lamp on the nightstand and soon the room was dark.

And I didn't know how she did it, but Lexi was quietly snoring just a few minutes later.

---

I WOKE up a few hours later, needing to go pee—thanks to my tiny bladder that was getting smashed smaller and smaller as the weeks went by.

I slipped out of bed as quietly as I could and tiptoed down the stairs—not wanting to use the bathroom upstairs and possibly alert everyone to my need to pee. So I went to the one by the master bedroom and flicked on the light.

I shrieked when I saw I wasn't alone.

Easton turned his back when he saw me, and I quickly flicked the light off so he could finish up.

"Sorry!" I hurried to say as I stepped out of the room, my heart racing from being startled and from the embarrassment of walking in on Easton while he was in the bathroom.

Out in the hall, I leaned against the wall and drew in some deep calming breaths. I heard the water turn on as Easton washed his hands.

"Uh, it's all yours," he grunted as he came out.

"Thanks," I said, not daring to look at him in the moonlight. I waited to turn on the light in the bathroom until after I had shut the door.

When I was done, I walked out to find Easton standing by a window and looking out at the snow-covered landscape.

"Sorry about earlier," I said, coming to stand beside him.

"Don't worry about it. I pee in the dark at home all the time and should have thought to shut the door here."

"It's so pretty out there," I said, changing the subject and gesturing to the scene before us. The sky was light after the big snowstorm and made it easy to see the snow-covered hill below.

"It is." His voice was quieter than it had been a moment before. "Everything is so peaceful on nights like this."

He stepped closer to the window and pressed his palm against the glass, like he was trying to feel the sight ahead of us.

I crossed my arms to fight away the chill coming in through the slight draft in the window. "Do you think we'll be able to get out of here tomorrow?" I asked, trying to figure out where the road was.

He removed his hand from the window and replaced it in his pocket. A hint of a handprint showed on the window for a moment before disappearing. "There are a couple of four-wheelers out back with snow-plow attachments, so we should be able to clear the road if it doesn't snow again."

"That's good." I shivered.

Easton looked at me. "You cold?"

I nodded, my teeth chattering.

"You should get back to bed where it's warmer."

But I didn't want to end the peaceful moment we were having together. For the first time since I'd left his tent all those months ago, things had been comfortable between us. I didn't want it to disappear just yet. I wanted to hold onto it for a little longer.

So instead of going up the stairs, I stepped closer to the wood stove, with my hands out in front of me, and let its radiating heat warm me.

Easton followed suit, and we stood side by side for a time. He flexed his hands against the heat. He had nice hands. They were lean and nimble and would serve him well when he became a dentist like he wanted to be. He kept his fingernails trimmed short and clean, and I couldn't keep the memory of what it had felt like to have him trace patterns along my arm from my mind. I missed holding his hands. They were strong and sure and made me feel safe.

"Remember how I was looking for my mom this summer?" His voice startled me in the moonlight.

"Yeah?" I asked. His mom had left their family when he was in elementary and had never tried to contact them since then. It had been really hard on their family, but I think out of everyone, Easton blamed himself the most for her leaving.

He looked at me carefully, like he was worried about how I'd react. "I found her."

"What?" I asked, surprised that he'd been able to find her after all these years. "You found your mom?"

He nodded. "I guess she started a band a while back, and I randomly came across one of their social media pages one day."

"Your mom is in a band?"

He shrugged and looked like he couldn't believe it, either. "I remember her singing when I was little, but yeah, I had no idea she was leaving us to become a musician."

"Does Lexi know about this?"

He shook his head. "I haven't told anyone."

He turned his back to the stove. I turned too, the front of my legs and torso feeling toasty warm.

We were quiet for a moment longer before he broke the silence. "She's doing a show in Ithaca next month. I'm thinking about going."

I peered up at him to watch his face. He swallowed, and I could tell it was hard for him to talk about his plans.

"I think that's a good idea. I know how you've been trying to figure out what happened to her for a long time."

He nodded, looking at the couch instead of at me. "I have questions. I'm not expecting her to come back or anything, but it would be nice to have answers about how she could leave her family behind. A loving mother wouldn't have been able to just abandon her children like that."

My limbs felt heavy because in a way he was describing

me. I was going to give away my baby and pretend like he or she was never mine to begin with. I was just as bad as his mother.

"Yeah, a loving mother wouldn't do that," I said, feeling a dark cloud settling in my chest. I closed my eyes and drew in a deep breath, hoping to push the guilt away.

I was too young to have a baby. I wasn't ready. The baby would be better off with a family who had their crap together.

I couldn't raise a child when I was still growing up myself, right?

Or was that just me wanting to take the easy way out of a difficult situation?

Was I just as selfish as Easton and Lexi's mom?

I shook my head. I needed to go to bed. I needed to rest from all these confusing thoughts swirling through my mind.

I touched Easton's arm. "I'm gonna go up to bed now. I'm exhausted."

He looked at me, his face half lit in the moonlight. "Please don't tell Lexi what I told you. I don't want her to get her hopes up."

I pressed my lips together before saying, "I won't." Then I let my arm drop from his and stepped away from the warmth of the stove.

"And Juliette?"

I froze, and then slowly turned back to face him. "Yeah?"

"Thanks for always being so easy to talk to. I know things have been awkward between us for a while, but I hope that this weekend can be kind of like a turning point for us. I hope you'll feel comfortable enough to call me your friend."

I nodded, thankful for the darkness because the thought of only ever being friends with Easton broke my heart all over again.

When I felt I could talk without my voice cracking, I forced a smile and said, "I'd like that."

At least as his friend, I'd get to claim a part of him—even if it wasn't all the parts of his heart that I wanted.

"I'm just going to add a few more logs to the fire then I'll head up too," he said. "Sleep well." He opened the door to the stove.

"Goodnight, Easton," I said.

"Night." He looked up briefly before turning back to what he was doing.

I walked up the stairs, and then toward my side of the bed, feeling colder and colder with each step. It was symbolic in a way —each step I took away from the fire made me feel colder, worse. Just like the more I put space between Easton and me, the lonelier I felt.

I pulled back the covers slowly, careful not to wake Lexi as I climbed into bed. She didn't even startle, which I was grateful for. I couldn't show her this part of me. The part that wished so badly that I could go back in time and re-do the past with her brother.

If I hadn't gone to Easton's tent that night, would we still be together now? Would he have waited for me to get back from Paris?

I turned on my side and watched as Easton appeared in the loft a moment later. He sat down on his bed, his back to me for a minute. I watched his shoulders rise and fall with each deep breath he took. He sat there for a while, and I couldn't help but wonder what he was thinking about. Was it about his mom? Maybe Mercedes? Or was it possible that he too could thinking about us and regretting the last time we'd been together in the middle of the night?

He seemed to draw in one more deep breath before lifting the covers on his side of the bed and climbing in with his back to his best friend.

My heart clenched in my chest one more time before I forced myself to roll onto my back and face the other way. We would be friends. That was better than what we'd been yesterday.

# CHAPTER EIGHT

CHRISTMAS CAME A FEW DAYS LATER, and with it I got a little Christmas present of my own. My belly officially popped out and there was no hiding it anymore. It was big and round, and my shirts definitely didn't fit. I needed to go shopping.

But more importantly, I needed to go to my grandma's. Like, *now*.

"Can I go to Grandma Irene's house tomorrow?" I asked my mom as she pulled our traditional Christmas morning breakfast—a blueberry French toast casserole—out of the oven.

She set the hot dish on the stovetop to cool. "Why?"

I turned to the side so she could see for herself. Her eyes got big as she took in my stomach.

"I think it's time for me to go into hiding."

She nodded, her face still showing her shock as she removed her oven mitts and put them in a drawer. "I'll call Grandma Irene after breakfast."

As we ate, I tried to figure out exactly what I would tell Lexi. I had thought I'd have a couple more weeks to warn her about my leaving to help my grandma, telling Lexi that she was getting old and needed someone to take care of her until we could convince her to go to an old folks' home.

But now that I looked how I did, I'd have to tell Lexi not in person but over the phone, after I was already in Buffalo, so she wouldn't see me looking like this.

Once Mom had finished eating, she went into her office down the hall to make the phone call, and I cleaned up breakfast as I waited. My grandma needed to say yes. If she didn't, it could ruin everything. My secret. My reputation. My mom's chances of getting re-elected.

This had to work.

I pushed start on the dishwasher, and my mom came in the kitchen with a frown on her face. The back of my neck felt sweaty.

"Well?" I asked, unable to take the suspense.

Her shoulders dropped. "Grandma Irene won't be able to take you until January fifth like originally planned."

"Why?" My voice came out louder than I'd expected as I felt panic creeping in.

Everyone would find out. I was going to be the town slut.

Easton was going to hate me all over again.

My mom touched my arm, sensing my anxiety. "It'll be okay. We'll figure something out."

"But why can't I just go to Buffalo now?" I asked. Grandma Irene was super conservative. Was this her way of punishing me for being a naughty girl?

"Apparently, Grandma planned a cruise with her sisters. She's already in Florida staying at Great-aunt Christine's house. They board the cruise ship tomorrow."

"How long is the cruise?" I asked. Some cruises were for only like three days, right? Lexi wouldn't get home from her aunt's house until tomorrow. I could avoid Lexi for three days. That could work.

"She'll be flying back to New York on the fourth."

I walked into the living room, needing to sit for a moment.

Mom sat down beside me on the gray couch, resting her hand on my knee. "We'll figure this out, Juliette. I'm the mayor for good-ness' sake, I should be able to come up with something."

I sighed, letting my head flop back against the back of the couch. "Should I just pretend like I already left?" I asked, peeking at my mom from the corner of my eye.

She seemed pensive. "How would you do that?"

I shrugged. "Well, I pretty much stayed home alone all last week, I could do that for another ten days."

Mom looked hopeful. "That could work."

I started formulating the whole plan in my head. I could tell Lexi that my grandma had an emergency, and that we had to go help her out. Then after a few days I could say that my grandma still wasn't doing great, and so I'd have to stay longer until she got better because my mom had to get back for work. It was an elec-tion year, and she couldn't have the city thinking she wasn't dedi-cated to her job.

I would start my online classes, and then figure out more excuses when the time came.

It wasn't honest at all and there was a huge chance that this would all blow up in my face, but desperate times called for desperate measures—and I was desperate right now.

---

"YOUR GRANDMA IS SO lucky to have you," Lexi told me a few days later as we video-chatted. I'd been hiding out in my house for the past four days, not going outside unless it was in the backyard for a few minutes to watch my dog, Patches, play in the snow. I was going a little stir crazy, not used to spending *so* much time by myself. But I only had a week left before I could go to my grandma's and have freedom again, so I would soldier through.

"Yeah. I haven't spent this much time with her since before my dad died, but it's been kind of fun. I had no idea she was so funny," I lied.

I was just thankful that Lexi was buying my story. Over the past few days, Mom and I had been busy setting up a corner in the spare bedroom to look like it might belong in a grandma's house. My mom, desperate to keep our reputation intact as much as I was, had gone to Goodwill several times this week to buy a bunch of "old lady" decorations. There was now an overstuffed floral couch along the wall, with a super ugly lamp and end table next to it. She'd found a painting of a country cottage to hang on the wall behind me to complete the scheme.

To say we were *all in* on this scam of ours was an understatement. It was do or die around here.

"Will you be back in time for school next week?" Lexi asked, adjusting the frames of her glasses on her face.

I pushed a frown onto my lips. "I don't know. She's really confused right now. I'm kind of worried she's getting Alzheimer's or something because she keeps asking me who I am."

It did run in the family. My great-grandma had it and so had her dad. It was likely that I would get it, too.

Instinctively, I placed my hand on my stomach. It was also likely this baby would get it and never know it was coming because he or she would be adopted.

What was I doing? How could I give a baby away without letting him or her know where they came from?

I shook my head. I couldn't think about things like that because it stressed me out, and stress wasn't good for the baby, either.

"Hey, I'll be right back. I need to go pee real quick," Lexi said before disappearing from the screen.

I scrolled through my photos from Paris while waiting. Lexi was famous for taking a long time in the bathroom.

I was just looking at a photo from one of the fashion shows I'd gone to when I heard Easton and Noah's voices through the speakers of my computer.

I clicked back to the video-chat screen, only to find the boys had walked into the kitchen at Lexi's house and were grabbing something to eat.

Not wanting them to see me on Lexi's computer screen, which she'd left unattended on her kitchen table, I scooted out of my webcam's view, leaving just the image of the old floral couch for them to see if they looked my way. Then I watched the screen from my hidden spot and went still.

Easton was wearing a teal blue t-shirt today—the one that really brought out the color of his eyes. He grabbed a container of leftovers from the fridge.

"I have to say, I'm surprised you and my sister have lasted this long," Easton said to Noah as he scooped some sort of casserole-looking thing onto a plate.

Noah sat at the bar with his back to the camera. "That's because she's your sister and you can't see how awesome she is."

Easton scrunched up his nose but didn't respond.

"Have you talked to Mercedes recently? How's that going?" Noah asked.

I craned my neck and turned the sound all the way up on my laptop, so I could hear Easton's response. What was the status of his relationship with her? I knew they were new, and he'd said once before that they weren't that serious, but he could have just been saying that so I wouldn't feel bad.

Easton gave a non-committal shrug and scooped some casserole onto a second plate. "She's great."

"Great?" Noah repeated. "Why am I not convinced?"

Easton continued looking down at what he was doing. "I don't know. I guess..." He sighed.

When he didn't finish his sentence, Noah prodded him further. "You guess what?"

Easton shrugged. "I guess I keep comparing her to someone else."

My pulse pounded in my temples.

"Who?" Noah leaned over the counter.

I held my breath as I waited for Easton to answer.

Easton still didn't look up as he said, "Just someone else."

"Oh, so we're keeping secrets from each other now."

*Thank you, Noah, for not just letting this slide.*

Easton put one plate in the microwave. "It's just a girl I was kind of dating this summer."

I leaned closer to my computer, my heart racing even faster.

Noah was quiet for a moment, seemingly shocked about Easton's revelation. When he spoke again, his voice sounded confused. "You were dating someone? How come I never knew about this?"

"We kind of wanted to keep it a secret."

"*You* had a secret forbidden relationship?" Noah asked, awe apparent in his voice.

"You say it like that's the biggest surprise of your life."

Noah laughed. "You're just not the type to sneak around with a girl."

Easton smiled—a genuine smile—and I wondered if he was remembering all the good times we'd had together. "It was fun. I mean, you know all about that since you and Lexi snuck around behind *my* back."

"We told you we were dating."

"Yeah, except you said it was fake."

"And it was." Noah shrugged. "Well, you know, until it wasn't."

"Me and this girl..." Easton looked off into the distance. "It was real. More real than anything else in my life."

My stomach muscles tightened at his words because I knew exactly what he meant. It *had* been real. So real that I'd been willing to do anything to keep from losing him.

Easton switched out plates in the microwave and pushed the hot one to Noah. "I'm not sure Mercedes and I have the chance to get there, you know."

"Do you think you and this other girl have a chance at getting back together?"

Easton didn't answer immediately. The microwave beeped, and after he got his food, he sat at the end of the bar. He dug his fork in, studying it for a moment before finally saying, "No, I don't think we do."

And my heart, which had blossomed with hope over the past few minutes, sunk into my stomach.

Lexi appeared on the screen again, her chair screeching across the floor as she pulled it out to sit.

"Hey, sorry about that," she said. "My dad stopped me on my way back from the bathroom. What were we talking about again?"

When she didn't see me on the screen, she said, "Juliette? Are you still there?"

I sucked in a deep breath and scooted in front of my computer again. "Yeah, I'm here." My voice squeaked.

Easton's head shot up in the background and he looked at the screen with horror on his face. "Wait...Juliette was there on your computer this whole time?"

Lexi looked over her shoulder to her brother. "Yeah. We were chatting before I went to the bathroom."

Easton continued to appear shocked, so I did the only thing I could think of and waved at him through the screen. "Hi, Easton. Hi, Noah."

He cleared his throat. "Uh, hi."

Noah glanced at Easton, and then at me, as if putting two and two together. A second later he moved from his spot at the bar to the kitchen table, sliding a chair right next to Lexi.

He leaned closer to the computer. "I'm guessing you overheard our conversation."

I stared wide-eyed at him, not knowing what to do. Should I slap my computer shut and run? Or would that make things more obvious?

He continued, "Think you can help me figure out who Easton snuck around with this summer?"

Lexi's jaw dropped, and she turned to her brother. "You were sneaking around with someone?"

Easton's eyes went wide. "Maybe."

Noah got a knowing look on his face, and I had a feeling he was more perceptive than I'd ever given him credit for. "So you never answered my question, Juliette. Do you have any idea who the secret girl might be?"

My forehead beaded with sweat. "I, um, I don't know. Y-your guess is as good as mine."

Noah and Lexi's eyes both narrowed, but they said nothing.

I needed to disappear.

I moved one hand to the lid of my laptop. "Anyway, I better go. I think my grandma wants to eat dinner soon."

Lexi looked really confused about what was going on. With a frown, she said, "Okay, I guess I'll talk to you later?"

"Yes." Definitely later. "See you." Then I shut the computer screen before they could ask me anything else.

I just hoped they wouldn't corner Easton, since he wouldn't be able to escape to his fake grandma's house like I had.

## CHAPTER NINE

THE NEXT FEW days dragged on as I tried to entertain myself. Mom and I had our own little New Year's Eve party, and all I could think about was how stupid it was that I couldn't go out for just one night of fun with my friends.

Why did I have to get so big while my grandma was away? Couldn't the baby have waited two weeks longer to make my pregnancy obvious?

At least I still had my video chats with Lexi. Those were the only thing keeping me sane at the moment.

"Happy New Year," Lexi said as soon as her face came into view on the screen of my laptop.

"Happy New Year," I mumbled. I was officially halfway through my pregnancy at twenty weeks and would start the new year off with a bang by getting an ultrasound done the next day. I'd find out if I was having a boy or a girl. And with the information, I'd make myself get more serious about finding adoptive parents for the baby. Time was ticking, and I needed to figure things out fast.

"Did you and your grandma do anything fun last night?" Lexi

asked. She had her hair pulled back in a ponytail today, and thankfully, was sitting in her room on her bed where Noah and Easton couldn't overhear our conversation.

"We watched movies, and she fell asleep before midnight, so nothing too exciting." I wanted to ask her about Easton, and if she and Noah had figured out who was the girl he'd been secretly dating. But since that would only make things more obvious, I asked, "What about you? Did you do anything fun?"

"Mercedes invited us to a party with a bunch of people from school, so yeah, that was fun."

*Mercedes.*

I couldn't think her name without tasting bile in my throat.

"So, are she and Easton getting serious then?" I asked, hoping I sounded way more unconcerned than I felt.

She shrugged. "I don't know. From what Noah said, it sounds like he's pretty stuck on this other girl from last summer."

Uh, oh. Why had I brought this up?

I nodded blankly, having no idea how to respond.

She narrowed her gaze. "Do you have any idea who the girl is? I mean, all summer he was with Noah or with us or at work. I don't know how he had time to fit in a secret relationship, too."

"Yeah, no idea," I said, my voice coming out way higher than it should have.

She pursed her lips and leaned back against the pillows on her bed. "Maybe it was someone he worked with."

"Maybe."

She nodded thoughtfully, pulling her hair out of her ponytail as her head rested against the wall. "Maybe I'll ask his boss if she remembers him flirting with anyone at Emrie's."

*No!* His boss, Margaret, was the *only* person who had known about us. And she'd been cool enough to keep our secret. Lexi could definitely not talk to her.

But telling her not to do that would only look suspicious.

She cleared her throat. "Speaking of Easton, you guys looked comfy at the cabin."

"We were just trying to keep warm."

She shrugged. "I don't know. I saw the way he was looking at you when you fell asleep on him. I think my plan is working."

"I think you need to forget your plan." It was making things awkward. Yes, it had been nice to be so close to Easton after all these months. And he was still an amazing guy. But Easton had said so himself that he wanted to be friends. Just friends. So even if there wasn't a secret baby in the mix, there wasn't a chance.

We'd already had our chance together, and it had been great. But things were different now, and we were different people. It was best for us to just look back on it with fond memories but keep an eye on the new future we both would have—separate futures where I had the baby and Easton knew nothing about it.

My phone rang.

"Hey, I'm gonna get this real quick, it's my mom," I said to Lexi. Then I muted my conversation with her and put Mom on speaker.

"Hey, Juliette, do you want to go to the mall in Syracuse after I get off work? We probably should get you some maternity clothes before you go to Grandma's."

I looked down at the t-shirt I was wearing, my Ridgewater High Basketball tee from last year. It was the only shirt that covered my belly these days. Yes, the fashionista in me died every morning when I had to get dressed.

I hated the thought of having to buy ugly pregnant-lady clothes, but it was a necessary evil now.

"Sure. That's a good idea."

"Great. We'll grab dinner while we're down there. I'll be home to get you around five-thirty."

"Okay. Thanks."

After we hung up, I turned back to my computer. I moved my

cursor to unmute my video chat with Lexi only to realize I was never on mute.

My throat closed up as I dared a peek at Lexi's face. One look and I knew I'd made a terrible mistake.

"Juliette?" she asked, before I could shut my computer down to run and hide. "Are you pregnant?"

# CHAPTER TEN

I DIDN'T KNOW what to do, so I did the same thing I'd done a couple of days earlier and shut down my laptop.

I couldn't believe I didn't double check to make sure I had really muted my conversation with Lexi. And why did I have to be lazy and put my mom on speaker instead of holding the phone up to my ear?

Now the very thing I'd tried to prevent over the past weeks was happening. Lexi knew I was pregnant.

And if Lexi knew, then it was only so much more likely that Easton would soon find out, too.

I paced around my basement, trying to figure out what I was going to do.

How was I supposed to trick my friend into thinking I wasn't really pregnant when she'd blatantly heard my mom say we were going to buy maternity clothes for me?

What other reason would I need maternity clothes for?

Lexi wouldn't believe me if I told her I was just getting fat and needed extra wiggle room in my clothes these days.

Ugh.

*Ding-dong.*

I paused. Who was at my door? The only people who usually came to my house were Lexi or the UPS guy. Did we have packages coming?

I tiptoed down the hall and to the front door. When I checked the peephole, I had to look down to see who was standing on the other side.

Lexi.

She'd run here in her pajamas.

Why was she here? Did she realize that I was home?

I leaned my back against the door, my breath coming in short bursts as I tried to figure out what to do.

I wasn't ready for this. I hadn't thought up a good-enough excuse yet.

Could I tell her I was maternity-clothes shopping for my cousin who was about the same size as me, and who was too embarrassed to buy them herself because people would know she was pregnant?

That probably wouldn't work.

So I did the next best thing: I turned the deadbolt to lock Lexi out.

Then I ran to the other doors in the house and locked them too just to be safe. Once done, I dashed back into the kitchen and sunk low by the cupboards to where I wouldn't be spotted.

But Lexi must have caught on to what I was doing, because a minute later, she was standing at the back door, looking in through the square of glass.

"I know you're in there, Juliette," her voice muffled through the door. "I saw you run past the living room window a second ago."

I sat as still as I could, only listening to the sound of my labored breathing.

"Open up, Juliette. Or I'm going to call the cops and tell them

I saw someone sneaking around your house when you're supposed to be in Buffalo and your mom is at work."

My shoulders sagged. I was caught.

"I know you're probably worried, but just let me talk to you."

I rubbed my eyes. How was I supposed to even begin a conversation like this?

*Hey, you know how you have those purity rings in your family? Well, it would probably burn off my finger if I tried to wear one.*

No. That made me sound like I slept around like crazy. It had just been the one time.

*So you've probably noticed how fat I'm getting. Surprise, you're going to be an aunt again!*

That wouldn't work, either.

She wouldn't really call the police, would she?

The glass in the door rattled when she knocked on it.

"You can't hide in there forever, Juliette. I know where you guys keep your secret key."

I blew out a long breath and pulled myself up to a standing position.

I guess this was happening.

So I walked back into the dining area, unlocked the door, and let my friend in.

My lips trembled and tears pricked at the back of my eyes as Lexi took in my appearance, her eyes pausing on my stomach. And then I looked down because I couldn't watch her reaction. I had never felt so exposed in my life.

"Oh, Juliette," Lexi said, her voice filled with pity. And that was all it took for me to completely break down. I'd cried a lot over the past few months, but this was the first time I had someone besides my mom's initial reaction to compound my feelings. If Lexi thought things were bad, they really must be.

"I'm so sorry. I had no idea." Lexi pulled me into a hug and rubbed my back. I clung to her, needing someone strong to hold on to.

She held me for the next minute until I was able to calm myself. Once I had gotten my sobbing under control, I wiped my eyes and gave her what I was sure looked like a watery smile.

"You'd think after seeing what Maddie went through, I would've known better," I said.

*That Easton would have known better, too.*

"When did this happen? How?"

I sighed. "I think you know *how* it happened."

She shook her head. "You weren't dating anyone when you left. When did it happen?"

*At your family's end of summer camp-out in your brother's tent.*

But I couldn't say that because I had to protect Easton.

"In Paris." Guilt stabbed at my chest like a knife. "It happened when I first got there."

Lexi was silent, like I'd completely stunned her. I'd always had a boyfriend, but as far as she knew, I'd never wanted to take things this far.

And I hadn't. Until that last night when I'd thought about leaving for Paris in a few days and how I didn't want Easton to forget about me while I was gone.

Well, that night had definitely been memorable.

When she was quiet for too long, I launched into the story I'd rehearsed in my head a million times. "I went to a party one night with some girls I met there. I was feeling lonely being in a new country, and this really hot guy came up and was sweet. And then we..." I let my words trail off.

I knew my story made me look bad, like I hadn't cared about the thing that should have been saved for marriage, according to Lexi's family. But I had to tell her a lie so she wouldn't find out how it really happened.

She swallowed, her eyes wide. "Does the guy know?"

I shook my head. "I didn't get his number or anything. Everything happened so fast."

"How long have you known?" I was grateful she wasn't saying anything about how slutty I sounded. Her sister may have gotten pregnant in high school, but at least it was with a guy she'd been dating for years.

"I found out in October."

"Have you been to a doctor yet? Do you know what you're having?"

"I went to the doctor when I first got home, and I have an ultrasound to find out if it's a boy or a girl tomorrow."

She was quiet for a minute. "Are you thinking of keeping it?"

"No."

She nodded, calmly taking everything in. Would she judge me for not wanting to keep the baby when her sister had?

"As you've probably guessed by now, my plan is to go live with my grandma, have the baby, place it up for adoption, and then come back and resume regular life."

"When do you go?"

"In a few days. My grandma is still on her cruise."

"So you've been hiding in your home ever since Christmas?" There was sympathy in her eyes.

My throat thickened with emotion as I thought over everything I'd done to keep my secret. "I popped out on Christmas morning. My mom and I thought it was best to lie low, so no one would find out. It's an election year, and a story about the mayor's daughter going to help her ailing grandma sounds a lot better than an out-of-control teen sleeping around in Paris."

"But we know you're not like that."

I cocked an eyebrow and pointed to my belly. "Most people will see this and make up whatever story they want to believe."

"I'm so sorry," she said.

I pressed my lips together and shrugged. "It's just a consequence for my actions, I guess."

"But a pretty difficult one."

That it was.

"I'm sorry I didn't tell you. I just..." I lifted a shoulder. "I didn't exactly know how."

She nodded. "It's okay. I'm sorry you felt like you couldn't tell me. I wish I could've been there for you sooner. No wonder you didn't want to go snowboarding."

I laughed, even though the conversation we were having was far from lighthearted. "I totally faked my headache."

"Do you think it would help to talk to Maddie? I'm sure she'd be happy to talk to you since she went through this a couple of years ago."

I felt the blood drain from my face. "I don't want anyone to know. Promise me you won't tell anyone. Not Maddie. Not Easton." *Especially not Easton.* "Not Noah. I just want to get out of Ridgewater for the next five months, and then come back and start over like it never happened."

Lexi looked worried, like she wasn't sure this was the best idea. But she nodded.

"I can keep a secret."

I gave her a hug. "Thank you."

# CHAPTER ELEVEN

"ARE you planning to know the baby's gender?" the ultrasound technician asked me as she pushed around on my way too full bladder.

"Um..." I said, trying to keep from losing everything in front of her and my mom. I had to pee so bad.

She must have seen my eyes turn yellow or something because she lifted the ultrasound probe from my belly and said, "You can go pee first. You won't need a full bladder for this."

"Thank you!" I said a little too loudly.

She chuckled and pointed to the bathroom. "Just lock both doors since the bathroom is shared with another room."

My mom helped me get down from the bed. Less than a minute later I felt *so* much better.

I would never take going to the bathroom for granted again!

The woman smiled when I came back in the room. "Better?"

"Yes," I said.

"Did you want to know the gender or not?" she asked.

*Did I?*

That would probably make everything much more real, and I

was already overwhelmed after what I'd seen of the baby today. He or she already had arms and legs and a head and chest. Putting a "he" or a "she" to it would just make things that much more difficult. I didn't want to get attached to the baby. I wasn't ready to be a mom.

But adoptive couples liked to know these things, and since I was already halfway through with the pregnancy, I needed to get more serious about my search for them.

Easton's baby deserved a great family. One who would love this baby as if it was their own. He or she deserved to have a mom like the woman I met at the doctor's office. Someone who thought this baby was a miracle and who would give it the best home possible.

"Yeah, I guess I'd like to know," I finally decided.

My mom took my hand in hers, giving it a reassuring squeeze.

And then I tried to relax as the image of the baby was on the wall in front of me again—well, at least it kind of looked like a baby. I just had to take the lady's word for it with all the parts she had pointed out, since I couldn't tell myself—to me it only looked like there was an alien in there.

She moved the transducer probe along my stomach, taking pictures and measurements as she did so. Then she put an arrow on the screen and typed B-O-Y.

My limbs went tingly as I realized what that one word meant.

The baby was a boy.

Easton and I had made a baby boy.

Instantly, the image of a newborn baby with my dark hair and Easton's bright blue eyes popped into my mind.

"It's a boy, honey," Mom whispered as she squeezed my hand.

I couldn't respond. I felt numb.

I had always thought having a boy first would be a great way to start a family. Boys could help protect their younger sisters, like Easton had done for Lexi and me when we were in elementary.

The technician wiped away the goo on my stomach and finished everything up while I lay there in shock.

I was going to have a boy.

Would he be tall like Easton? Would he be as good at lacrosse as Easton was?

I shook those thoughts away. I wasn't supposed to think about those things. They just made this so much more real. I couldn't get attached to the baby. I couldn't imagine a future for him. Because I wasn't going to be part of that future. He wasn't mine to keep.

Unless...

No. There was no "unless." There was only adoption. That was the only option. I would be barely seventeen when the baby was born. I still had another year of high school. And then I had my dreams of working in the fashion world. I couldn't do all those things with a baby on my hip, or a toddler running around my legs.

And this baby deserved to have two parents. Even if I kept the baby and Easton found out, our son would still live in two separate homes. That wasn't fair to a kid. One week here, one week there. Never knowing which parent he'd be spending the holidays with.

No. I needed to find a couple who'd been married for a long time. One who'd tried to have kids but couldn't. A family that was stable. Mature. Patient. Smart. Grown-up.

Not me.

Not Easton.

Not us.

I had grown up without my dad. He was never there for the daddy-daughter dances. He'd never been there to teach me how to play basketball. He hadn't been there to give me advice about boys.

He had died. And yes, I couldn't predict the future. But I could do what was best with the information I had. I could give my baby what I had always wanted. A mom *and* a dad.

The nurse handed me a long strip of photo paper with three images she'd taken of the baby. She added, "And here is a flash drive with a few more."

"Thank you." I took the USB stick from her outstretched hand and couldn't help but notice the concern in her brown eyes.

She too knew that the baby deserved more than I could give him.

I carefully folded the ultrasound photos in half, setting them inside my purse. Then Mom and I got up and left.

Before we could reach the exit doors that led to the parking lot, I asked my mom, "Is it okay if I walk home?"

It wasn't too cold today, and I wouldn't mind the exercise after being trapped inside my house for the past week and a half.

"Are you okay, Juliette?" There was worry in her eyes.

I pulled my lips into what I knew was an overwhelmed smile. "I will be after some fresh air and exercise."

She nodded. "Just be safe, okay?"

She was probably worried I was going to throw myself in front of a car.

I couldn't pretend like that hadn't come to my mind a few months earlier.

But I would be okay. I still had options—even if they were hard.

"It's only a few blocks."

I PULLED my coat as far across my torso as I could and tied the belt. It barely stretched across my stomach. Maybe I should have asked my mom to buy me a new coat along with all the maternity clothes we'd bought yesterday.

It started to snow about halfway through my walk home. I pulled my hood over my head and tipped it down to keep the snow out of my face.

The wind picked up about half a block later. I was starting to regret this walk home.

A car pulled along the curb beside me a little later. And since it was starting to get dark I quickened my pace, not liking the thought of creepers trying anything on me.

My heart raced when the car slowly rolled along beside me.

"Juliette?" a male voice called out.

I turned my head to see that it was a blue mustang. It rolled to a stop, and Easton leaned over the center console. "Is that you, Juliette?"

He looked surprised to see me. But then I remembered that he thought I was at my grandma's house a few hours away from Ridgewater.

I quickly put my purse on my other arm, hoping it would help hide my stomach before he could see it.

Once my belly was safely blocked from his view, I pulled my hood away from my face. We'd already made eye contact, so I couldn't just pretend like I hadn't heard him.

"Yeah, it's me."

He blinked, like he still wasn't sure he was seeing things right. After a moment of hesitation, he said, "D-do you want a ride home?"

I looked ahead. I still had three blocks to go, and the snow was falling faster and faster by the minute...but getting a ride home meant being close to him. And if I was close to him, it was likely that he would notice how much I'd popped out.

"No thanks. I'm okay." Then I turned my attention back to the path ahead and continued walking.

He kept pace along beside me. "Come on, Juliette. It's getting dark. Let me give you a ride."

"I need the exercise. I'm fine."

"So I guess you didn't really want to be friends after all?"

I sighed. Why did he have to play the friend card?

I swiveled to face him again, biting my lip as I tried to figure out how to respond.

"You said at the cabin you wanted to try to be friends, right?"

I nodded.

"Well, friends don't let friends walk home alone at twilight when it's snowing and they're still three blocks from home. Especially when they live on the same street."

He had me there.

I adjusted my purse again and turned to face him straight on. "Okay. Fine. I'd love a ride."

He grinned and pushed open the passenger door.

I stepped off the curb and climbed into his car. I buckled myself in, making sure that my belly wasn't too obvious from my sitting position. When I finally looked around his car, I was instantly assaulted with the memories of the last time I'd been in it. It had been late August, just five days before I was supposed to leave for Paris. We had gone out for a drive to talk about how things would work when I was gone. But instead of talking through the logistics of everything, we'd made out for hours instead. Kissing was much better than talking about being separated for months.

I pushed the thoughts away and turned to Easton, hoping he wasn't remembering the same things I was.

"Thanks for the ride," I said.

He was looking at me with a confused expression. "When did you get back from your grandma's?"

"Um, yesterday. I, um, had to come back to pack more of my things since it looks like she'll need my help for a while longer."

He frowned. "Really? So you'll miss school?"

I swallowed the brick in my throat. "Yeah."

He still looked confused. "Why doesn't she come stay at your house if she needs help?"

"Um..." I scrambled for an answer. "She and my mom don't really get along, so we thought this was best until we can convince her to go to a retirement center."

He nodded and pulled onto the road.

Hopefully, he'd bought it.

"What are you going to do about school then? I was looking forward to hanging out with you more."

It was then I remembered the conversation I overheard between Noah and Easton in the Stevens's kitchen last week. About how Easton and the girl he'd dated had had something special, and he didn't think he and Mercedes had a chance at getting there.

Did he want to see if we could work things out?

I cleared my throat. "Did you mean what you told Noah?"

His hands tightened on the steering wheel and he let out a cough. "What do you mean?"

I drew in a deep breath, hoping it would give me some bravery. "About me and you."

He pinched his lips together. "So you really heard everything, didn't you?"

"Yeah." I stared straight ahead. It was easier to have conversations like this when you didn't have to look at each other.

He slowed the car as he turned a corner. "Well, don't you think it's true?" I felt him look at me.

"That we had something special? Or that there's no chance of it working out?" I asked.

"I don't know. I guess either one."

I sighed and looked at him carefully, not sure how I should answer. "I don't know. I guess both. We had something special. But you were right, we're better off as friends."

He nodded slowly, seeming to take in what I said.

We sat in silence for a while, each lost in our own thoughts. But there was a question that had been plaguing me for a long time and I needed an answer. "Do you think things would be different if we didn't..." I couldn't finish the sentence.

He glanced at me again, sadness in his eyes. "If we hadn't taken things too far?"

I nodded.

"I don't know. Maybe. I guess we'll never really know, though. We only have what actually happened."

"I guess that's right."

He pulled onto our street and drove all the way to the end, making a U-turn to stop in front of my house.

"Thanks for the ride. I really appreciate it." I reached for the door handle, but when I tried to push it open, it didn't budge.

"Oh sorry, it's been having issues lately. Let me help." He undid his seatbelt and then leaned across me to grab the handle. A whiff of his cologne met my nose. He smelled like happiness and summer.

Cold air blew through the crack in the door and he slowly pulled himself away, his shoulder brushing across my stomach.

"Thanks," I said, surprised by our sudden closeness and really hoping he hadn't just felt the baby.

"No problem." He pulled away farther, and our eyes locked for a moment. His blue eyes were different than they'd been a moment before, but very much the same way they'd been months earlier when he was telling me he wanted to kiss me.

My stomach muscles twisted. Could he feel the electricity in the air?

My breath came out in shallow bursts as we stared at each

other for a moment longer. And then his eyes dipped down to my lips.

Was he thinking about kissing me?

I unbuckled my seatbelt and turned my head away. He was dating Mercedes, and I wasn't about to get in the middle of anything.

Plus, he'd just said himself that things would never work out between us.

I opened the door wider and set one foot on the ground, ready to leave.

"Hey," he said, his voice startling me. "Don't forget your purse." I turned back to him—he had picked up my bag and was holding it out to me.

"Thanks," I said, taking it from him.

But his face had gone white. Confused, I looked down at my purse. And then I saw what he'd seen. The ultrasound photos.

I yanked the bag away from his grip and put it over my shoulder, ready to bolt.

"Are you pregnant?" His voice stopped me, and my insides felt hollow.

No, no, no, no, no. He could not have just found out.

My heart thundered in my chest. I needed to get out of here now.

I needed to go, but his hand shot across the space between us and grabbed my arm so I couldn't leave.

His voice came out louder, like he was barely keeping it together. "Are you pregnant, Juliette?"

I couldn't breathe. What was I supposed to say? He wasn't supposed to find out!

I looked back at his face, which was full of anxiety and disbelief, and maybe even a little anger.

"Please tell me." His grip on my arm got tighter and his voice got even louder. "Are. You. Pregnant?"

He looked like he was on the verge of a freak-out. Like I had the power to completely crumble his entire world with whatever I said next.

I put a hand on my stomach, rubbed it, and sighed, "Yes."

"Yes?" His whole body sagged, and he ran his hands through his hair. "No." He blinked his eyes shut like he wished he hadn't just heard what I'd said. Then he turned back to me, his eyes searching mine for hope that things weren't as bad as they seemed. He swallowed hard before asking, "Is it—is it mine?"

It was like all the life and hopefulness he'd ever had was blown out like a candle.

I couldn't do this to him. Just watching him struggle for air was more than I ever wanted to see in him.

He didn't need this burden.

I shook my head fast. "No, Easton." I touched his arm, hoping he could hear me over whatever was going through his mind right then. "It's someone else's. Someone from Paris."

"Really?" He looked at me like he didn't believe me, but there was a flicker of hope in his eyes. As if whatever I said next was his lifeline. "It's not mine?"

"No. The t-timing would be off for him to be yours."

"But we..."

I shook my head. "Like I said, the timing is off. I'd have to be further along." Tears bit at the back of my eyes as I spit out so many desperate lies.

He finally relaxed against his seat. And I sucked in a deep breath, relieved that he'd taken my story so easily.

But then he turned back to me with narrowed eyes. "You slept with another guy?"

The hurt in his tone was almost as bad as the fear had been earlier.

"It just happened. I-I'm sorry I don't really have anything else to say other than the fact that we were broken up, and I was feeling lonely in Paris."

He clenched his jaw. "How long did—" he started, but then he shook his head like he didn't want to finish that thought.

"I know it looks bad," I hurried to say. "That's why I'm going to my grandma's house. I didn't want anyone to find out."

"I can't believe you would do that. Did what we have not mean anything to you?"

The tears spilled from my eyes now. "It did. Of course it did, Easton." Now I was sounding desperate, and I was mad at myself. All the feelings from that night came rushing back. The utter lowness I had felt when he had rejected me after something that had seemed so special.

I blinked my eyes shut. I would not cry in front of him. He didn't need to know how much he'd hurt me then, and how much he still had the ability to hurt me again.

"I thought you were different," he said. "I thought at least I had given away that part of myself to someone who knew how special it was."

"I did." My voice cracked.

He shook his head. He wasn't listening anymore.

And I was just so lost with this conversation. First, he was scared that the baby might be his, then he was relieved that it wasn't, and now he was mad at me for getting pregnant by another guy.

What did he want from me?

"I'm sorry, Easton."

He looked straight ahead, the muscles in his jaw flexing. "I'm sorry that you're pregnant, Juliette. Sorry if anything I did made you feel like you had to do that."

I sniffled, urging my tears to stop falling down my cheeks. He didn't need to see me like this. I had already cried too many tears over Easton.

"I-I'm going to go now," I said. "Thanks for the ride."

I dared one last look at him, but he wasn't looking at me anymore. Instead, he was shifting his car into drive again, ready to leave me and my mistakes far, far behind him.

"I'll see you around," he said.

I climbed out and stepped onto the sidewalk with shaky legs. The only thing keeping me from curling up on the curb and crying like a baby was the knowledge that my grandma would be home in a couple of days, and soon I would really be able to escape to her house and leave everyone in Ridgewater behind.

# CHAPTER TWELVE

WITH TEARS STREAMING DOWN my face, I ripped off my coat as soon as I got home. A minute later, there was a knock on the front door.

I was not in a place where I wanted to see anyone, so I ignored it and hung my coat in the closet.

The knock came again, this time followed by a voice on the other side.

"Will you please open up, Juliette?"

It was Easton.

What more did he want to say? How much more hand sanitizer did he want to rub into the wound?

I didn't want to talk to him anymore, so I didn't answer. Instead, I walked toward the kitchen to self-medicate with ice cream.

But apparently, he didn't care about what I wanted, because a second later, the front door pushed open and Easton stepped inside, his chest heaving like he'd just run a race.

When our eyes met, I saw pain reflected in his.

Was he expecting me to apologize some more?

I crossed my arms. "What do you want, Easton?"

I probably would have come across more threatening if my voice hadn't wobbled and it didn't look like I'd just been bawling my eyes out.

He stepped closer, shutting the door behind him.

"I—" He lifted his hands in a helpless gesture. "I need to apologize to you."

*You bet you do.*

He came even closer until there was only a couple of feet between us. "I'm sorry for what I just did back there." He sighed. "That was about the worst way I could have reacted."

I pinched my lips together, hoping it would keep me from bursting into tears all over again.

He must have noticed how unstable I was because he closed the distance between us and pulled me against him, wrapping his arms around me.

"I feel like such a jerk."

"You should," I said, my voice muffled against his shoulder.

He shook his head and just pulled me tighter against him. "I'm so sorry, Juliette."

I blinked my eyes shut, hoping it would stop my stupid tears from spilling out even more. But it didn't help.

"It'll be okay." He rubbed my back, and I could feel his heart beating so fast in his chest. "If someone said any of those things to Maddie when she was pregnant, I would have punched them in the face. You didn't deserve that."

I buried my face in his chest as a sob wracked my body. He kissed my head then nuzzled his cheek against my neck.

"I didn't mean those things," he whispered. And maybe I was just being delusional, but he really sounded sincere.

I pulled back and wiped under my eyes. My fingers came away black. I must totally look like a raccoon right now.

"I think I need a minute." I sniffled, keeping my eyes down so he wouldn't see what a mess I was. "I'm going to go wash my face."

He nodded and let me go.

I washed my makeup off and just stayed in the bathroom for a while, not sure I wanted to go back in the living room to face Easton again. It was great he came back to apologize, but that didn't make me forget his initial reaction.

I splashed my face with water one more time, took a deep breath, and then made myself go back out to face him.

I found Easton sitting on the gray couch in the living room, his fingers strumming rhythmically on the armrest.

"Sorry, I had to wash off that mess." I sat on the other end of the couch, tucking one foot under me.

"I've always thought you looked good without all that makeup, anyway."

I ducked my head down, not sure how to take his compliment. "Thanks."

His gaze drifted toward my belly. Was he trying to figure out how far along I was?

I grabbed a throw pillow off the couch and covered my stomach with it.

He cleared his throat awkwardly. "So, I guess what you said about going to your grandma's house meant you probably weren't planning to keep the baby?"

"No. I don't think so."

He nodded and picked at the couch cushion. "It's probably easier to just move on like it never happened, huh?"

Easier?

I didn't think anything was *easy* about this.

"Does the Paris guy not want the baby then? Is he pressuring you to give it away?"

Of course, the only reason I could possibly dream of giving away a baby would be because someone else was telling me to.

Not because that's what I thought was the best decision for myself and my baby.

I wanted to roll my eyes at him.

But I knew I should have expected this, because this was how things worked in his family. His sister had kept her baby.

"The guy actually doesn't know about the baby. I decided that for myself."

His eyebrows raised. "You didn't tell him?"

I looked down again and spoke carefully, hoping he wouldn't be able to detect that I was lying. Everything depended on Easton believing the baby wasn't his. "I don't have a way to contact him."

"You don't? Isn't he tagged in those photos with you?"

So he'd done a little research on Evan. "That was just a friend. This other guy was a one-night thing," I said, continuing with the same lie I'd told Lexi.

He went still, stunned that I could have a one-night stand. Should that make me feel better?

He regained his composure a moment later. "Doesn't the guy need to sign away his rights or something for the adoption? I thought I remembered Maddie talking about that."

I shrugged. "I watched a YouTube video a while back where the girl said something about the father having thirty days after the baby is born to come forward and claim his parental rights or something. After that, I think the adoption process goes pretty smoothly."

I probably needed to do more research, but the girl in the video made it sound straightforward, anyway.

I was hoping it was true.

"You'll have to keep the baby for those thirty days, though. Are you afraid that you'll bond or something? I know Maddie couldn't give Grant away once she saw him."

Which was something I was terrified of. I couldn't get

attached to the baby. "I think the baby would go into foster care at that point."

He blew out a long breath. "Sorry you have to make all these decisions by yourself."

I nodded. It would be nice to decide these things with Easton's help. But I knew this was the way it needed to be. I'd seen how scared he'd look for that small instant when he thought he was going to be a dad. His whole life had probably passed before his eyes.

I felt a little guilty lying to him, but I could ignore that feeling for now. I'd be miles away soon, and the next time I was back in Ridgewater, all of this would be a thing of the past.

# CHAPTER THIRTEEN

"ARE you sure you want to go to your grandma's?" Lexi asked as she helped me pack my suitcase a few days later. I was set to leave for Buffalo the next morning. As soon as Grandma Irene landed in New York, she'd call us, and then my mom and I would hit the road.

"Would you want to go to high school looking like this?" I turned to the side so she could get the full view of my belly. It wasn't humongous yet, but it was definitely noticeable. And it would only get bigger and bigger as the months went on.

She looked at my stomach for a moment before saying, "It's not that bad."

"It's not that bad *yet.*" I grabbed a shirt and stuffed it into my suitcase. "But I've seen pictures of my mom when she was pregnant with me, and we're not the kind of ladies who stay petite and small with the babies stuck in their rib cages." I shook my head as the image of what my mom had looked like when she was pregnant popped into my head. "We carry low and we carry big. Pretty soon it's *all* gonna be hanging out, and I don't want everyone seeing me like that."

"You could carry differently," she said, always the optimist.

I cocked an eyebrow. "And I could also carry the same."

"I guess I wouldn't know if Maddie carried the same as my mom did, since my dad burned all those pictures of her when she left us."

"Yeah. Maybe you should get knocked up like me to see if you and Maddie are the same."

She threw a pair of socks at my chest.

But the mention of her mom had me thinking about what Easton had said about trying to meet her. Which then had me thinking about Easton and our last conversation.

"Did Easton say anything to you about me?" I folded a pair of maternity pants.

She frowned. "No, why?"

I shrugged. "I saw him on Tuesday, that's all."

Her hazel eyes went wide behind her glasses. "Does he know you're pregnant?"

I looked down, not wanting her to see anything on my face that would lead her to believe that Easton was a bigger part of this story than I'd led on. "After my ultrasound appointment, he saw me walking home. He gave me a ride and accidentally saw the photo of the baby poking out of my purse."

"Well, he didn't say anything to me about it. But I guess he's pretty good at keeping secrets, since he still hasn't budged on telling me who was the girl he secretly dated over the summer."

I purposely avoided looking at her for a moment.

"Who do you think it is?" She leaned closer.

My phone started ringing, saving me from trying to figure out how to answer her question. My grandma's name was on the screen. I swiped to answer. "Hi, Grandma."

"Hey, sweetie." Her warm voice sounded through my earpiece. "I have some bad news."

Bad news? "What is it?" I asked. Was her flight delayed or something?

"We just docked in Florida, so this is the first I've been able to contact you. But my sister Christine had a stroke while we were on the cruise. She's okay now, but I don't feel good about leaving her alone."

"Oh no, Grandma. I hope she's okay," I said. I supposed one more day wouldn't be such a terrible delay.

"She's okay. But I'm going to have to stay at her house for at least a few weeks, just until she gets on her feet. As you know, Uncle Vearl died a couple years back, so I'm really all she has right now."

Disappointment fluttered through me. I had to wait another few weeks before I could go? I was already going stir crazy. I couldn't imagine looking at the same boring walls of my house for another three weeks.

"Couldn't you bring her to your house? She might like a change of scenery, right?" I asked as a last-ditch effort.

"I'm afraid that won't work, sweetie. She's comfortable at her own house. I'm really going to just have to stay here right now. It doesn't make sense to make her travel all that way when her home is here."

But it made sense to *me*, because *I* needed somewhere to go. I had nowhere else. My mom's sisters would definitely not understand my situation. They cared a lot about how they presented themselves to the world—more than anyone else I knew. They were even worse than my mom.

My grandma spoke again. "I'm really sorry, Juliette. I promise to call you as soon as I feel like it's safe for me to leave her."

I sunk onto the bench at the end of my bed. "Okay. I understand. Take care of Aunt Christine. Tell her that I hope she gets better soon."

We ended our call. I dropped my phone onto my bed, with no idea what I was supposed to do now.

Lexi watched me carefully. "I'm guessing that wasn't good news?"

I sighed. "No. I'm stuck in Ridgewater for another few weeks. I can't hide out in my house forever. I'm going to start pulling out my hair."

She bit her lip and sat next to me on the bench, mulling over something. After a moment, she said, "Would it be so bad to go to school?"

"Yes!" I blurted. "They'll eat me alive in there."

"Well, I'm here for you, and apparently, Easton knows, too." She put her arm around my shoulder. "So if nothing else, you can come hang out at our house after school if you need a change of scenery."

I leaned my head on her shoulder. "Thank you for understanding. You're the best."

She patted my stomach. "Anything for you two."

———

IT ONLY TOOK two weeks of online school and endless hours of having to entertain myself to realize that there was no way I was going to keep this up. Grandma's house in the picture or not, I thrived on being around other people. That was what brought me to life. And after talking to my doctor, we both decided that it was probably best for me to go back to school. She worried I might become depressed, and that was hard on me and the baby.

So I pulled up my new stretchy pants, put on my cutest boots, tried not to think about how horrendous my roots were looking these days, and went to school.

The first day back was horrible. There was no way to put it besides saying it was one of the worst days of my life. Every fear I had had about showing up to school with my new growth came true.

The second day was just as bad. I would walk into my classes, sit in the back, and hope that no one would look my way. But apparently, no one had anything better to do with their lives besides talk about the girl who'd gotten herself knocked up in a foreign country.

Which was exactly why I was eating my lunch in the back corner of the girls' locker room.

*Disgusting, I know.*

Still, it was better than listening to everyone's whispers and assumptions on how I'd gotten myself pregnant.

My phone buzzed with an incoming text.

Easton: **Where are you eating lunch?**

Having nothing left to be ashamed about, I told him the truth.

Me: **The girls' locker room.**

Easton: **Gross.**

Me: **Yep.**

I took another bite of my sandwich and contemplated my life.

Easton: **Want to get out of here?**

Me: **What do you have in mind?**

Easton: **I know how much you like bowling.**

The bowling alley had been one of our favorite sneak-away spots last summer, since it was on the other end of town and no one from school ever went there.

It was tempting. But...

Me: **Wouldn't that ruin your perfect attendance record?**

Easton: **Says the girl eating her lunch in the moldy locker room. Let's get out of here. I only have PE and Physics after lunch.**

Was it completely stupid of me to consider this? We had said

118

we'd try to be friends—not that we'd really done a great job of it so far.

I looked around the dingy locker room.

Me: **Okay, I'll meet you at your car in five.**

---

WE GOT a lane at the bowling alley and put on the rental shoes I doubted the disinfectant spray really did much for.

"I don't know if you realize this, but I'm kind of a bowling pro now," Easton said, as he typed our names into the computer.

"Oh really? Because I don't know if that's humanly possible with how bad you were before I left." I smiled as I tied my shoelace—something that was getting harder and harder to do these days with my growing belly.

"You just watch and be impressed." He grabbed his ball and walked up to the lane. He stood there for way longer than I thought necessary, as if he was sizing up the exact position he'd throw the ball down. Moving an inch to the right, then an inch to the left.

"I think you're too far on that side," I called to him, jokingly.

He moved a centimeter to the right again then turned back with a grin. "Better?"

"Maybe. I mean, I guess you're the pro now so maybe I should've just kept my mouth shut."

His grin broadened, and the sight of him smiling at me did funny things to my chest. He had a great smile.

"Watch and be amazed," he called back over his shoulder, shooting me a wink. Then he pulled his arm back and flung the ball down the lane.

He knocked down two pins.

"You're a pro, huh?"

He turned back to me and raised his hands. "So I might've exaggerated a bit. But those two pins...they didn't stand a chance." I laughed, and his face brightened at my laughter.

I had missed this. Just goofing around with Easton.

His ball came back, and he went up to finish his turn. This time he knocked down three.

"See if you can beat that." He dusted his shoulders off in a proud gesture.

I raised my eyebrows. "Five pins is pretty impressive for one round."

He sat on the bench, spreading his arms across the back, and gave me a challenging grin. "I think that might be the high score of the afternoon."

I shook my head with a smile and grabbed my ball. It was one of the pink balls that the little kids used. I thought I could handle something heavier, but Easton wouldn't have it. Apparently, he wanted me to keep my baby safe.

I guess it was sweet in a way.

I threw the ball down the lane with much less finesse than Easton had. But finesse didn't matter as much as I'd thought, because my little pink ball knocked down seven pins on its first roll down the lane.

I spun around and faced him, my mouth open in surprise. "Who's the pro now?"

He clapped his hands and leaned forward, laughing. "Just show me up, why don't ya?"

Which is exactly what I did. By the end of the game, he had bowled eighty-five to my ninety-seven. Not my best game, but definitely not my worst. And the best thing to come from the bowling game was the perma-smile on my face. It was amazing how you don't realize how depressed you are until you're happy again. I had a feeling my doctor might prescribe more visits to the bowling alley if she found out about today. Easton had always been good at cheering me up when he wanted to.

"You wanna grab something to eat?" he asked as we put away our balls.

"I guess I could eat." It was only two-thirty, but I could always eat these days.

We went to the bowling alley's restaurant and ordered food.

"I've been craving one of these all week, so this is perfect," I said before taking a bite of my pastrami burger. And just like I'd imagined, it was delicious.

He took a sip of his soda. "Are pregnancy cravings a real thing?"

"Totally." I covered my mouth with my hand as I finished chewing. Then I washed it down with some root beer. "You wouldn't believe how many lemons I've eaten this month."

"Lemons?" He looked at me like I had suddenly turned orange with purple stripes.

I nodded, dipping a fry in my nacho cheese sauce. "I used to think they were gross, but the lady I lived with in Paris always had lemons with salt for an afternoon snack."

Easton scrunched up his face. "Salt on lemons? How is that good?"

"Trust me. It's delicious. In fact..." I looked over to the guy at the service bar then back to Easton. "I'll be right back."

At the counter, I waited for the twenty-something guy to finish filling a soda cup for the one other person who was at the bowling alley this afternoon.

He looked up at me as he put the lid on top. "What can I get for ya?"

"Do you have lemon wedges?"

"For your drinks?" he asked.

"Not exactly."

He looked at me curiously but shrugged like he didn't really care before grabbing two lemon wedges and placing them in a small plastic container.

When I returned to the table, Easton eyed the lemons for a moment. "What are those for?"

"Instead of explaining the delightful combination that is salt and lemon, I figured you should just experience it for yourself," I said with a smile.

With a wary glance, he picked up one of the wedges. I showed him how to sprinkle the salt evenly in a decent layer all over the lemon's surface, and then watched as he did it himself.

"On the count of three," I said, holding mine close to my mouth. "One, two, three." And then I bit into it, my mouth puckering with the sour but satisfying taste.

He hesitated for a moment, waiting to make sure I would follow through before taking a bite himself.

"Ahhh." He made a face and spat the lemon out. "That's just horrible." He grabbed his soda and gulped it down.

I laughed. "You're such a baby."

He shook his head. "How can you like that?"

I shrugged, still laughing at him. "It's delicious."

He licked his lips, like they still tasted sour. "I'll give you all my lemons from now on."

"Fine with me." I grinned.

He piled the wrappers and plates together on the tray and stood to throw it away. "Ready to go?"

"Sure." I dipped one more fry in the nacho cheese sauce, popped it in my mouth, and followed him outside.

He drove me back to the school to where my car was parked.

"Thanks for cheering me up." I unbuckled my seatbelt.

"It was fun. I've missed hanging out with you."

"Me too," I admitted. "Don't be surprised if I try to convince you to take me out again tomorrow."

I covered my mouth when I realized how that sounded. Like I'd thought this was a date.

"I mean..." My mind scrambled for a moment. "I didn't mean like a date. I know this wasn't a date. We're just friends. You're dating Mercedes."

"Actually, I'm not."

"You're not?"

He shook his head. "I thought you heard."

"Heard what?"

"That she's dating someone else."

"What? Who?" I furrowed my brow. I hadn't heard any of this stuff.

"A guy from your grade, Mark Lancaster."

"Mark Lancaster?" My jaw dropped. "But they hate each other."

He shrugged. "Well, they don't anymore. I guess Christmas break changed that."

"Weird."

"Not that weird." He shrugged. "I mean, *we* hated each other until about seven months ago, right?"

He had a point there. I rubbed my stomach absentmindedly before realizing I couldn't do things like that when talking about us. If I did, he would pick up on it and wonder why. And I couldn't have him figuring it out.

I cleared my throat and looked at him. "Sorry she cheated on you. That has to sting." I watched for any sign of pain in his eyes. Had she hurt him?

He shrugged like it really didn't bother him. "We weren't exclusive. Just went on a couple of dates. I'm really not that worried about it."

"Well, you're better than me. I'd probably egg Mark's house if I was you."

"Does that mean you approve of me egging your Paris dude's place?"

I froze. So the thought of me sleeping with another guy had really bothered him a lot.

I guess that made sense. When I found out he was dating Mercedes, I'd wanted to cut off her hair in her sleep or claw at her perfect porcelain skin with a fork.

Yeah, I'd blame those vicious thoughts on my out-of-whack pregnancy hormones. I wasn't normally a violent person, I promise.

"If I find out his address, I'll give it to you."

He gave me a sad smile. Did the idea of me being with someone else really make him that sad?

Guilt flooded me, but I pushed it away.

Him being sad about me hooking up with someone else was much better than him being devastated because he was the real father.

"How's the adoption process going, anyway?"

I shrugged. "I found a website with links to lots of prospective parents' profiles, but I haven't really looked."

"I'm going to Ithaca Saturday night to try to see my mom, but I could help you look at some profiles that afternoon. I'm a good judge of character."

It would probably be good to let Easton have a say in who raised his baby.

"Sure, that would be great."

I would just continue to ignore the little voice in my head that told me he deserved to know the truth.

# CHAPTER FOURTEEN

"THESE PEOPLE LOOK NICE." Easton held his phone out Saturday afternoon so I could look at the couple he'd been reading about.

Easton, Lexi, and I were all hanging out at my house, browsing different adoption websites in search of the perfect family for my baby.

I took his phone from him to check out the couple. On the screen was a photo of a nice-looking man and woman. They held each other in a sweet embrace as they smiled up at me.

"They do look nice," I said. I scrolled past the photo to read a little more about them. They were in their early thirties and had been married for seven years. They were hoping to adopt a baby boy since they already had a two-year-old girl who they'd adopted from South Korea two years ago.

I continued reading until another photo popped onto the screen. This one was of them with their daughter who looked like she was laughing.

"Their little girl looks happy, I guess." I rubbed my stomach hoping to feel some sort of inspiration from the baby. I didn't nec-

essarily believe in fortune tellers, or voodoo magic, but if the
baby kicked like crazy when I was looking at a particular couple, I
would take it as some sort of sign.

I had no idea what I was doing here and could use all the
inspiration I could get to help me find the right couple.

But so far, the baby just seemed to be sleeping through the
whole thing because nothing had happened yet, even though
we'd gone through thirty profiles.

Easton's deep voice interrupted my reading. "They live in
Pennsylvania, which isn't too far to visit every so often if you do
an open adoption."

I nodded, overwhelmed at everything I needed to consider.

Did I really want an open adoption?

As if sensing how overwhelmed I was, Easton took his phone
from my hand. "How about I text you the link, so you can just add
it to your list? You don't need to decide right now."

I sighed. "Thanks."

A second later my phone buzzed with the text from him.

"Do you guys think I should do an open adoption?" I looked to
Lexi and Easton for reassurance.

"It's really up to you," Lexi said. "I think Maddie said they
were a good thing. Right, Easton?".

He nodded. "There are pros and cons to it just like everything
in life."

"Pros and cons?" The way he said it made it sound like he
thought there were more cons than pros.

"One of the biggest pros is that you get to choose the parents
yourself, which is why we're looking at profiles, right?" he asked.

"Yeah," I said.

"Getting to talk to the parents ahead of time can help you feel
more comfortable giving your baby to them. And then after that,
you can have contact—however much or little you and the adoptive parents decide on. I think this will show the kid they weren't

just dumped somewhere randomly because you didn't care about him."

"Dumped?" Lexi interrupted him. "Not sure that's the best word choice here."

Easton shrugged. "Sorry. Um...I guess what I'm trying to say is that it can help the kid know where they came from and why they were adopted in the first place."

I nodded. "Yeah, I was reading forums online a while back about kids who had no idea where they came from, and they had a really hard time dealing with some abandonment issues."

Easton looked thoughtful. "Either way you go about it is tricky. The whole situation is hard. But there are a lot of positives that come from open adoption, if that's the way you feel you want to go." Wow, he really must have done a lot of research on this when Maddie was pregnant. I knew he had kind of been her support system and gone to a lot of her appointments with her before she dared tell their dad, but I guess I didn't realize just how much he had learned about the process.

"But closed adoption is okay, too," Lexi added. "If you don't feel you can handle all this stuff, or it's too overwhelming for you, you can do that, too. There are loving parents waiting for a baby to love just the same. And maybe you could still write a letter to him or something, explaining why you did what you did."

"You think that's allowed?"

She shrugged. "I'm not sure, but it sounds like it should be."

I leaned back on the couch, feeling overwhelmed. Maybe I should just let my mom pick for me.

Easton touched my arm. "Remember, you still have a few months. You don't have to make all these hard decisions this minute. Give yourself some time."

"I just want what's best for him." I rubbed my stomach and stared at the ceiling, suddenly exhausted.

He gave my arm a squeeze before pulling his hand back. "We're here to support you."

I searched his eyes. He was being so sweet about this—both he and Lexi were.

Maybe it would be okay to tell him the truth. He'd probably be better at choosing the couple for me, anyway.

If he wouldn't try to make me keep it, that is.

Lexi glanced at her watch. "Well, I better get going. Noah's taking me on a date tonight."

"What are you guys doing?" I tried not to feel jealous of the fact that she had a boyfriend to do fun things with. It had been way too long since I'd been on a date.

She picked up her phone from the coffee table and pushed it into her back pocket. "He's taking me to dinner, and then we're going to play laser tag."

"Sounds fun." I forced enthusiasm into my voice. I didn't need to be jealous of my best friend. She deserved to have a great boyfriend like Noah. I was happy for her.

She bent over to give me a quick hug. "I'll see you later. Let me know what you need me to do for you."

I hugged her back. "Thanks. I will." And then she left.

I turned back to Easton, wondering why he hadn't left with his sister. There was a nervous expression on his face.

Was he nervous about being alone with me in my house again?

It was then I remembered what he had planned to do tonight. He was going to go see his mom.

He rubbed his hands along the sides of his jeans. "I guess I should probably leave. My mom's band is playing at eight, and you never know how the roads will be."

"Yeah, you don't want to risk missing it," I said.

He nodded, but he didn't look up.

"Are you nervous?" I asked.

He chuckled awkwardly. "A little. But I'm sure I'll live." His lip quirked up into a half smile.

"Would it help if I came?" The words were out before I thought them through. He wouldn't want me to go. We were friends now, sure, but not really the please-come-with-me-because-I'm-going-to-find-my-mom-who-I-haven't-seen-in-a-decade type of friends.

But his shoulders seemed to relax at my offer. "You wouldn't mind?" His tone was so hopeful I couldn't take it back.

I pressed my lips together. I didn't really have anything better to do. "Sure, why not? What are friends for?"

And that seemed to settle it.

I was going to meet my baby's grandma tonight.

***

EASTON WENT HOME to change his clothes before we left, wanting to look his best when he saw his mom.

I changed out of my sweatpants, deciding on a fitted navy-blue dress and heeled boots. There was no hope for hiding my belly anymore, so I might as well make it look as cute as it could be.

Plus, if I talked to Easton's mom, I wanted to make a good first impression—well, as good a first impression a pregnant teen could make.

I left a note for my mom, telling her where I would be and that I'd be home by midnight.

Soon we were on our way, driving to Ithaca mostly in silence. I could tell he was nervous about meeting his mom, so instead of trying to make conversation I knew he wouldn't be able to concentrate on, I watched him as we drove. It was dark outside, so only the lights from the dash or the oncoming traffic lit his face, but I couldn't help but admire him. He was so good looking, and I was still super attracted to him.

He had a nice nose—not too big, not too small. His jaw, while not as pronounced and squared as Noah's, was strong and slender. And I wished I could run my fingers along it one more time to remember how it felt.

His shoulders were broad, and his arms toned from years of chopping wood in his backyard.

"How are you feeling now?" I asked as we entered the city limits. The GPS on his phone said we'd arrive at the concert venue in eleven minutes.

"Honestly?" He glanced over briefly. "I feel like I'm about to throw up."

"Sorry about that."

He shrugged. "Hopefully, I won't chicken out. This is kind of a once-in-a-lifetime chance, I think."

I nodded. "Do you know what kind of band she's in? Is it a rock band, jazz, or a blues band?"

"I think it's more like a folk band. The pictures I saw online made them look like hippies."

I raised my eyebrows. "I cannot picture your dad being married to someone like that." His dad, a former drill sergeant, was all about structure and following the rules.

Easton merely nodded, his hands gripping the steering wheel tighter. "Which is probably why they're not together now. I think my dad was way too strict and she was too free-spirited for them to get along very well."

"Makes sense."

We drove through the town a little way until we came to a parking lot behind an older brick building. The sign outside was lit up with the words: "The Cornell Brew."

I had expected a much larger place, but maybe his mom was

just getting started in this musician thing. I guessed everyone had to start from somewhere.

We climbed out of the car and headed into the coffee shop. A tenor voice and a banjo greeted my ears as soon as we stepped inside the crowded venue. College-aged students with large mugs sat on couches and on just about every available seat they could find. And on the small stage was a college-aged guy with black-rimmed glasses, a white button-down shirt, and a banjo.

Easton turned to me. "Do you want something to eat?" The anxiety in his eyes was obvious. He was so nervous. I wanted to wrap him in a hug and tell him everything would be okay.

But since I didn't know whether he'd accept a hug or not, I simply nodded and said, "Food would be great."

I ordered an Italian club sandwich at the counter, along with a bottle of water, and was just pulling out my wallet to pay when Easton handed the cashier a ten-dollar bill.

"You don't have to buy it for me. I can get it myself," I told him.

He shook his head. "You're helping me out. It's the least I can do."

My chest warmed at his generosity. "Thank you."

"No problem."

It was then I realized he hadn't ordered anything. "Are you not hungry?"

He shook his head. "I can't really eat right now."

I couldn't eat when I was nervous, either.

We grabbed a tall, round table in the back corner. Easton wrung his hands as he looked anxiously around the room. His mom's group wasn't set to go on until eight, so we still had about five minutes.

"This sandwich is delicious," I commented, hoping to distract him for a moment. "You want some?"

I knew he was nervous, but I didn't want him to pass out from low blood sugar before his mom even came out. He had a fast metabolism and got lightheaded when he exercised without eating. This situation was probably similar to that.

"I'll get something to eat after."

The banjo guy finished his final song, and then a middle-aged woman went to the stage.

"Is that her?" I whispered to Easton.

He squinted his eyes for a moment, like he hadn't seen her yet. But when he realized I was talking about the woman on the stage, he said, "No, that's not her. My mom has bright red hair now—at least the pictures online made it look red."

The woman on the stage thanked everyone for coming and had us give the banjo guy one last round of applause.

When the clapping died down, she leaned closer to the microphone again. "We're excited to have September Road, a folk band out of Rochester here to sing for us tonight. Let's welcome them to Ithaca."

The crowd clapped politely, and soon, a lady with bright red hair appeared on the stage with two other guys wearing black hats. His mom looked younger than I'd expected, but still about ten years older than her bandmates.

"Thank you all for having us," Easton's mom spoke into the microphone, her voice surprisingly low, and she looked just like Lexi without the glasses. "We're excited to play for you tonight."

I watched Easton for his reaction to seeing and hearing his mom for the first time in over a decade and noticed his face had gone white. I reached over and placed a hand on his knee in what I hoped was a comforting gesture.

He looked at me and gave me a small smile before covering my hand with his own and squeezing it.

Their set lasted for half an hour. Easton gripped my hand tightly the entire time, not relaxing for a second. It was hard to watch him as he watched his mom, a mixture of hope and fear in his eyes.

This better not turn out to be a bad idea.

There was a thirty-minute break between their set and the next group. Once they finished, they put their instruments away and went to mingle with the crowd.

"I guess it's now or never." Easton sighed heavily when people started moving around and chatting with each other.

"Do you want me to come with you?" I asked, since he still had a firm grip on my hand.

He seemed to think it over for a moment before shaking his head. "This is something I should do on my own."

"I'll be here if you need me."

He finally let go of my hand and stood.

I flexed my fingers to get the blood flowing back through my veins properly as I watched him weave his way toward the stage. His mom was in the center of the crowd, talking animatedly with the people around her. A line had formed to greet her and her band, and Easton joined the end of the line.

He glanced back at me as if looking for reassurance, so I waved.

I hoped, for his sake, that she'd somehow recognize him after all these years. It would be hard if your own mother didn't know who you were—though he did look a lot different than he had in elementary when she left his family.

I took a sip of my water as I waited for him to near the front of the line. I must've taken just one sip too many because I suddenly had to go pee.

I sat in my seat and crossed my legs, hoping that I could put off going to the bathroom for a little longer. Easton needed me. I couldn't be in the bathroom when he spoke to his mom.

There were still two people ahead of Easton when the baby

sat on my bladder just right, making me feel like I was going to explode.

*Mean baby.*

I rushed to the bathroom, hoping I'd make it back in time to see how his conversation went. But there was an endless line in front of the women's bathroom, and of course, no line for the men's.

I tapped my hand on my thigh and shifted my weight from side to side as I waited. Why had I drunk so much water?

When I finally made it out of the bathroom, I scanned the room for Easton. But he was nowhere to be seen and his mom was already talking with another group of college-aged kids.

I walked around and searched the crowd, but I couldn't pick out his light brown hair. After making a few circles around the room, I grabbed my coat from my chair and gave him a call.

His phone rang and rang before eventually going to his voicemail. But that made sense because the room was loud, and he probably couldn't hear the ringer, anyway.

After another few times around the room without seeing him, I decided to check outside.

A cold breeze whipped at my cheeks as I opened the door, the bell ringing above my head. I walked down the sidewalk and turned the corner to head toward the parking lot. It was then that I saw him sitting on a bench behind the building.

"Easton," I called to him as I approached.

He looked up at me before wiping his arm across his eyes.

Oh, no. Something was wrong.

# CHAPTER FIFTEEN

I QUICKENED my stride and sat down on the bench beside Easton, putting my hand on his knee.

"What's wrong?"

He shook his head but didn't say anything, and when I looked at him, it broke my heart. His lips were trembling as he stared straight ahead at the street lamp, tears streaming down his face.

"Oh no, Easton, what happened?" I instinctively put my arms around him.

He didn't say anything at first, just clung to me like I was his lifeline as his body shook with the light sobs he was trying to suppress.

"Easton?" I asked.

He shook his head and pulled himself away, and this time, he looked at me with his watery eyes.

He swiped a hand across his face. "She didn't want to talk to me."

"What?" I went still, not believing what I thought he'd just said. "She didn't want to talk to you? How—? Why—?"

He shrugged, tears trickling down his cheeks and his lips still quivering with emotion. "She told me I shouldn't have come. She didn't want to see me or be reminded of her past."

I shook my head and raised an eyebrow. "That doesn't make any sense."

He let out a shaky breath and raised his hands at his side. "She said this wasn't the place to talk to her, and that I needed to move on with my life and forget about her."

"How could you forget about her? She's your mom."

"I don't know. And I didn't really know what to say to her, either." He sniffled. "I didn't expect her to respond the way she did. I thought things would go so much better."

I sat there in shock for a moment. "I'm so sorry. Never in a million years did I think it would go like that."

He nodded, and his tears slowed. "I don't know why I even tried this. I haven't seen or heard from her in forever. Of course, she didn't want to see me."

How could his mom treat him like this? He was her son. Her only son.

*Just like the baby I was carrying was my son, too.*

Was this how my baby would feel when he found out he was adopted? Was I as bad as Easton's mom?

I put my hand on his shoulder and rubbed his back, pushing those thoughts away. This was different. She was in her twenties when she had Easton. She'd been married to his dad.

"Don't question yourself," I said, not knowing if I was talking more to myself than to him. "You had good intentions. Of course you were curious. I would be if I were you."

He nodded again. "My dad always said we should just forget about her. But I never understood why."

Would my baby's adoptive parents tell him to forget about me, too?

We were quiet for a moment, and then he said, "You know what the worst thing is?"

136

"What?"

"When I asked her if she had ever thought about us, or regretted leaving us, she said she never did. She never regretted it even once."

My heart hardened in my chest. "I think I'm going to go slap that woman right now."

He reached out and grabbed my hand before I could stomp off. "It won't do anything, Juliette."

"It'll make me feel better. How could she say that to you? I wanted to give her the benefit of the doubt all these years, but maybe she really is just a horrible person."

He sighed and slumped down against the bench. "I don't think I'll be missing her much anymore."

"Wanna get out of here?" I asked.

"Yeah, let's go home." He stood and held his hand out. I hesitated, not sure what he meant by this gesture. We had held hands in the coffee shop because he was nervous. Was this just like that again? Or was something else behind it?

I took his hand and let him help me to my feet, deciding that I didn't need to figure it out right now.

We were quiet again on the ride home, each lost in our own thoughts. I didn't really feel like bringing up what had happened back there with his mom but figured he was probably thinking about it. So we listened to music all the way back to Ridgewater. The baby started kicking, so I put my hand on my stomach to see if I could feel it. His kicks had been getting stronger and stronger lately, and it was kind of fun...if not scary at the same time.

Easton glanced at me and down at my stomach. "Is the baby kicking?"

I nodded. "I think he liked my sandwich too, because he's been kicking like crazy."

"It did look tasty, though I'm not sure how it tastes second-hand." Easton smiled, and I was glad to have a lighthearted moment after such a heavy one. "So, you put your hand on your stomach—does that mean you can feel the kicks on the outside now?"

I looked down at my stomach briefly before turning back to him. "Yeah, it's been pretty fun to feel him getting stronger. It no longer feels like little fluttery movements. Instead, it's more like these tiny little punches."

"I think I remember Maddie talking about that. I always wondered what it would feel like to have something moving around inside. But I guess I'll never really know."

I laughed. "Yeah, let's hope you never figure that out. Because I think you look a lot better as a guy."

"Just like you look a lot better as a girl."

I couldn't keep my cheeks from blushing at his comment and was thankful for the dark.

He cleared his throat. "I'm proud of you for going back to school this week even with how hard it's been. You aren't regretting it too much, are you?"

"Kind of." I sighed.

"Yeah?"

I shrugged. "Honestly, I'm hoping some other scandal happens on Monday to make everyone forget about me."

"We could always announce that I tried to talk to my long-lost mom this weekend and got turned away."

I let my eyes linger on his face, our eyes locking in understanding for a moment. "I guess that's one way to remind me that I'm not the only one who has problems, huh?"

"I was joking, Juliette." He reached over and grabbed my hand, intertwining his fingers with mine. "But you're really strong, you'll get through this. And for what it's worth, I'm here if you need me."

Our hands fit so perfectly together, and I couldn't help but think his hand in mine just felt right.

"Thank you." And the meaningful look on his face made my stomach do a flip. He was being so sincere and sweet even after what he'd just experienced.

He held my hand the rest of the way to my house, and I found myself watching the clock, wishing that the drive home would go on and on. This moment was just too nice to say goodbye to.

But the lights of Ridgewater soon appeared, and I knew this peaceful and happy moment was coming to an end.

Why couldn't time just stand still when things were good and fast forward through the hard times? As soon as Easton dropped me off, things would go back to normal, and we'd go back to being awkward friends.

I wanted more.

A few minutes later, we pulled up to my house. and Easton parked his car in front of my yard. My heart deflated, knowing it was time for me to unbuckle and say goodnight. I released my seatbelt and put my hand on the door handle.

He cleared his throat. "Is it okay if I walk you to your door?"

My chest lightened. Maybe he wanted to hold on to this moment as much as I did.

Or maybe he just wanted to make sure I didn't slip on the ice and hurt the baby. He'd been doing a lot of that this week.

Before I could answer, he climbed out and jogged around to the other side, and then opened my door.

"Such a gentleman." I smiled at him.

"I don't know if I'd go that far." He winked. He didn't take my hand again as we walked up the sidewalk to my house, and I tried not to feel sad about that. It had probably just been a fluke in the car and at the coffee shop.

I tried the doorknob on the door to see if it was unlocked, but it wasn't. My mom had probably stayed late to help clean up the community event.

"Do you want to come inside for some hot chocolate?" I asked as I searched my purse for my keys.

Easton glanced at the front door, a wary look on his face. "I should probably go home."

*Shut down.*

Ouch, that hurt.

I couldn't look at his face, feeling my cheeks burn with embarrassment. "Okay. Well, thanks for walking me to the door."

*Where are my keys?* I dug through my purse more urgently. I needed to get inside and hide now.

He cleared his throat. "I-it's not that I don't want to, but, um, I'm just trying to follow my dad's rules of not being alone in a girl's house."

Okay. Maybe he wasn't completely shooting me down.

"That's probably a good rule," I said when I couldn't think of anything else.

"Yeah."

When I didn't find my keys in my bag, I dug through my coat pockets. But they were empty.

"Is something wrong?" he asked.

"I must have left my keys in my room."

"So you're locked out?" he asked.

"I'll have to go through the garage, I guess."

I typed in the code and the garage door lifted. Easton followed me inside.

I tried the door that went into my house, and thankfully, the knob twisted open. "Success!" I said before turning back to him. "Thanks for making sure I got inside okay."

"Thanks for coming with me to Ithaca. It was good to have someone there."

"Anytime."

And now would be the time for me to go inside my house.

But my boots seemed glued to the cement step. Saying goodbye or goodnight to Easton had always been hard.

He didn't seem in a hurry to leave either, because he wasn't stepping away. He just looked at me with those soulful eyes of his.

But why?

I sighed. It didn't matter why. I was going inside now. I would lift one foot up, and then the other, and leave Easton alone in the garage.

I turned away from him.

"Hey, can you wait just a second?" Easton's voice startled me before my foot could come unglued.

I turned back to him, and I hated that I probably looked super hopeful.

He shuffled forward until he was standing on the step just below me. "Can we just keep this between you and me?"

This? What was he talking about?

Was he talking about me and him...?

I shook my head. "I don't want to have any more secret relationships, Easton. It never ends well."

His brow furrowed. "Secret relationship?"

"You wanted to keep this between just us." I pointed to myself and then to him.

That was what he'd been talking about, right?

Realization dawned on his face. "Oh, I was talking about us going to visit my mom. I was just making sure you weren't going to tell Lexi."

"Ooooh," I said. "Well, that was awkward."

He smiled. "What did you think I was talking about?"

"Um, nothing."

I turned to head inside, horrified at how good I was at digging holes for myself to step in. But he grabbed my hand, stopping me.

"Did you think I was suggesting another secret relationship

with you?" His voice was low, making my bones melt and shake at the same time.

"I just misunderstood you. Don't try reading into it." Even though he was only touching my hand, my whole body burned.

I wanted him.

He joined me on the top step. "You said you weren't into secret relationships, but what about an out in the open one?"

I pinched my lips together, feeling my eyes go wide. What was he suggesting?

*Was* he suggesting something?

Or was my brain just hallucinating right now?

Were pregnancy hallucinations a thing?

I needed to look that up online.

He inched closer and shut the door to my house before I could escape through it.

"Do you ever wish we could go back in time?" he asked.

I met his gaze, which was so intense it scorched my insides and scrambled my thoughts.

But regardless of whether my brain was working at full capacity or not, my mouth had always been great at mumbling a bunch of nonsense. So before I knew what I was saying, I blurted, "Um, yeah, I think it would be cool to go back in time. I'd love to see if cavemen were real or watch Jane Austen as she wrote her novels and see if there was an actual Mr. Darcy who inspired her —" I drew in a deep breath, hoping the oxygen would help.

"I'm not talking about time-travel. You know that's not what I meant, right?" Easton stepped even closer to me.

"Y-you didn't?" I stumbled backwards and lost my balance.

Easton reached out and grabbed me before I could fall. "No, I didn't."

"Then what did you mean?" My voice came out in a whisper.

His blue eyes pierced mine, and I almost melted into a pile of goo as he spoke. "The thing I want most right now is to pretend that we could go back in time. Back before the camping trip. Back before I said and did a lot of stupid things." He lifted his hand to my cheek and ran his thumb gently across my skin, making it tingle. "Back before I broke your heart."

"Me too," I squeaked. Oh, how I wished I could go back in time. More than I could ever let him know.

And all I could do was just stand still, watching him with scared eyes because I was so breakable right now. Everything in my life was such a mess, and Easton had the ability—with a single look or word—to either put me back together or completely crush me to pieces.

"I miss us, Juliette." His voice was low and husky. "Miss how I felt when we were together." He rested his forehead against mine. "Can we just pretend..." He released a shaky breath, his minty breath warm on my face. "I want to pretend for just a minute..." And then his lips were on mine, just the lightest of touches, but it was enough to send a pulse of electricity across every nerve ending in my body.

And it might have been completely stupid of me, but I stopped thinking about all the reasons why we couldn't be together and kissed him back.

I missed us too, and I wanted to pretend that everything was okay. Just for a moment.

I curled my fingers into his hair and pulled myself closer to him. And when he wrapped his arms around my waist, it felt even better than I had remembered.

He kissed me again, soft and slow, his lips weaving a spell over my mind that I didn't have the willpower to resist, and we fell into an easy rhythm as our mouths seemed to remember exactly what to do.

His hands pressed into the base of my back as they'd done many times before, telling me he was strong and secure. I could trust him.

"Tell me you missed me, Juliette," he whispered against my lips.

"I missed you," I admitted. I'd missed him so much.

He deepened the kiss and my brain went foggy. It was like I was waking up from a bad dream and nothing had actually gone wrong between us.

His hands moved in slow circles along my spine until they came to rest on my hips.

It was then that I immediately snapped back to reality and remembered why I couldn't kiss Easton.

I was pregnant. I needed to keep my distance, not jump into his arms.

"Stop. Wait." I pushed myself away from him.

He went still, so still it was like he was a statue, and when I stepped back farther to create space between us, I saw pain reflected in his eyes.

"What's wrong?" he asked, hurt apparent in his voice.

I shook my head, trying to reign in my emotions and not burst into tears over the fact that the last few moments had been perfect but couldn't ever be repeated.

"I can't pretend with you, Easton," my voice cracked with emotion.

"Why?"

"Because things are different now. I..." I drifted off, knowing I couldn't explain.

"Is it because you're pregnant?"

I looked up at him, scared that he had figured it out somehow. "Yes..." I said cautiously.

He took my hands in his. "That doesn't matter to me anymore. I know I reacted badly at first, but I got over it. It wasn't my place to feel betrayed. We weren't together."

I shook my head. He was being too nice.

"Don't shake your head like you don't think I'm sincere," he said, misunderstanding me.

"I'm not."

"Then why are you still pushing me away?" He ran his thumbs over mine. "I understand that what happened between us made you do things you wouldn't have normally done. But we could be great together. I'll help you get through this. Then once you've placed the baby up for adoption, it'll be like this never happened. Things can go back to normal."

I looked away, feeling the tears press at the back of my eyes. "You don't understand, Easton. It can't go back to how it was before."

I needed to just leave him before all my secrets came spilling out. I drew in a shaky breath. "I think you should leave."

I pulled my hands from his and opened the door to my house and went inside. But he followed right behind me, flicking on the light in the kitchen. "I'm not going until you tell me what's actually going on." He ran a hand through his hair and sighed heavily. "Is it the Paris guy? Are you in love with him?"

"No. Of course not."

He didn't look like he believed me. "Then why? I felt the way you were kissing me back there. That was real. As real as any kiss we've ever shared."

"It was pretend."

Anger flashed in his eyes and his jaw flexed. "Are you ever going to forgive me, Juliette? I said I'm sorry. I don't know what else I can do." His head fell back as he looked up at the ceiling in defeat.

"I know. It's me."

He lifted his hands at his sides. "How is it you? Because I've seen the way you've looked at me. It hollows out my stomach and makes me crazy at the same time."

"I'm not the same girl I used to be."

He stepped closer. "How?" This time he was demanding, and his voice was getting louder, angrier. "How are you so much different? Is it because I'm not cultured enough? Because I don't speak another language and haven't ever been to a foreign country like you?"

I shook my head, so frustrated because he wasn't just letting this go easily. "It's because I'm tired of lying to you. And if we were together, it would just get even worse."

"You're lying to me?"

"Of course I am." I threw my hands in the air. "Do you really think I could sleep with some guy in Paris when I was still in love with you?"

His jaw dropped, and I covered my mouth before I could say anything more.

"What are you saying, Juliette?" His eyes tightened with fear.

I had said too much. I had just told him I hadn't slept with a guy in Paris.

I shook my head, my hand still over my mouth. How could I ruin all my months of planning in a matter of seconds?

Easton stepped closer. "Are you saying that the..." He pointed to my stomach and swallowed. "Are you saying that...that the baby is mine?"

My heart raced and my chest felt tight, making it hard to breathe, and then everything suddenly went black.

# CHAPTER SIXTEEN

"JULIETTE!"

I opened my eyes to find Easton hovering above me.

*What?*

I looked around and realized that I was lying on my back on the kitchen floor.

"What happened?" I asked, my voice coming out confused and disoriented.

"You passed out." Easton took my hands in his and helped me to a sitting position, so I could lean my back against the kitchen island.

"I passed out?" I scrunched up my face, trying to remember what had happened, but there was nothing. Just a blank space in time that didn't exist anymore.

He leaned back on his haunches. "One minute you were talking, and then the next you collapsed to the ground before I could catch you."

I rubbed the back of my head where I must have hit it on something. "How long was I out?"

"Only a few seconds."

So weird. I'd never done anything like that before. The last thing I remembered was... I closed my eyes and groaned. The last thing I remembered was Easton finding out that the baby was his.

"Is something wrong?" he asked, unnerved by my groaning.

I dug my fingers into my hair. "I'm just remembering what was going on before I passed out." Maybe it was another one of those fight-or-flight reflexes. Instead of facing Easton when he found out the truth, my body had decided that it was better to blank out on him.

Well, at least it had seemed to calm us both down.

He cleared his throat, breaking me out of my thoughts. "So, I know this is bad timing and everything, but I'm going crazy here." He inhaled through his nose and released a breath through his lips. "Is that baby really mine?" He pointed to my stomach.

Instinctively, my hands went to my belly as if it could help protect me somehow. "Yes."

It was his turn to collapse now. But instead of fainting like I had, he simply dropped from his haunches on to his butt in the middle of my kitchen.

He was silent for a moment, probably processing this information. But then he looked sideways at me with an almost hopeful expression. "You're not just trying to find a guy to help you since Paris guy is impossible to find?"

I tried to force my feelings of frustration down because I knew I had brought this upon myself. "It's yours. I'm farther along than I told you originally, and you're the only one I ever..." I let my voice drift off, raising my eyebrows so he'd get the hint that I hadn't had sex with anyone besides him.

He lay all the way back on the tile floor, placing his arm across his eyes, like he was trying to block everything out.

"Sorry," I said when he didn't say anything for a long time. "This was the last thing I wanted to tell you."

We didn't talk for a long while. He just stayed on his back, looking up at the light on the ceiling, seeming to process everything. Was he scared?

Worried about what his dad would say? Did he officially hate me?

I looked down at my stomach, rubbing it gently with my hand. And then I realized I hadn't felt the baby move for a while. Had my fall hurt him?

Easton turned his head to the side again and watched me.

"What?" he asked.

"I haven't felt the baby move since getting home."

He sat up faster than I'd ever seen him move. "Do you think he got hurt when you fell?" His voice sounded urgent.

I frowned and touched different spots on my belly to try to find the baby, but there was nothing. "I can't feel him." I looked up at Easton, feeling scared. "What if I just killed him?"

Easton scrambled to his feet. "We better get you to the hospital."

I nodded and let him help me to my feet. Everything needed to be okay. Easton already found out about the baby. This drama would all be pointless if the baby just died in the end.

We didn't talk on the way to the hospital. Easton just drove as fast as he could, skipping stop signs and looking over at me every few seconds.

His expression became increasingly worried with each shake of my head that told him I still hadn't felt the baby move.

The lady at the emergency room told us to go straight to the labor and delivery wing, and before long, the nurses had a room ready for me.

"Any movement yet?" Easton scooted his chair to the edge of my bed.

I shook my head. "No."

The nurse came in a second later, wheeling an ultrasound machine behind her.

"How long has it been since you felt the baby kick?" she asked as she got the machine set up to use.

I tried to remember.

"You felt it on the car ride home from Ithaca, right?" Easton leaned closer and gripped my arm with his hand.

I nodded.

"Did you feel anything after?" he asked.

I tried to remember what had happened afterward. Easton had walked me to the door. We'd gone in the garage. He'd kissed me.

I felt my cheeks burn at the memory of the short kiss.

And then I'd remembered the baby and my secret, and I'd gone into the house.

"I don't remember feeling it after that," I whispered, nervous to know that was the last time the baby had ever moved.

The nurse looked slightly worried at my answer.

Did that mean she already knew? Was that something that always happened when pregnant ladies fell?

"How far along are you?" she asked.

"Twenty-four weeks."

"And you just fell to the ground, without tripping or getting pushed?" She eyed Easton.

Did she think he was abusive or something?

She totally did.

I tried to keep the annoyance out of my voice when I spoke. "Yes, I just passed out without any warning." Did she seriously think that just because I was a pregnant teen that it must mean Easton and I were horrible people?

*Hello, sometimes people just make mistakes, lady!*

I had to work hard to keep from growling at her for passing judgement.

The nurse nodded and had me lift my dress, so she could do

the ultrasound. Thankfully there was a blanket covering my lower half so Easton didn't get too big of an eyeful.

A few seconds later, the familiar black-and-white image was on the ultrasound machine's screen.

I held my breath as I waited for the verdict.

She turned the volume up on the machine, and a moment later, I heard the most beautiful whooshing sound ever. The baby had a heartbeat.

Tears pricked at my eyes as relief washed over me.

"He's okay," I whispered, looking at Easton.

But Easton didn't look as relieved as I felt. Instead, he stared at the screen with a strange look on his face. And I realized what this moment probably felt like to him. Until earlier this evening, he had no idea that the baby was his, and now he was looking at his baby for the first time.

I reached over to take his hand, hoping to offer comfort in what had to be a super confusing and overwhelming moment.

The baby was more developed than he'd been the last time I'd had an ultrasound. His hands were bigger, legs were stronger— everything about him was just more like a real baby than it had been before.

The nurse seemed to check a few more things before wiping the goo off my stomach and putting the ultrasound transducer back.

"I can't see anything wrong, but it would be a good idea to contact your doctor on Monday to talk about any concerns you may have."

"Thanks," I said. Then I looked warily at Easton, still not sure how he felt about this whole thing. He was just staring blankly ahead at a painting on the wall.

The nurse eyed him curiously. She'd seemed suspicious of my fall earlier; was she thinking he was disappointed that the baby seemed fine?

I couldn't keep my brain from being so paranoid about what she might be thinking now.

But she said nothing; instead, she turned her attention back to me. "If you have any worries about not feeling the baby move, you can always try the orange juice trick before coming in next time."

"The orange juice trick?"

"Yes. If your baby is being less active, you can drink a glass of orange juice and then lie down on your left side so you can do your kick counts. The juice usually excites the baby and will get him moving around a little bit more."

Okay, the juice trick. I would try to remember that for next time.

There were so many things to worry about.

I made ready to leave, glancing back at Easton to see how he was doing. He didn't look like a zombie anymore, but he still didn't look too good.

The nurse walked us to the door and down the hall toward the nurse's station. "I do recommend that you take it easy for the next few days. Try and stay down as much as you can. And if you notice any spotting, be sure to call your doctor immediately."

I nodded. "Thank you."

She went behind the counter and typed something on the computer. I was about to leave when I recognized another couple standing at the nurses' station. It was the woman I'd seen at my first appointment, Nadia. And she looked extremely distressed. Much different from how she'd been at the doctor's office that day.

"I think I'm having contractions," Nadia said to someone at the desk.

"How far along are you?" the nurse with curly blonde hair asked.

"Only thirty-two weeks." Nadia's face was pale and contorted in pain as she touched her stomach.

My nurse must have noticed that I was staring at Nadia and her husband because she stepped from behind the counter and gestured at the doors. "The exit is that way. Have a good night."

Not missing the blatant hint, I tore my gaze away from the worried couple and let Easton lead me down the hall. I looked back for one last glance at Nadia, only to find her doubled over in pain again.

Her baby was trying to come much too early. She was only thirty-two weeks along.

What if that happened to me?

I really hoped everything would be okay.

# CHAPTER SEVENTEEN

I TOOK it easy the next day, doing homework and watching a lot of TV, and trying not to move around too much in case it made me start spotting or go into pre-term labor like Nadia did. Besides being worried about the baby, I was also super sore. It took me a while to figure out why I hurt so much, but eventually, I realized it was because I'd fallen from a standing position on the hard tile floor, so of course I'd have bumps and bruises...even if I had no recollection of it. But the doctor said I shouldn't need to worry as long as it didn't happen again, so she gave me the go ahead to go back to school on Tuesday.

Things went better than they'd gone the first week, but I still had a lot of people staring at me as I walked down the halls.

I hadn't talked to Easton since Saturday night and Lexi had said nothing about him either, which made me think he hadn't told his family what he'd found out from me.

I felt super guilty about how he'd found out. He'd just been rejected by his mom, and then to find out he had fathered a child —and all of these happening in one night...

He was probably a mess.

I sat at a lunch table with him and Lexi, but he might as well have not been there because he was so distracted for the first twenty minutes, and then he started just kind of glaring at me.

"I'm going to head to class early," I said to everyone after receiving another uncomfortable glare from Easton.

"Is everything okay?" Lexi asked, looking at my half-eaten lunch.

"Yeah, I'm not very hungry today," I said.

"Do you want me to come with you?" She gave me a worried look.

I forced a smile onto my face, only eyeing Easton for a moment. "I'm fine. Just ready to get to class."

I emptied my tray into a garbage bin and escaped through the exit that went past the auditorium.

"Hey, Juliette."

I turned to find Easton jogging toward me.

I paused. He'd been so hot and cold that I had no idea what to expect from him this time.

He came to a stop in front of me. "I need to talk to you."

*Oh no. What does he want?*

"Okay," I relented.

He looked around for a moment before leading me into the hall by the band room that hardly anyone ever went in. He stopped me in a little alcove and then turned toward me.

"What did you want to talk to me about?" I asked, eager to get this over with.

He crossed his arms. "I've been thinking about things over the past couple of days and can't figure out why you tried to keep the baby a secret from me. Do you not think I'd be a good father? Were you scared of me?"

I stepped back, shocked that he'd assume those were my reasons. "Of course not."

"Then why didn't you tell me? When have I ever done something that would make you think you had to go behind my back and give my baby away?"

"Because I know you." I lifted my hands helplessly at my sides.

"What's that supposed to mean?"

"Do you want the truth?" I asked.

"Of course."

I leaned back against the brick wall. "I knew you'd want to do the *honorable* thing and keep the baby."

"And what's wrong with that? It's my baby. I should raise it."

I shook my head. "But that's not what I want to do. Do you think I *want* to be a mom at seventeen?"

"No." He crossed his arms. "But that's how life works. Things happen, and you have to adjust."

"This is exactly why I didn't want to tell you." Anger began to simmer in my veins. "I don't want to be pressured into doing something I'm not ready for."

He was quiet for a moment, and I could see the cogs working in his head as he pieced everything together.

I was nervous when he turned back to me. "Were you really going to give away my baby without telling me?" he asked.

I looked away, wiping a tear from my eye as the reality of this new situation came crashing over me. He was going to do just what I had feared. He was going to try to get me to keep the baby.

"I'm not ready to be a mom." My lips started to tremble. "I can't do it."

He just watched me for a while, not saying anything as I tried not to cry. I couldn't be a mom. Not a good one, anyway.

Instead of showing empathy for me, though, his voice was bitter. "You shouldn't have made the decision for me. I deserved to know."

I looked up at him through my teary eyes. "Well, you know now."

"Yes, I do."

We were silent for a while as I tried to stop my tears from falling. I couldn't go to class looking like this.

I glanced at Easton, wondering why he wasn't leaving.

He took a drink from the water bottle he'd brought with him. "So how much longer do you have?" He eyed my stomach.

"What do you mean?"

He peeked around the corner, up and down the hall as if checking to make sure no one was within hearing range. Then he turned back to me and lowered his voice. "When's the baby due?"

I swallowed. "May eighteenth."

He twisted the cap on his water bottle. "That's just a month before graduation."

I nodded. "Yup."

"Would you be more open to keeping the baby if we were together?" He looked at me through his lashes.

I shifted against the wall, feeling uncomfortable. I'd thought about that a few times as I'd daydreamed about us getting back together. I still cared for him and thought he was a great guy...possibly one of the best guys I knew when he wasn't worried about the consequences of having sex too young.

But getting together because you loved each other was one thing. Getting together because you were having a baby was an entirely different thing.

So I drew in a deep breath and said, "I don't think so. I would still only be seventeen, and I think this baby deserves to have parents who are married and committed to each other for the rest of their lives. I grew up without my dad and I don't want that for my baby."

"But I'm willing to be a dad," he said, irritation in his voice.

"The problem is that you aren't willing to let me try." He ran a hand through his hair. "I just don't feel like adoption is the right thing to do when he can be with his biological parents. It'll be hard, but I'm sure our families will help. My dad did a lot for Maddie and Grant. He can do it again. We can do this."

Okay, now I was getting frustrated. He had known for...what? *Three days* that the baby was his?

I'd had months to think about it and had done research into the different options ahead of me.

I narrowed my eyes. "Why were you so supportive of adoption before and now you're suddenly saying it's a bad thing?"

I mean, he'd been so sweet earlier, helping me look for prospective couples on Saturday afternoon. Now it was becoming this horrible thing in his eyes.

"Because it's *my* baby and not some foreign douchebag's. And that single fact changes *everything*."

---

EASTON AVOIDED me for the next few days. He found a different table to sit at during lunch, and whenever I went over to hang out with Lexi, he always found a reason to leave the room.

It was unavoidable to escape each other entirely, though, because the Stevens's house and our school weren't *that* big.

So I became a master at scanning the halls for Easton and taking different routes when the situation deemed necessary. This was why I stopped when I came to an intersection on Friday and looked both ways to make sure Easton wasn't within sight. The coast was clear, so I joined the throng on their way to the lunchroom. I was starving today, so instead of waiting to get in line with Lexi and Noah, I continued with the crowd toward the main lunch line.

And just because I couldn't ever be completely lucky, I ended up getting stuck standing behind a group of senior basketball players: Chance Clemont and his minions, who were known to play basketball hard during the week and party hard on the weekends.

Currently, they were ragging on each other and talking about their celebration plans for after tonight's home game—most of which involved hooking up with girls at the unchaperoned party Chance was throwing.

I tried to ignore them, looking at my phone as I waited for the line to inch forward. They'd gone through their list of cheerleaders who they thought would be fun to invite, when I heard my name.

"What do you think about inviting Juliette Cardini?" Chance asked, and when I peeked at him, I caught a quick smirk on his face.

"Juliette Cardini? Who's that?" Trey Pratt, the point guard, asked.

Chance said, "Oh, remember the hot forward on last year's girl's JV team?"

"The one who got knocked up?" Trey asked, seemingly not aware that I was right behind him.

"I'm right here, guys," I said, hoping they'd stop talking about me once they realized Chance had only brought up my name because I was standing right there.

"Oh, I didn't notice you." Chance winked.

I wanted to punch that stupid smirk off his face. "Well, now that you know I'm here, you can stop talking about me."

Chance stepped closer, forcing me to retreat, my back against the wall.

He raised his eyebrows and dipped his head lower until he was invading my personal space bubble. "What do you say?

Wanna come to my party and let us show you how things get done in the good ol' United States?"

"Get done?" I asked, wishing I wasn't trapped between him and the wall and that he'd just turn back around and bug someone else.

He shrugged. "Well, I just figured that since you slept with all the guys in Paris, you'd be up for something this weekend. I mean, it's not like you can get pregnant again."

My mouth dropped, shocked that he would say something like that, but nothing came out.

He stepped even closer, taking advantage of my inability to respond or move, and whispered in my ear, "You can't tell me you're not interested."

Finally, my body decided to work again, and I pushed him away. "Get away, Chance. I wouldn't even share an Uber with you."

Anger flashed in his eyes. "So just how many guys did you have to sleep with to get pregnant, Juliette? Five? Ten? Twenty?"

"Shut up." I crossed my arms, daring a glance around the room and noticing that we had drawn a crowd.

He raised his eyebrows. "What, you don't like people talking about what a slut you are? Why did you keep the baby, anyway? Were you in love with this foreign douche? If it was mine, I'd tell you to—"

Chance didn't finish his sentence because suddenly Easton was yanking him away.

"Leave her alone, Chance," Easton bellowed.

Chance's jaw flexed and he turned on Easton, getting right up in his face. "Why do you care what I say to her?"

"Because it's not right to talk to a girl like that."

"Ooh, Easton Stevens coming to stand up for his little sister's best friend. Always playing the hero," Chance said in a mocking tone. Then his expression became more serious. "We all know you wouldn't touch her with a ten-foot pole. Not now that she's infected with some other guy's baby. You have your *purity* rules and all."

Easton moved closer, and the look in his eyes had me scared about what he would do to Chance.

When he spoke, his voice was low and threatening. "Be careful what you say. You have no idea what you're talking about."

"Really? I know exactly what I'm talking about." Chance stepped toward Easton, towering over him.

"You need to leave Juliette alone. She's *nothing* like what you're saying."

Chance glanced over at me then back to Easton. "She certainly looks like she slept around Paris."

"I said to stop it." Now they were only inches apart. Easton's jaw tightened.

"Why?" Chance challenged him.

"Because that's *my* baby you're talking about, Chance." He pushed Chance hard, forcing him back.

A hush fell over the crowd, and Chance's grin broadened as he caught his balance. "You're Juliette's baby-daddy?" He laughed. "Mr. I'm-Too-Righteous-To-Hook-Up was already getting it with his sister's friend? This is too good."

I didn't know what I was supposed to do. Easton had just admitted, in front of a huge crowd, that he was my baby's dad.

Before I could do anything, Easton did something I'd never seen him do before. He punched Chance in the face.

My whole body shook as I watched Chance wipe at his nose and Easton push his way through the crowd and head for the exit that led to the parking lot at the back of the school.

"Easton. Wait!" I called as I chased after him, my heart pounding in my ears.

He didn't turn around, so I went as fast as I could down the sidewalk to try to catch him as he stormed away.

He turned on his heel to face me. "Please stop running, Juliette. I don't want you to slip on the ice and hurt the baby."

I stumbled to a stop just before crashing into him. "Please talk to me," I said, out of breath.

"I don't think—" he said before we heard another voice behind us.

"Easton? Juliette?"

I turned to find Lexi with a shocked look on her face. I blinked my eyes shut, knowing what was coming.

"Is it true?" she asked sadly. "Are you the girl...?"

This was about the last way I wanted her to find out.

She would never trust me again.

My mind scrambled for some way to explain without looking like the worst friend in the world. But there was nothing, because I really was that bad of a friend. I had snuck around behind my friend's back to date her brother. Lied to her for months. And then I'd told her that the baby was some other guy's.

She had trusted me, and I'd completely ruined it.

I sighed and held my hands up when nothing came to my tongue.

Easton stepped beside me and slipped his arm around my shoulder—like he was going to steady us both in the storm we'd created.

"It's true, Lexi." His voice was solemn. "The baby is mine."

Lexi shook her head, and I could see that she was struggling to keep her emotions under control. "How...?"

I stepped forward. "I wanted to tell you..."

She wiped at a tear beneath her glasses. "Why did you lie to me?" She shook her head again and crossed her arms over her chest as she shivered. "How could you both lie to my face for months?"

"I'm sorry," I said, lamely. "I didn't want to."

Noah came out the door, his expression worried as he looked from Lexi to Easton and me. Then Chance and his gang came out behind him, apparently ready to watch a possible showdown.

"We'll talk to them later," Easton's voice was in my ear as he eyed Chance. "Let's get out of here." And then he took my hand and pulled me toward his car.

# CHAPTER EIGHTEEN

EASTON and I ended up at the bowling alley ten minutes later, not talking as we drove. We ordered food from the same guy who'd been working the grill last time, and then sat in our regular booth.

Easton sighed and slouched against the faded red booth, letting his head rest against the top of the seat. "I'll probably have to tell my dad tonight, now that the whole school knows, huh?"

He looked so lost right now that I wished I could make him feel better. But there was really nothing I could do. We had made our bed, and now it was time to sleep in it—no matter how messy it was.

"Do you want me to come with you?" I offered.

He closed his eyes and shook his head. "I don't think he'll like having an audience when I drain the life out of him."

I dipped a fry in the nacho cheese sauce, imagining Mr. Stevens when Easton told him. This would kill him. I could just see that big man collapsing onto their living room couch when Easton told him the news.

"You sure you don't want me there?"

He sighed and sat up straight again, taking one of my fries. "No, I'll do it myself."

"I guess that means I'll have to tell my mom who the real father is."

We locked gazes for a moment, each of us probably picturing how our separate conversations would go. I had a feeling mine would probably go a lot better than his. For him, his dad would get the bombshell that another one of his children had made a baby. For my mom, she was just going to find out who my partner in crime actually was.

Maybe she'd be relieved—if Easton came around to my plan, we wouldn't have to deal with the thirty-day waiting period before someone could adopt the baby. He'd be able to sign his rights as soon as possible.

Unless he convinced me to keep the baby...which I had a feeling he would not give up on anytime soon.

"So, do you want to go back to school after this?" Easton asked as I took a bite of my pastrami burger.

I chewed and swallowed. "I don't know. We kind of made a big scene back there."

He set his soda down on the table. "Chance Clemont is a jerk."

"Yep."

"I can't believe he had the gall to say that stuff to you. He's lucky I didn't throw him down."

I smiled at the image that came to my mind of Easton tossing Chance to the floor. Chance was a couple inches taller than Easton. But Easton was built like his dad and had muscles to go along with his height where Chance was still a bean pole.

"I bet you could take him," I said.

He returned my smile and held up his hand with his finger and thumb an inch apart. "I was this close to doing it."

I took a sip of my water. "Thanks for stepping in for me. I appreciate it."

He nodded, his expression going more solemn. "I couldn't stand by and let them talk to you that way, especially when I knew none of what they were saying was true."

I dipped my head down, having a hard time meeting his gaze. He was such a great guy. He'd risked his reputation to save mine. "Well, I appreciate it."

We both reached for a fry and electricity crackled where our fingers touched.

I looked shyly away as I dipped my fry in the cheese sauce.

Easton cleared his throat. "Now we have to smooth things out with Lexi and Noah."

I released a long breath as the image of Lexi's betrayed face came to mind. "I think we really hurt her."

He balled up his hamburger's wrapper and tossed it on his plate. "She'll get over it."

He said it like it was a sure thing, but I didn't know. I had betrayed her trust and lied to her so many times already. Could I really hope she'd be willing to forgive me again?

I checked the time on my phone. Lunch period was long over, and it was already fifteen minutes into the next period.

"Do you want to head back to school? Or do you think the bowling alley is a sufficient enough lesson on the laws of physics for today?" I asked.

He glanced at the bowling lanes and then back to me. "I think bowling might just be the lesson I need today." He gathered up our trash. "We can worry about facing the new rumors at school tomorrow."

EASTON and I stopped by Emrie's on our way back to the school so we could pick up a pint of Lexi's favorite ice cream. I figured that if I was going to beg for forgiveness, it might be a good idea to show up with some ammo.

I waited for Lexi at her locker, holding the ice cream in front of me. "I'm sorry, Lexi."

Her eyes stopped on the ice cream for a minute before she pulled some books out and dropped them in her backpack. Then, as if I was invisible, she shouldered her bag, shut her locker, and turned to walk toward the parking lot.

I hurried after her. "Are you not even going to acknowledge me now?"

She shrugged as I got in step with her—thankfully, she was short and didn't have as long of a stride as I did.

"I don't know why you're so worried about me talking to you now. Apparently, you haven't been so keen on talking to me about stuff for the past six months. Not the important life-altering type of things, anyway."

I groaned and put my hand on her arm to stop her. "Please, just talk to me."

She turned to face me, her arms crossed and her toe tapping on the shiny tile floor impatiently.

"You have any more lies you want me to hear?"

I wanted to roll my eyes but didn't, because I knew I deserved it.

"Can I just give you a ride home and talk to you for a few minutes? I promise I won't bother you after that. I just need to explain."

She pursed her lips. Then she grabbed the ice cream and spoon from my hands and said, "Fine. But not until after I've eaten this entire thing."

I gave her a small smile. "Thank you."

LEXI WAS true to her word. She didn't say anything until she had eaten the entire pint of ice cream.

For a girl who was so small, it was amazing how much she could pound down when she wanted to.

I pulled up to the curb in front of her house and she opened her door to climb out. Was she going to just take her ice cream and run?

But she turned toward me and said, "You might as well come inside and talk. That ice cream made me thirsty."

So I followed her into her house.

Lexi grabbed herself a glass of water, and then we went downstairs to talk in their family room. She looked like she had a lot of questions for me, but instead of asking any of them, she just stared at her glass of water and rubbed the condensation off the sides.

I cleared my throat and decided it was probably best to just get started. "So I pretty much wanted to tell you that I'm really sorry that I never told you about Easton and me dating."

She nodded. "Yeah, that is quite interesting. And I've been wondering all afternoon, when exactly did you and Easton date? He was always either at work or with Noah or us together. There aren't that many spare hours in a day."

"It started last July."

I didn't say anything more, but then she looked at me like I was stupid. So I continued, "And as for how, I guess I just have to say we were really good at sneaking around right beneath everyone's noses. It's not as hard when everyone thinks you hate each other."

"But that still doesn't tell me *when* you actually had the time."

I looked down and picked at a loose string on the couch cushion. "Remember how I didn't have a job and my mom was always working, and you spent a lot of time babysitting Grant?"

"Yeah."

"Well, on one of those bored-out-of-my-mind days, I decided to get some ice cream and see how annoying I could be to Easton while he worked."

"So you started secretly dating Easton behind my back just because you wanted to annoy him?"

I shook my head. "No, that's not what it was like. Yes, I did want to see how far I could push his buttons while he was at work, because I knew he couldn't treat a paying customer rudely and still hope to keep his job. But, I don't know, after a while it was just fun hanging out with him."

"Why didn't you have me tag along with you?"

"Part of me just wanted to get used to doing things on my own for a change. I knew I'd be in Paris soon, and so I wanted to get used to being more independent."

"Except you weren't really by yourself, were you? You just replaced me with my brother."

Wow, she really was mad at me. I had never seen her like this before. Usually she was so nice to everyone, always going out of her way to make things better for people.

"I can see why you'd say that."

"So, was sleeping with my brother part of your endgame? Were you trying to see how far you could take things before you went off to Paris?"

What? Did she seriously think that?

My mouth hung open for a moment before I could respond. "Do you really think that about me, Lexi?"

She shrugged one shoulder, a frustrated look on her face. "I don't really know what to think about you anymore, Juliette. You've told me so many lies."

My jaw tensed, and tears pricked behind my eyes. "It was

nothing like that. Yes, we did sneak around behind everyone's backs, and I regret that. I wish I could go back and do things the right way, but the fact is that I can't. All I have is now. Which is why I'm trying to fix things."

"Only because you got caught though, huh?"

"Maybe this was a mistake," I said, readying to stand.

Lexi set her glass on the side table. "Juliette, wait. I'm sorry, I didn't really mean any of those things. I'm just mad right now."

I stared at her, not understanding what was happening. Finally, I swallowed and said, "I'm really sorry for all the lies I told you. I can't say enough how sorry I am."

She looked at my stomach and her expression softened. "I know, Juliette. I'm sorry that I'm being so mean right now."

I nodded. I could understand some of that. Hurting people hurt people. I had hurt her, and so she wanted to hurt me back.

"So from what I'm hearing," Lexi said. "You and Easton had this super-secret forbidden relationship that was exciting, and you just wanted to keep it that way because it was fun?"

"Yeah."

She nodded. "I guess I can't really fault you too much for that, since I kind of did the same thing with Noah just a few months ago."

"Except you didn't keep it a secret from me." That was how we were different.

She was nice enough not to say "well, duh" to me.

Instead, she asked, "Did Easton know all along that the baby was his?"

I shook my head. "He just found out on Saturday. I had hoped to quietly have the baby and not ruin anyone's lives in the process."

"And are you two secretly dating again?"

I shook my head again. "We pretty much broke up when this

happened." I pointed to my stomach to show that we'd taken things too far and the guilt afterward had ruined us.

She nodded her head solemnly. "But do you wish that you were still together?"

She watched me for my reaction, and I knew what was written all over my face. I still cared about her brother. And yes, I wished we could be together.

"I'll take that sad look on your face as a yes, you're still in love with my brother."

I nodded, a wave of emotion rushing over me. I missed Easton. I missed us. I missed how I felt when we were together. I missed how he used to look at me, and hold me, and kiss me. I wanted that so much.

But things were so messy between us it was hard to think that they could ever work out.

So I changed the subject.

"On a scale from one to ten, how badly do you think your dad will react when he finds out he has another grandchild on the way?"

Lexi sighed. "I'm thinking a ten, though seventeen might be more accurate."

I bent over and put my hands on my face, rubbing up and down it to relieve some tension. "That's what I was afraid of."

"Yeah, pretty sure he'll put me on birth control after this. Even though Noah and I have no plans of needing it in the foreseeable future."

"Sorry about that."

She nodded. "Yeah, I guess we can just thank my dad and my mom's amazingly fertile genetics."

I couldn't help but wonder if my parents would've had more children if my dad hadn't died so young, since apparently, I was super fertile, too.

*Guess I'll never know.*

"How many times did you and Easton..." She didn't finish her sentence; her cheeks turned pink instead.

"Just once."

"And how was it?"

I raised an eyebrow. "Do you really want to know?"

Her cheeks turned darker. "I guess I probably don't. It's better not to know some things about your brother."

# CHAPTER NINETEEN

MY MOM WAS next on my list of people to confess to, and while the initial news that Easton was the father of my baby seemed to shock her, she took it in stride. I think me getting pregnant by one of Ridgewater High's honor students was at least a better story for her to spin to the public than the story of a reckless daughter abandoning all her morals once she was out on her own in Paris.

School was difficult for the next few days as students spread rumors about how I must have *made* Easton sleep with me. It was hard not to walk down the hall without hearing whisperings of how I seduced him into being my secret boyfriend and how I'd thrown myself at him, because otherwise it'd have never happened since he was such a good guy.

It sucked that everyone automatically tried to give him a pass in this whole situation, but I guessed that was just how things went sometimes.

It was getting to the point where I was tempted to go to one of the alternative high schools when thankfully, the gossip mill changed. One girl in my grade's dad had apparently disappeared without warning, and since the FBI were involved, Eliana Costa and her missing dad were suddenly the talk of the school and the whole town.

I felt bad for her but couldn't pretend like I wasn't relieved to have some of the pressure off of me.

I continued to go to my doctor's appointments, and the baby kept growing as the weeks went on—which was good, but also scary. The bigger he grew, the bigger he'd be when I had to somehow push him out of me.

"Mind if I join you?" Easton was sitting on the front porch of his house when I walked by one evening.

I had started going on walks once the weather got better, because April in New York was a beautiful thing. The snow had melted for the most part, and blossoms were blooming on all the trees.

"Sure." I stopped at the end of his driveway and waited for him. "I'm going to the park."

He nodded as he joined me, and soon we were headed down the sidewalk again. "I was hoping you'd go on another walk today."

"'Another walk'? Does this mean you've been stalking me this past week?" I asked with half a smile.

He laughed. "No, I'm just observant and have seen you walking past my house pretty much every day after I got home from lacrosse practice."

I didn't know how I felt about him keeping an eye on me. Over the past couple of months, we had come to a sort of truce. We were cautious friends. That was probably the best way to put it, anyway. We spent time together when I was with Lexi, and we had been getting along okay after the big showdown at school where he told everyone about our secret. But we didn't really talk about the baby, or what would happen when he was born. It was just easier not to argue.

"Did you ever tell NYU what your plans are for next year?" I asked him as we came to a stop at the intersection. We waited for a red car to drive past, and then hurried across the street.

"I told them I was coming, so they'd hold my spot. But..." He shrugged. "I'm also considering taking courses online so that I can stay close to you and the baby."

I rolled my eyes. "So you're still set on keeping the baby?"

He nodded. "Yeah."

"But what if I don't want to be a mom right now? How does that work into your plans?"

We turned the corner and headed south toward the park.

"Then I guess I'll be a single dad. My dad, as you know, isn't excited about the prospect of becoming a grandpa again, but he says he's willing to help out and support me where he can."

"But what if I want my child to have two parents—a mom and dad who are in love and committed to raising their child together?"

He kicked a rock off the curb. "Well, I haven't really figured that part out yet. But, I'm not planning to be single forever."

I stopped in my place. *He's thinking about finding another girl?* In all my thoughts of the future, I had never imagined this as a possibility.

"You're going to get married?" I swallowed the huge lump that had formed in my throat. "To someone else?"

He stuffed his hands in his pockets and turned to the side to face me. "I think that's usually how most people intend their life to go. Don't you plan to get married someday?"

"Yeah, I guess so." My eyebrows scrunched together. "I mean, not like right now or anything. But when I'm a little older and have more of my life figured out."

He nodded and continued to walk down the path, so I quickened my step to catch up. "I plan on the same thing, too."

We were quiet for a while as we walked past the old houses

that were painted green and blue and purple. And I tried to imagine this future that Easton talked about. The future where he married someone, and where I married someone else.

I shook my head. I didn't like that. I didn't like that at all.

Easton couldn't fall in love with and marry some other girl. No one else would ever be good enough for him. He was amazing. Smart. Strong. Kind. Thoughtful. Loving. Had a great work ethic. A strong sense of duty. And his eyes... I dared a quick look at him and my breath caught in my throat. Looking into his eyes was like looking into the ocean. They were cool blue—vibrant, yet peaceful and very much alive. He made me feel alive, yet calm and secure at the same time. He always had.

He was like the perfect guy. How could I find another guy just like him for myself? Someone who would be a great husband and be a great dad when the time came that I was ready to have kids.

I realized then that in the back of my mind, maybe I had always planned to end up with Easton when we were done with high school and in college or in our careers. Like a small piece of me had always expected that he would always be there in my future, kind of like how he'd always been there for me in the past.

I studied him as we approached the entrance of the park. He couldn't marry some other girl. He couldn't raise *our* baby with someone else. How could that even be a thing in his head?

He turned around and caught me staring at him. "What?" he asked.

I let my head fall back and looked up at the clear blue sky for a moment. "I don't know. I'm just so confused right now."

"What are you confused about?"

I shrugged. "I don't know, everything. My future. You. Me. Where we stand and what I want."

He nodded and looked down, his heels scuffing the sidewalk

as he lazily stepped one foot in front of the other. "I'm confused, too."

And for the first time since finding out I was pregnant, I wasn't certain I was making the right decision. Maybe finding another family for this baby really wasn't the best choice after all. Maybe I'd been wrong all along, and I needed to raise this baby with Easton. Maybe my future would be harder, yet still an amazing thing. Because if keeping the baby meant that I got to keep Easton in my life forever, wouldn't that be worth it?

I felt the baby rolling around inside and I placed my hands on my belly to feel him kicking. I cared about this baby. I wanted him to have the best future he could have. Was it possible that his future was actually meant to be with us?

We walked onto the bridge that led to a nice grassy area with the gazebo in the middle. But instead of continuing on to the gazebo, we stopped at the top of the bridge to look at the river below.

Easton leaned his forearms against the wooden railing and turned his head to the side, seeming to study me. "So what are you thinking about now?"

I gripped the rail with my hands, bracing myself against it. "I don't know, I'm wondering..." I bit my lip, not sure I really wanted to say what I was thinking about aloud because that meant I was seriously considering it. And I knew Easton would jump on any chance he had to get me to come to his side.

I closed my eyes. An image of him with our baby and another girl that wasn't me came to mind. A twinge coursed through my chest. I couldn't let that happen. I couldn't let some other girl raise my child with Easton.

I pushed the thought away and released a heavy breath before I spoke. I looked at him. "I guess, I'm starting to wonder if adoption really is the best choice for us."

I watched Easton carefully as his eyes widened and the first signs of hope showed on his face. "So you're actually going to consider keeping him?"

I swept a fallen blossom off the wood railing, hesitating for just a moment before saying, "I guess I am."

He put his arm around me and pulled me against him, kissing the top of my head. "I'm going to try really hard not to get my hopes up about us doing this together, Juliette. But I can't pretend that having you consider it as an option makes me more hopeful for the future."

# CHAPTER TWENTY

I STOPPED by Emrie's after dinner on Friday night. Lexi and Noah were out on a date, but the weather was so nice that I didn't feel like going home yet.

The hope of spending time there with Easton as he worked might have factored into my decisions a little.

Things had been good between us after our conversation in the park, and I daydreamed a lot about how things would be if we ended up together after all of this.

Like I had told Easton, I was entertaining the idea of keeping the baby and raising it with him. I still wasn't sure it was exactly what I wanted. But I had another month and a half to figure it out, so hopefully I'd have the clarity I needed by mid-May to make the best decision for everyone involved.

I stepped inside the ice cream shop to find Easton, with his little paper hat and apron on, wiping one of the tables clean. His uniform was dorky, but he still looked cute in it—it was hard for Easton to not look cute.

He looked up when he heard the bell jingle. And when he

saw me, his broad smile warmed me from head to toe. He was happy to see me.

"Hi, Juliette."

"Hi." I looked around the ice cream shop suddenly nervous. As I took in the old photos and classic 50s-style décor, I felt a sense of *déjà vu* from last summer. I cleared my throat before I could start fantasizing about kissing Easton in a booth. "I'm here to sample all your new flavors." I smiled, hoping he'd remember with fondness—instead of pain—all the times that I had done that last summer.

He finished wiping off the table and grinned. "Margaret created six new flavors since the last time you sampled them all."

"Six?" I raised my eyebrows, impressed. "Margaret's been busy."

"That she has." He walked past me to go behind the counter, and I joined him on the opposite side of the display case. "So, which ones are new?"

He pointed to a brown one that looked like it had caramel and chocolate chunks inside. "This one is Chocolate Mudslide, which is probably the ice cream flavor closest to what they serve in heaven." He winked at me.

I returned a smile, feeling giddy at his playfulness. "I'll definitely have to sample that one."

"This one is Orange Dreamsicle, another good choice." He pointed to an orange-colored ice cream. "And the others are Raspberry Mango Sorbet, Vanilla Bean Moose Tracks, Tahitian Paradise, and Chocolate Cinnamon Bear." He pointed to each one as he named them.

My ears perked up at the mention of Chocolate Cinnamon Bear. "You already know how addicted I am to chocolate-covered cinnamon bears, so I think I'll try that one first."

"That's what I was thinking when I suggested the idea to Margaret a few months ago."

"So you were thinking about me?" I asked, feeling brave for a moment.

His cheeks turned an adorable shade of pink, and I couldn't keep my smile from growing bigger.

He shrugged as he grabbed a small spoon from a red-and-white container by the register. "You might have crossed my mind once or twice while you were in Paris." He scooped some ice cream onto the sample spoon.

He wasn't looking at me. Was he embarrassed?

I decided not to say anything more about it.

He held the sample for me so I leaned close to the counter to take it, but my belly hit the glass way sooner than it had months earlier since it was huge now. Easton noticed my new situation and smiled as he extended his reach. Our fingers brushed in the exchange, and my skin tingled as my nerves remembered what it was like to touch Easton.

It'd been way too long since we touched, and I wanted to find an excuse to touch him even more.

It was like last summer all over again. He must have totally seen through my excuse of sampling every single flavor from the first time I did it.

I put the spoon in my mouth then slowly pulled it out, savoring the taste of the chocolate and cinnamon combination. "Okay, yeah, I definitely want a scoop of this one."

"I thought so." He winked.

I tried the other five flavors and had him add a scoop of rasp-berry mango sorbet to my cone as well. I was eating for two—it was only fair to the baby that I eat two scoops, right?

I looked around the room, trying to decide where I wanted to sit as Easton filled my order. There was only one other couple in the room in a booth in the back.

I didn't want to assume that Easton would join me in the booth like he always had last summer, so instead of going over to one of those, I walked toward the bar. I gripped onto the counter and had to stand on my tippy toes to reach the seat. In the past I'd always just plopped myself up there, but with a huge belly, it wasn't nearly as graceful an experience as I'd hoped. Instead, I had to scoot way back on the stool just to get my belly to fit behind the counter. And even then I had to hunch over to stay on my seat.

So classy.

"This thing is getting way too big." I pointed to my stomach as Easton scooped my ice cream into the waffle cone.

"I think you look great, Juliette." He glanced up from his work.

I leaned my elbows on the counter. "Pretty sure I look like a whale right now." It was hard to see all the girls at school wearing the latest spring fashion and not be able to be the trendsetter anymore. It just wasn't worth updating my wardrobe when I wasn't going to fit in my clothes for much longer.

At least I really hoped my belly would shrink back down after the baby was out.

Easton set the scooper back in its bowl of water. "You don't look like a whale, Juliette." He handed me my cone. And then he looked me over, a small smile forming on his lips. "You're beautiful."

My insides wanted to warm at his generous words, but there was no way he could think this was beautiful. I had gained thirty pounds since last October. Most days the muscles below my belly were just so tired and sore that I didn't want to get out of bed.

"You know it's not good to lie, right?" I said.

He shook his head and smiled. "I'm not lying, Juliette. You really are beautiful."

I rolled my eyes and licked the melting ice cream before it could drip down my fingers. "Well, you're only saying that because you have to."

He raised his eyebrows and crossed his arms. "Pretty sure I have freedom of speech and so, no, I don't have to say anything if I don't want to."

"Well, you did this to me, so I'm pretty sure that you do."

He gave me a frustrated look before leaning over the bar so our faces were only inches away from each other. "If I didn't think you looked totally hot right now, then why am I having such a hard time remembering why I shouldn't just take you out back and kiss you like I used to?"

I froze as chills raced up my spine. He couldn't be serious. Could he?

But when I met his gaze again, his eyes were intense, and I got the feeling that maybe he really meant what he was saying.

I swallowed hard and spoke as calmly as I could, hoping he couldn't see how flustered his words had made me. And I pretended to be my old, bold self and said, "Maybe you should try it sometime."

His gaze fell on my lips for a second, making my heart bang against my ribs. "Maybe I will."

I couldn't breathe. Seriously, I needed to get oxygen into my lungs or I might faint from the way he was looking at me.

Would it be so bad if I grabbed his hand right now and rushed away to the back room?

The couple in the corner seemed like they'd be talking for a while, and no one else was in here.

Easton glanced at the couple as well. Was he thinking the same thing I was?

But then the door jingled behind us and broke the staring match we were having. A middle-aged couple walked in with two young children and a baby.

Before going to help the family with their orders, Easton whispered to me in a voice that no one could hear. "I get off at nine-thirty. I'm up for a late-night walk in the park if you are."

My cone almost slipped from my hands as the words and their possible implications washed over me. But I switched my grip and worked to rein in my excited emotions so I could say, "Come by my house when you're off. I'll be ready."

EASTON KNOCKED LIGHTLY on my front door right at nine forty-five. I pulled on my oversized hoodie, which was the only warm jacket that could fit me these days, and met him on the porch.

"Ready?" he asked, and there was an anticipation in his eyes I hadn't seen in way too long.

"Ready," I answered. I was more than ready to see where things could go between us. More than ready to kiss him again if that was on the table.

I leaned back into my house to tell my mom I was going out for a walk with Easton.

"Just be back by midnight, okay?" she called back.

"I will," I told her before shutting the door.

"My dad expects me home by eleven, so you should definitely be back by midnight," Easton said as we strolled down the sidewalk.

"You still have a curfew even though you're eighteen?" I asked.

He shrugged. "My dad may know that I can't get you pregnant *again*, but that doesn't mean he's still not paranoid."

"I guess that makes sense." Though I had noticed his dad loosening up a little. Lexi had been sure that he was going to put her on birth control after he found out about Easton and me, but he'd surprised her by not saying anything about it. It seemed like maybe he'd realized that hovering over his kids constantly had made them *more* likely to sneak around and not less.

We made it to the park about fifteen minutes later, walked across the bridge and stopped in the little gazebo. The park was technically supposed to be closed at dark, but hopefully we wouldn't get caught breaking the rules.

"How was the rest of work?" I asked Easton as we sat down on a bench.

"Good. That family who came in while you were there ended up making a huge mess, and the baby wouldn't stop crying...but aside from that it was slow."

I frowned at his mention of the baby crying. Would *our* baby cry a lot? I'd never been very good with Grant when he had cried as a newborn. I wasn't the "baby whisperer" like Easton had been.

"What are you thinking about?" Easton reached over to touch my knee, breaking me from my thoughts. "I can tell from the look on your face that you're thinking about something."

I shrugged and played with the strings on my hoodie. "I'm wondering how much our baby will cry."

"Probably only when he's hungry, needs a diaper change, or is tired."

"Yeah?" I asked hopefully. That didn't sound so bad.

But then Easton continued, "Or when he's uncomfortable, has gas, or is just having a grumpy day."

I shook my head. "So pretty much all the time then?"

He gave me a lopsided grin and squeezed my knee. "No, not all the time. And usually they're better for their parents because they know them and are used to their voice and smell." He looked down at my stomach. "Our baby is already used to hearing your voice all the time, so that'll give you an advantage when he's out."

"*If* we don't go the adoption route, that is." I raised an eyebrow, reminding him I still hadn't decided on whether I was keeping the baby.

Easton made a face that told me he didn't like what I'd said, and I worried I may have ruined the moment. But instead of jabbing back, he said, "Yes, if you decide to raise him, then you'll have a head start over me. I mean, I still haven't even felt him kick yet."

"Is that something you want?" I asked hesitantly. "To feel the baby kicking?"

He nodded. "Yeah, of course."

"All you had to do was ask," I said. Lexi had felt the baby kick tons of times as we'd hung out—I should have known Easton would have wanted to feel the baby, too.

"I didn't know if you'd be okay with it," he said.

Which made sense. We'd had an emotional barrier between us for the past couple of months.

As if on cue, the baby started thumping around.

"He's kicking now, if you want to feel," I said, hoping Easton wouldn't feel weird about touching my stomach.

"Can I?" There was an anticipation in his expression that made my heart squeeze in my chest.

"Yeah." The baby kicked again, so I quickly lifted my hoodie over the top of my belly, leaving just my stretchy T-shirt exposed.

He scooted closer and held his hands over my stomach before asking, "Where is he?"

"He's been kicking me here." I took his left hand in mine, trying not to feel too nervous about touching him again, and placed it on the lower right side of my stomach. "And here." I directed his right hand to the center of my stomach.

Easton went still and seemed to concentrate on what he was feeling, and I watched him for his reaction, hoping the baby would cooperate.

"Is he kicking?" Easton asked after a while.

I shook my head. "Maybe he has stage fright."

But the baby must have liked hearing my voice or something, because he kicked again.

"Did you feel that?" I asked, looking up and feeling hopeful.

He frowned and pressed his hand to my stomach a little harder. "No. Which hand would have felt it?"

I moved his left hand an inch higher. "He was just right there. Maybe he'll do it again."

We sat motionless for a moment, waiting. But after a full minute, there was still nothing.

"I don't think he likes me very much." Easton met my gaze.

"Maybe I should have drank orange juice before coming on this walk," I said, remembering the trick the nurse had told me at the hospital.

"Does it usually take this long?" he asked after another long moment.

"Sometimes. Did you ever feel Grant kick when Maddie was pregnant?"

He made a face. "No. That would be gross."

"How?" I asked. Did he think this was gross and he was just being nice?

"She's my sister and I was, like, fifteen. I wasn't going anywhere near that if I didn't have to."

"I guess I can understand that." And I was relieved he didn't seem to think me or my stomach was gross.

I felt a thump again. I watched for Easton's eyes to light up, but he must not have felt it.

So I moved his right hand slightly higher and then covered each of his hands with my own, putting enough pressure on them so that he should feel the baby kick the next time—if he kicked in the same spot, anyway.

Easton bent his head down close to my stomach, letting his mouth hover just an inch away from it, and then said, "Come on, baby. It's me, Easton...your dad." He glanced at me for a second as if to check on whether I was okay with him talking to the baby. My face heated up because it was such an intimate situation to be in, but I nodded for him to continue. "Come on, baby. You know you want me to know that you're real, right?"

The baby kicked me hard, right near where Easton had been talking to him, and Easton looked up with excitement in his eyes. "Was that him?"

I nodded.

He got the biggest smile on his face. "I felt him."

Then the baby started kicking like crazy, like now that he'd broken the ice with Easton he wanted to completely show off all the acrobatics he could do inside my belly.

"Whoa," Easton said when my stomach moved like a wave. "That's crazy."

I smiled, feeling super connected to Easton and the baby in this moment we were sharing. "It's pretty cool, huh?"

He nodded. "So cool."

The baby kicked again, and the expression on Easton's face melted my heart completely. He was in awe of what we'd made.

He pursed his lips together and looked at me carefully. "Thank you for taking such good care of him." His voice was gravelly. "Thanks for giving this baby a chance. I know it hasn't been easy, but for me, this one moment has made everything we've been through, everything with my dad and everyone at school, worth it."

If I wasn't already sitting, my legs would have turned into jelly because of his sincerity. I'd never had anyone look at me like this before, like I was this amazing person who was doing something great.

And for the first time since finding out I was pregnant, I did feel like I was doing something good. I was growing a baby. I had created life, and this baby had the chance to grow up and do great things in the world.

If I could bottle up this emotion that I was feeling and sell it, I could probably be a very rich woman. It was a different kind of high than I'd experienced before. *Love.* Love for Easton. And love for the baby.

I would give anything to make this moment last forever. And when I saw the love reflected in Easton's eyes, my whole body tingled.

I needed to be closer to him. And before I could really grasp what was happening, we were gravitating toward each other. I closed my eyes and leaned in even closer, my lips anticipating the moment they would brush against his.

But before we could kiss, a flashlight shone right in my eyes.

"The park is closed at dark." A gruff voice sounded from behind us, breaking me out of the trance I'd fallen under. I turned to see a white-haired cop just a few feet away, with his arms crossed. He was not happy to see us. "You two should not be here right now."

# CHAPTER TWENTY-ONE

EASTON and I walked home from the park after being interrupted by the policeman, neither of us saying anything about the almost kiss.

At least I thought we had almost kissed. I couldn't really know for sure, though, since it hadn't actually happened.

Hopefully, it hadn't all just been in my imagination, anyway. If so, I really might need to look into pregnancy hallucinations.

"Thanks for going on a walk with me." I pulled my house key out of my pocket as we stepped onto the front porch of my house.

He dipped his head down. "I'm glad we went. It was cool to feel the baby kicking. He seems so much more real now."

"He does." Which was scary and kind of exciting at the same time.

I wanted to ask how he felt about the baby now that he had felt him kick. But I wasn't sure whether I really wanted to know his answer because I still wasn't sure what I wanted it to be. A huge part of me was still overwhelmed with the thought of keeping the baby and raising him. There were so many things in my life that were not known yet. And most times, when I did think about keeping the baby, I mostly envisioned Easton...and then the baby as an afterthought.

That probably wasn't the best sign for someone on the precipice of becoming a mother.

"I better go," Easton said. "My dad is expecting me."

"Good night," I said, even though I didn't want to say goodbye just yet.

"Good night, Juliette. I'll see you tomorrow." And before I knew what was happening, Easton stepped closer and gave me a quick kiss on the cheek.

My skin warmed and tingled where his lips had been, and I couldn't keep the smile off my face. I covered my cheek with my hand and was happy to see him return my smile.

"Sleep well." He looked at me bashfully before stepping off the porch and disappearing into the night.

I SLEPT in the next morning after having tossed and turned most of the night. It seemed like my best sleep came after six a.m., so I was grateful that it was Saturday and that I didn't have to get up early for school.

The doorbell rang below as I brushed my teeth after my shower. A moment later, my mom's voice called up the stairs, "You have a visitor, Juliette."

I frowned and set my toothbrush back in its decorative holder, wondering who would be at my house on a Saturday morning.

I walked down the stairs in my pajamas. Standing in the frame of the front door was Easton, holding a huge curved pillow-type thing in his hands.

"Hi, Easton." I gave him a confused look.

"Good morning. How did you sleep?"

I made it to the bottom of the stairs. "Rotten for the first half of the night, and okay for the last half."

"I assumed that might be the case." He stepped forward and held out the pillow to me. "I heard you talking to Lexi earlier this week about how you have to use about a zillion pillows just to get comfortable. So I went online and found this. It just came in the mail this morning."

The white pillow was shaped like a funky-looking pair of stuffed giant pants. "What is that?"

He smiled. "It's a maternity pillow. According to all the pregnancy forums online, this is a lifesaver."

I took the pillow from his hand and checked the tag, which showed a picture of a woman lying on the bed with the pillow tucked under her head, behind her back, and then also between her legs. It was like she was sleeping with an upside-down "U."

But she had a soft smile on her face that would lead anyone to believe she was sleeping peacefully and dreaming wonderful dreams.

Easton cleared his throat. "Anyway, I just thought it might be something worth trying out." Now he looked uncomfortable. I didn't want him to regret bringing this to me.

So I put a grateful smile on my face. "This is super thoughtful. You're the best." I hugged the pillow to my chest. "I'm excited to give this a try tonight."

He nodded and smiled back, relief on his face. He stepped back. "Anyway, I'm just on my way to work, but I thought I'd drop that off first in case you wanted to take a nap this afternoon."

My chest warmed. "Thank you. I really appreciate it."

After he left, I shut the door and leaned against it, sighing and hugging the pillow. Easton really was a great guy. I would be the luckiest girl in the world if things ended up working out between us.

My mom came into the room, concern in her eyes. "What was that about?" She was sipping a mug of hot chocolate.

I held out the maternity pillow for her to see. "Easton brought this over for me."

"And what is that?" Mom furrowed her brow.

"It's a maternity pillow. Easton said it should help me sleep better."

She nodded and blew into her mug. "That was very thoughtful of him."

"He's a thoughtful guy."

Mom pinched her lips together, as if hesitating in saying what she was thinking.

"I know you're thinking something, Mom. What is it?"

"I'm just wondering where you're at right now. You and Easton have been spending a lot of time together this week, and I'm worried that's what made you change your mind about things." She sighed. "I know the Stevens family, and I know how strongly they feel about stuff like this."

"Easton's not a bad guy, Mom."

She leaned against the wall that split the entryway from the kitchen. "I never said he was a bad guy."

"Then what are you saying?" I asked, suddenly defensive.

"I'm just saying I remember the pressure that Maddie went through when she was pregnant, and I just—" She waved her hand in the air. "I don't want you to feel pressured into keeping the baby if that's not what you really want."

Had she been, like, eavesdropping on my conversation with Easton earlier this week? How could she even know I was rethinking things? I hadn't told anyone about it.

"A few weeks ago, you told me you wanted to find an adoptive couple that both you and Easton agreed on, but have you even been looking, Juliette?"

I looked down, not wanting to answer her.

"I know this is a hard decision," she continued. "But the baby will be here in less than six weeks, possibly even less if he comes early. You need to make these decisions now."

I leaned my head back against the door and sighed, feeling overwhelmed at all the decisions I had to make and the ticking time bomb that was about to go off inside me. I blinked my eyes shut and released a long breath. "I know, Mom. I'm trying to figure this all out. There's just a lot."

When I opened my eyes again, she was looking at me with understanding and compassion in her face. "I know it's not an easy thing, honey. But I want you to think really hard and long about what you want. Just you. You're the one who needs to make this decision for yourself, and you're the one who'll have to live with that decision for the rest of your life. I know you and Easton have a history, and he is a nice boy. But that is just one piece of the puzzle. Raising a child is hard. It's not something that should be taken lightly. It's a big decision to make, and once made, you'll have to live with the consequences, both good and bad."

"I know how consequences work, Mom." I was pregnant, for goodness' sake.

"I know, Juliette." She came to me and put a hand on my shoulder. "I just want you to think long and hard about why you would keep the baby versus why you'd place him up for adoption. It's a big deal. And I'm here to support you with whatever you decide. But I do feel like I need to remind you that raising a child is an eighteen-year-and-beyond commitment. If you're going to do it, I want it to be for the right reasons."

"So, in other words, right now you're thinking I'm considering it for the wrong reasons?"

"I think you might be trying to please someone else because you're afraid of losing him."

I looked down, feeling my cheeks burn because she was spot on. My mom knew me better than I thought.

She dropped her hand from my shoulder and shrugged. "Having a baby brings in a lot of difficult things—and having raised you on my own for the most part, I can tell you that it wasn't easy. I had your dad for the first few years of your life, but then I was doing it on my own, and I can't tell you how many times I wished to have him back—because I loved him, yes—but also because it would've been so nice to share the difficulties of life with someone. I just don't want that to happen to you. I don't regret having you, but I can't pretend like it was always easy. I just want you to keep that in mind."

"Of course I don't think it'll be easy. That's why I'm really thinking this through."

She pulled me into a hug. "I just want what's best for *my* baby. I want you to live the life you wanted to live, without regrets."

"But what if I decide I want to place the baby up for adoption, and Easton decides he wants to keep him?" Tears pricked at the back of my eyes. "Am I supposed to just pretend like it doesn't affect me, and like the baby was never mine?"

Mom pulled away and looked me square in the eyes. "I think it's important for you to talk to Easton about why exactly he wants to keep the baby. There's a big difference between doing something out of duty and doing something because that's what you really feel inside your soul is the right thing for you to do."

I shook my head, not wanting to think about all these things. I wiped at a tear that had escaped out of the corner of my eye and sighed heavily. "Making adult decisions is hard."

She nodded. "I know, honey. That's why I'm so worried about you having to make them while you're still just a teen."

I shook my head and hugged my maternity pillow to my chest. "I'm gonna go back to bed for a while," I said, suddenly feeling exhausted.

A minute later, I dropped the pillow onto the bed and

climbed in the middle of it, letting its softness comfort me in my confusion.

I couldn't deny that what my mom said made sense. Was I only entertaining the thought of keeping the baby because I was afraid I'd lose Easton without the baby tying us together? Or did I really want to be a mom to this sweet boy?

The uneasy feeling inside my stomach told me I knew the answer. I was only considering keeping the baby because I didn't want to lose Easton. But deep down inside, I knew I wasn't ready to be a mother. At this point in my life I couldn't give a baby what he needed: a mom who wanted to be a mom.

I was such a horrible and selfish person.

Did I really not have a single maternal bone in my body?

I closed my eyes as guilt washed over me. I knew what I needed to do. And doing it would risk fracturing the already unsteady surface Easton and I were standing on.

I needed to have another hard conversation with Easton and see if we could work things out in a way that was best for everyone.

I just hoped I wouldn't lose everything in the process.

# CHAPTER TWENTY-TWO

I MEANT to talk to Easton about our decision for the baby all the next week, but whenever we had a moment alone, I lost all my nerve because he was being so sweet about everything.

On the days he didn't have work, he would come over after his lacrosse practice and go for a walk with me because he knew I wanted the daily exercise.

I had signed up for a childbirth class a couple of months ago, which started on Tuesday. And instead of me going with just my mom, Easton asked if he could come too, because he wanted to know how to help me when it was time to have the baby.

He was being everything I'd ever imagined my future husband would be, and I didn't have the heart to rip the rug out from under him and tell him I didn't think I could raise our baby with him.

So I kept going through the motions, promising myself that *tomorrow* I would talk to him about it.

Tomorrow was always a better day to do it than today.

But as the days went on, I was running out of tomorrows.

When Friday came, I knew I had to force myself into it. So I went up to Easton in the hall between first and second period, and asked, "Do you want to go to dinner and a movie with me tonight?"

"Dinner and a movie?" he asked, his eyes brightening. "Like a date?"

I shrugged, hoping to come off like I didn't care how he answered, even though my insides were freaking out. "If you want to call it a date, then yeah."

He furrowed his brow. "Wait, but aren't I supposed to be the one to ask *you* out?"

That would be nice. But he was a high school guy, and they didn't always catch the hints their female counterparts tried to give them.

I cleared my throat. "It's the twenty-first century. I'm pretty sure it doesn't matter who does the asking."

My heart raced as I waited for his answer. I hadn't really considered what I'd do if he turned me down.

Thankfully, he didn't make me wait too long. The corners of his lips lifted up. "I'd love to go out with you tonight."

I smiled, and his smile broadened.

And when I remembered why I was asking him out on the date—the grin on my face faltered.

We had to talk about the future.

---

"CAN you believe this is the first time we've been on an actual date in public without worrying who might see us?" Easton asked after the waiter took our orders. We had decided to go to Texas Roadhouse for dinner since it was next to the movie theater.

"Usually, people like to go on at least one official date before they get pregnant, but I guess that was way too old-fashioned for us."

He laughed, and I was happy we could joke around for a moment.

It would be a good idea to let him get food in his stomach first before breaking the news that I couldn't keep the baby.

"So I've been thinking about how we'll work everything out once the baby's here, and I was wondering if you've thought of any names for him yet?" He stabbed his steak with his fork and sawed at it.

I looked down at my grilled chicken salad, trying to figure how to answer. How was I supposed to tell him that I didn't think we should have a say in what the adoptive parents named our baby?

I turned my fork in my hand. "I haven't really thought of any names."

He nodded thoughtfully as he chewed his food. He swallowed and said, "I was thinking it should be a super manly name. You know, I don't want teachers or other people getting confused by one of those names that can be used for either a boy or a girl, like Jordan, or Jaden. You know, names like that."

I swallowed my bite of salad. "Yeah, I agree." *I guess.*

"What do you think of Titan? Or Brody?"

I made a face. I did *not* like those names.

He noticed my expression and shrugged. "*Or* there are always names like Braxton or Cody."

"I like Cody. That's cute."

His face lit up, happy that I had liked one of his suggestions.

Before he could get his hopes up though, I hurried to say, "But I don't really want to get attached to any names right now."

His brow furrowed, and I worried I had just said too much. We still had the rest of dinner and a movie to get through. I didn't want to ruin the night right from the start.

Why had I suggested going on such a long date?

Probably because I really liked Easton, and I wanted to spend as much time with him before I pushed him away for good.

So I said, "What I meant was that I've heard people say that babies come out looking completely different than they had expected, and they want to name the baby after seeing what he looks like."

Easton seemed to relax. "Okay. I'm fine with making a list and then seeing what name fits his cone-shaped head best."

"Cone-shaped head?" My voice came out louder than I had planned and people at the other tables turned to look at us.

Easton smiled. "Yeah, Grant's head was so long when he was born. He looked like an alien."

"Is that normal? Or just a Stevens's family trait?"

Easton laughed. "I think it's normal. They have to squish themselves out somehow."

I crossed my legs as the image of a huge baby coming out of me popped into my head. This was going to hurt so bad.

"Is something wrong?" Easton asked. He was way too perceptive sometimes.

I played with my food for a moment. "I'm just imagining childbirth. I think I want them to knock me out while it's happening."

He reached across the table and touched my hand. "You'll be just fine. I'll be there to help you through it all."

I looked at his face, and he had such a sincere expression that I believed him. Everything would be okay. He would make sure of it.

But when he removed his hand to go back to eating, the anxious thoughts resumed. I couldn't think like this. I would not be raising this baby with Easton.

I pursed my lips and focused on my food for a moment. How was I supposed to handle this? Easton was set on keeping the baby.

But why? Out of duty, or because he truly wanted to be a dad at eighteen? I needed to do what my mom suggested and ask him why he was so against adoption.

But before I could ask, he started talking again. "I spoke to Maddie earlier, and she said we could have Grant's old clothes for the baby."

"That's really generous of her."

"She also said that Grant just switched to a toddler bed, so we can use his crib, too." He shrugged, like he had this all figured out. "I was wondering if you wanted to maybe put it in your room or something."

My eyes widened. Hearing how much he'd already planned for the baby was making things way too real.

He must've noticed the alarm on my face because he said, "Not that I expect you to keep the baby with you every single night. I mean, I guess if you want, I could have a crib in my room and you can get one at your house. We could kind of trade-off every night, so we could at least get some good sleep every other day."

I took a drink of my water, overwhelmed by everything he was suggesting. We would both still have at least another month of school once the baby was born. He would be preparing for graduation and beyond. His dad worked all day. My mom worked all day. Lexi was in school just like Easton and I were. Who would watch the baby for us while we were at school? And even then, how would I get my homework done after that? Even if we found a babysitter during the day, I'd still have homework and he would have work at Emrie's at night.

Easton may have thought through some of these things, but had he thought through *everything*? Did he have a solution for all the different scenarios that would need attention?

Yeah, sure he talked about taking online courses instead of going to NYU, but I still couldn't imagine expecting that from him. He would have to go to an actual school at some point if he still wanted to be a dentist. He couldn't just do all that hands-on work from the comfort of his kitchen table.

And how was I supposed to go to fashion design school and get an internship for one of the famous fashion designers in New York with a baby in tow? It was super expensive to live in Manhattan. How could I get an apartment big enough for me and the baby? And who in their right mind would want to hire an eighteen-year-old with a baby to work the long and odd hours required for fashion shows?

The more I thought about it, the more I felt myself slowly dying inside. And that wasn't how I should feel. The baby deserved someone who was excited for him to come. Not dreading it. He deserved two parents like I'd always wanted. A stable environment.

I drew in a deep breath, hoping to calm my crazy thoughts. "How about we just focus on this moment right now and have a good time at the movie? We can figure all this stuff out later."

Easton scooped green beans onto his fork. "I think it's important to have these conversations, but I guess it's okay to have fun for one night." He winked at me. "What movie did you have in mind, anyway?"

It probably didn't really matter what I wanted because I knew I'd just be thinking about all these things during the movie.

"I'm up for whatever you are."

"Really? That means you don't mind watching the latest kiddie show?"

"I like kiddie shows."

He studied me for a moment, and I got the feeling he didn't believe me, but that was okay. We would enjoy our dinner-and-a-movie date. And then I would pull the rug out from under him when I dropped him off at home.

# CHAPTER TWENTY-THREE

"I HAD A GREAT TIME TONIGHT." Easton unbuckled his seatbelt after I stopped my car in front of his house.

"Me too," I said.

*Just tell him you can't keep the baby. It's now or never.*

Or it was *now or later*...and now would be much better than telling him later when I was handing the baby over to a social worker.

His hand hesitated on the door handle.

"So are you going to walk me to the door or what?" he asked with humor in his voice. "You did ask me out on the date."

I smiled nervously before clearing my throat. "Actually, do you want to hang out a little longer?"

His eyes widened, and then a grin stretched across his lips. "Hang out?"

"I was thinking it would be fun to grab a blanket and look at the stars."

He raised his eyebrows, and I wondered what he was thinking I'd meant when I'd said *hang out*.

"I'll grab a couple of blankets from inside and we can head out back," he said.

His dad was sitting in their living room, watching some crime show when we walked inside.

"We're just going to head out back for a while," Easton told his dad.

Mr. Stevens eyed me, his gaze taking in my stomach for a moment before he said, "Just don't stay out too late. You have work in the morning."

I tried not to worry about how he probably thought I was trying to seduce his son again.

Easton grabbed two quilts from the family room downstairs and led me out back.

Their backyard was awesome. It had tons of trees around the perimeter, but there was a small hill right in the middle of the lawn that Lexi and I had spent many summer nights reclining back on and just looking at the night sky.

Easton spread out a red-and-blue quilt on the grass. Then he opened the other one and placed it across our legs as we huddled together on the ground.

"Do you know what this reminds me of?" Easton asked after we'd settled in. It was chilly outside, but every point of contact between us was super warm. I probably should have suggested we do something else, since my brain was having a hard time remembering why I'd suggested we come out here in the first place. Instead, it kept thinking about how nice it was to be cuddled up beside Easton and how it would be so easy to forget all my worries and just kiss him instead.

It would certainly *feel* nice, anyway.

But I needed to focus on what he was saying instead of the way his mouth moved as he spoke.

"What does this remind you of?" I asked, once I remembered his question.

"It reminds me of when we got snowed in at Noah's cabin."

I smiled. "That seems like so long ago."

He nodded. "A lot has changed since then, and yet, not a lot has changed at the same time."

I knew what he meant about the things that had changed. He knew I was pregnant and that he was the father.

But what did he mean by what hadn't changed?

"Are there things you wished had changed since then?"

He looked at me, and it was a quiet look that made my stomach muscles tighten.

"I wish you trusted me more."

"I do trust you."

"I don't know." He shrugged and trained his gaze at the night sky. "It feels like you have all these walls up and that you're afraid to let me in again."

I looked up at the sky as well. It was super clear tonight, and the stars were bright. The expansiveness of the universe made me feel so small. Was I making a much bigger deal out of these things than necessary? Did my choice really not matter that much in the grand scheme of things?

I spoke in a quiet voice. "I'm not trying to have a ton of walls. I just..."

"You're just worried I'll hurt you again?" He peered over at me.

I shook my head. "I'm worried *I'm* going to hurt and disappoint *you.*"

He reached his arm around my shoulder, pulled me closer to his side, and kissed the top of my head. "You couldn't ever disappoint me, Juliette. You are amazing."

I nuzzled my head into his chest, knowing what he was saying was so far from the truth. But I didn't correct him because I wanted to pretend like everything was going to work out between us, just like he had wanted to pretend we could go back in time that night a couple of months ago.

I breathed in his cologne, letting his familiar scent calm me. We could get through this. If we were meant to be, our deep feelings for each other would get us through this difficult time.

They just had to.

He laid down on his back and I curled up against him on my side, letting his arm pull me even closer to him as I rested my head on his chest. We were quiet for a while, watching the sky above us. It was a chilly night, but beneath the blanket I felt warm—I didn't want this moment of peacefulness to ever end.

But I knew before the night ended that I would have to tell him I couldn't keep our baby. It would just keep getting harder and harder if I continued to put it off.

I sighed and let my fingers trace along the design on the front of his hoodie.

Easton lifted his head slightly from the ground to look at me. "Is something wrong?"

I sighed again, focusing on the way my fingers were tracing along his chest. "I have something I need to talk to you about...but I kind of don't want to talk about it."

He let his head fall back to the ground again. "What is it?" He sounded wary.

My hand stilled on his chest as I tried to figure out the best words.

But no good words came, so I said, "I don't think I can keep the baby."

There was a sharp intake of breath, and when I dared peek at Easton, his jaw was set and his eyes had hardened.

"You still want to give away my baby?" The look he gave me was one that I'd expect someone to give a friend who had betrayed them on the deepest extent possible.

But he had to have known this was coming. I'd told him all

along that I didn't think I could be a mom while still in high school.

I looked away, focusing on the shadow of a tree instead of him. "I just don't think I can do it. He deserves to have a mom and a dad."

He sat up, forcing me to sit as well. "Why don't you get it, Juliette? I'm willing to be a dad," he said loudly, the frustration in his voice obvious. "I'm willing to be there for our kid so he can have two parents. The only problem is that *you* don't want to help me."

I shook my head, feeling tears surge to my eyes. "I can't do it, Easton. Every time I think about the future and trying to take care of a baby while still going to school and college, I feel the life go out of me. I don't want to resent our baby. I don't want to be like your mom and feel like I'm so trapped that I end up just leaving someday."

Easton pulled his head back. "But you're not my mom. You're different."

"I don't think I am. I think I'm the same."

He blew out a frustrated breath. "But I have everything figured out. Our families are supportive. Maddie did it with Grant."

"And she did a great job. She was lucky to have so many people to help her."

"Those same people will be there to help you."

I looked away. He wasn't listening. He was so set on his way that he couldn't see mine.

After a long moment, he said, "I should have a say with what happens to my kid. He's mine just as much as yours." He sighed. "But if you aren't willing to help me, I'll raise him on my own. I'll deal with the consequences of my actions instead of taking the easy way out."

Was that what he thought of this? That there was only one right way to deal with consequences?

I glared at him. "You think this is easy?" I scoffed. "I've never had to do something so hard in my life."

His expression softened, and he turned toward me. "But what if things do work out between us? I ..." He sighed and brushed some hair behind my ear. "It'd kill me to know that I gave up our first child. If we ever got married, how could we explain to our kids that we already had a baby together but that they wouldn't know him? How do you think that would make them feel? They'd probably always wonder if we were going to give them away, too."

"Not every kid feels the way you do about your mom." I shook my head, my lips trembling with all the emotions I was feeling. "Things have been so up and down between us. It's not fair to bring a baby into such an unstable environment when there are other options. There are lots of great couples out there who could give our baby everything he needs."

"But we aren't always going to be high school students." He took my hand in his, running his thumb across the back of my fingers. "We're going to grow up, too. People do this all the time. We can do it, too. I have faith in us."

I stared at our hands. This was probably the last time he'd ever willingly take my hand in his.

When I spoke, my voice came out just above a whisper. "But what if I just want to be a regular high school student?"

His thumb stopped, and his grip tightened. "Then I guess you can sign over all your parental rights if you don't want to do this. I plan to take responsibility for my actions."

He was so narrow-minded right now. All he could see was his way of thinking and he was ignoring everything else.

But life wasn't always black and white. Sometimes you had to live between the shades of gray.

I touched his arm gently. "Sometimes taking responsibility is admitting you can't do something and making a hard choice."

He shook his head and pressed his lips together. I watched his whole demeanor change as a storm of emotions crashed over him. And I knew there was something even deeper behind his reasoning that he hadn't told me about before. This was more than just a sense of duty to him. More than living with the consequences of his choices.

There was something raw inside him that kept him from seeing any other alternatives.

I touched his arm gently. "What is it, Easton? What aren't you saying?"

The muscles in his jaw flexed, his eyes vulnerable. "Do you remember what I looked like after my mom turned me away in Ithaca?"

I nodded as the image of him completely breaking down on the bench behind the coffee shop came to mind. It had been gut-wrenching to witness. I'd watched an almost-grown young man, completely fall to pieces.

"That's why I don't want to give my baby to someone else."

"I don't understand."

"I don't want my son to ever feel like I did." His voice broke and there were tears in his eyes. "I don't want him to ever think I didn't want him."

And then the strong boy at my side broke down and cried.

He lifted his head and spoke through his tears as his jaw trembled. "Is it so wrong that I don't want my son to go through the same thing I did?"

I put my arms around him and pulled him close, my heart breaking for him. This was why he'd been so stubborn about the whole thing. It all stemmed from his feelings toward his mom and his fears that he would do the same thing.

I rubbed his back. "You're nothing like your mom, Easton.

The very fact that you're willing to raise a baby on your own shows just how loyal you are to those you love."

He pulled away and wiped at his eyes. "I don't just love the baby, Juliette."

I went still, not daring to let myself interpret what he could be saying. "You don't?"

He gently traced his thumb along my cheekbone. "Of course not, Juliette. I never stopped loving you."

My insides swelled when the meaning of his words crashed over me. *Easton loves me?*

He had never stopped loving me just like I had never stopped loving him.

My voice was raspy when I spoke. "I love you too, Easton."

His eyes filled with so much hope it felt like my heart would burst.

He took my hands in his, his eyes earnest. "We can do this, Juliette. We can raise our baby together."

"No." My stomach went to my throat, and it felt like it was choking me. "I can't, Easton. I can't do this. Our baby deserves more than I can give him right now."

He sighed. "What if we got married?" He watched me cautiously. "You've been so worried about the baby having two parents who are married. This would fix that."

I looked down, my pulse pounding so hard in my body.

*Get married? Right now?*

Before meeting his gaze again, I asked as calmly as I could. "Would you be talking about marriage if there wasn't a baby on the way?"

This was a serious conversation, and he needed to really think it all through. Not just throw out a proposal because he thought it would fix everything.

I held my breath as I waited.

His brow furrowed. "No. We're young and in high school."

I nodded, my chest constricting. "That's right. We have a lot of growing up to do."

He shook his head, finally understanding. "But there *is* a baby involved. I'm sure we'd get around to getting married, anyway. You just told me you loved me."

My heart felt heavy, and I couldn't help but feel so sad about this whole situation. "That's not the kind of proposal I want." I made myself look at him. "I want a guy to ask me to marry him because he can't imagine going through life without me. Because he's so in love with me. *Me*...not a baby. You would feel like I trapped you."

"But I wouldn't."

I drew in a deep breath. "I would. I'm not ready for that. I have things I want to do. I can't get married and raise a baby when I'm still growing up myself. I still have a whole year of high school after this. You'll be in college. That's different. But can you imagine going to high school and being a dad at the same time?"

"But you can do it," he said, almost desperately. "You're amazing, Juliette."

"But I don't want to. That's the missing ingredient in this whole situation. I don't want to give up all my plans when the baby can go to a great home with parents who are so excited to have a chance at raising and loving him."

His eyes hardened. "I'm keeping the baby. And if I have to, I'll put a block on the adoption."

I touched his shoulder, just feeling so hopeless about everything. How could two people who cared about each other have such differing opinions?

He stared at me, like he thought I might change my mind after hearing his ultimatum.

But instead of giving in to make him happy, I said what I knew deep down to be true. Something that had been there all along, just waiting for me to finally figure it out.

I took a deep breath and spoke my truth. "I really don't feel that the baby was sent here to be with us. I think he just had to come through us to be with someone else."

Easton opened his mouth, like he was going to say something. But after a moment, he just shook his head and stood.

"That's where I think you're wrong, Juliette," he said as he gathered up the blanket, making me shiver as the warmth was taken away from me. "I don't understand why a baby that was meant for another couple would be inside of you right now. I think that's just a cop out to make yourself feel better about your selfish decisions."

I put my hand to my chest as his words and their meaning washed over me. Easton really thought I was a horrible person. And I didn't know what I was still doing sitting on the grass. So I rolled over onto my knees and hefted me and my huge belly up to a standing position.

"Wait, Juliette." He stood in front of me before I could waddle up the hill. "I didn't mean it. Can we just talk about this a little more?"

I crossed my arms. "I don't think there's anything more to talk about. We obviously see very differently on this subject, so I think the best thing to do now is for me to just go home before you say any more things that you'll regret."

So I left, and he didn't come after me this time.

# CHAPTER TWENTY-FOUR

"YOU SURE YOU don't want to come to the lacrosse game?" Lexi asked me after school on Tuesday as we made ourselves an afternoon snack at my house.

"I have that birthing class tonight, so I really need to get home and do my homework." It was kind of true. I really did have a class...but if I wanted to go watch Easton and Noah play in their game, I could have. I didn't have *that* much homework tonight.

She raised an eyebrow. She was cutting an apple into little wedges. "You're sure you aren't just pretending to be busy so you don't have to be within ten yards of my brother?"

So she had noticed how much Easton and I had been avoiding each other since Friday night. "I don't think he'd like me watching him. If they lost the game, I have a feeling he'd blame it on the bad vibes I was sending him."

"What exactly happened between you two?" Lexi pushed her glasses up higher on her nose. "I thought you asked him on a date. Then the next thing I know you're avoiding each other like the plague."

I shrugged as I pulled the almond butter out of the fridge. "Our date didn't turn out so great."

"Why? Ever since I found out about you two, I've been watching my brother. I've never seen him look at anyone the way he looks at you. I'd almost say he's in love with you."

"I know." I swallowed the thick lump in my throat. I scooped almond butter out of the container and plopped it into a cereal bowl to dip my apple slices in.

"You know?" She paused.

I nodded. "He told me he loved me."

Her eyebrows squished together, and she pointed the knife at me. "And what? You told him you didn't love him back? Is that why things are so awkward?"

I put my hand out carefully to lower the knife she still didn't realize was about to poke me in the stomach. "No, I told him I love him, too."

"What?" She noticed what she was doing with the knife and set it on the counter. "Then why are you not talking to each other?"

I blew out a long breath. "Because when he suggested we get married and raise the baby together, I told him no."

Her eyes got wide and her mouth dropped open. "He did *what?*"

I thought over what I'd said and realized how crazy it sounded. What normal high school girl gets proposed to by her dream guy and turns him down?

Like hardly anyone. No one besides me that I knew of.

I leaned against the granite counter. "He only asked me to marry him because he thought it would convince me to keep the baby."

"Why would he even suggest that? Is he crazy?"

I sighed and dropped a handful of dark chocolate chips into

my bowl. "I don't think he really thought it through. It just kind of happened."

At least I hoped that was the case. I never considered how my rejection would have been for him if he'd been serious.

But he hadn't been serious...

Right?

I sat at the kitchen table and dipped my apple slice in the almond butter, followed by the chocolate chips. "Anyway, I think we kind of went to the point of no return."

Lexi joined me at the table. "Do you think he'll be at your birthing class tonight?"

"I doubt it." Which meant, I'd probably be there alone with all those other happy couples who were actually mature enough to take care of their babies—since my mom couldn't make it tonight.

"I can probably get out of babysitting Grant if you want someone there with you."

"No, that's okay. I think they're just teaching us breathing exercises. I'll be fine on my own."

---

I FOUND a seat in the back of the class hoping none of the other expectant parents would notice that the teen-mom was partner-less.

But I should have realized that today was the one day I needed someone there with me, because once we were all settled in, the instructor told us we'd be practicing focus techniques and ways that a support partner can comfort their pregnant partner during labor.

Which meant, I would look like a fool standing in the corner, pretending like I had someone there to fulfill that role.

"We'll start with a standing position," the instructor said. "In this first position, the partner in labor will wrap her arms behind the support partner's neck and then lean on him. This is a great position to help ease the pain of the contractions, and your support partner can massage your back to make you more comfortable."

I watched the other couples move into the position, kind of like they were slow dancing. Everyone was distracted with the exercise. They probably wouldn't notice if I slipped out of the room, right?

I was planning to get an epidural, anyway. I didn't need to know these positions if I would be numb from the waist down.

The instructor seemed to notice that I was standing alone, and she walked over. She asked, "Do you have someone coming tonight?"

I bit my lip and shook my head. And my hormones must have been really out of whack or something because I suddenly felt like crying.

Which was stupid. My mom would be there when I was going through the actual labor and delivery part. It wasn't like I would be all alone then.

"My mom is still at the city council meeting."

The instructor nodded, but there was a look of pity in her eyes.

Of course, everyone felt bad for the pregnant seventeen-year-old in the room who wasn't smart enough to keep her legs closed.

"We have a volunteer on duty right now. I could ask her to help you if you wanted."

Was she suggesting I hugged on some stranger? What was the politest way to say, "Heck, no!"?

I swallowed the lump in my throat. "I think I'll actually sit this one out. I'm sure my mom will know what to do."

"We'll be going over some breathing techniques, so I really encourage you to stay. You can have a seat if you don't want to take part in this portion."

I noticed that the rest of the class was watching me. How humiliating.

Out of the corner of my eye, I saw a tall figure fill the open doorway. Was everyone in the hospital coming to gawk at me now?

But on second glance, I realized it was Easton. He had shown up.

I tried to wipe the moisture from my eyes as an overwhelming sense of relief washed over me. I didn't have to be the lone person in the room anymore. When our gazes met, Easton nodded and strode toward me. He looked like he had just showered after his game, his hair slightly wet and combed to the side.

"Sorry I'm late. The game went into overtime."

I was speechless for a moment as my mind tried to wrap itself around the fact that he was even here.

"I didn't expect you to come."

He looked around at what all the other support partners were doing and pulled me closer so his arms were around my waist.

I hesitantly reached my arms toward his neck, and my body was stupid enough to like how close we were, even though we were supposed to be experiencing irreconcilable differences.

"Even if we don't agree on everything, I'm still going to be there when the baby is born," he said quietly in my ear. "If you'll let me, that is."

I nodded and tried to keep my heart from swelling in my chest, telling myself he was only doing it for the baby, not me. "That's fine. Thanks for showing up."

The instructor spoke again. "Now support partners, this is a great time for you to help provide relief to your partner by massaging her back. If your baby is posterior, it can cause painful back labor and the right amount of pressure can go a long way in reducing the pain."

She taught us how to breathe during contractions and then reiterated how important it was for us to have a focus image.

I had no idea how she expected me to picture the sandy beaches of Hawaii when I was screaming my guts out...but I drew in a deep breath and tried to picture the beach in Kauai where my mom and I had gone on vacation two years ago. I imagined the way the waves had lapped gently at the shore and how it felt to dip my toes in the water.

I relaxed against Easton as I got more into the meditation, letting the way his hands were rubbing across my back soothe me. My back had been hurting a lot lately, thanks to the huge counterweight it had to support constantly, so the massage felt amazing.

The instructor spoke again. "Support partners, your main job during labor is to make sure she's as comfortable as she can be. Labor can be incredibly overwhelming, and she really needs to hear your voice, so she knows she's not alone in this process. Touching her and kissing her, or just holding her hand, are all great ways to comfort her and help her know you're there for her when the contractions become intense."

At her mention of kissing, my eyes opened, and the image of the beach was gone. Easton wouldn't try kissing me, would he?

We went through a few more standing and sitting positions, ending with one where Easton sat in a chair while I sat backwards on another so I could lean my back against his chest.

"You'll most likely be on the hospital bed for this position, but this will give you an idea of how this works."

Was I really going to be doing all these things with Easton when the baby came? Or would my mom be in this spot?

I scrunched my nose at the thought of sitting like this with my mom. As awkward as things were with Easton, it would be way weirder to have my mom do these things with me. We weren't *that* close.

"Just rest your head against your partner's shoulder and take a deep breath in through your nose," the instructor said. "And then out through your mouth."

I did as she said, noticing how good Easton smelled right now. He wasn't wearing any cologne, but his soap smelled heavenly.

The instructor turned on some calming music and we just kind of sat there for a while.

"This is a good position for massaging your partner's shoulders and gently rubbing her stomach as the contractions come. Just make her feel loved and appreciated," the instructor said.

Easton's hands softly touched my belly. "Is this okay?" he asked.

"Yeah." I closed my eyes and tried to ignore the feelings of attraction that were coming over me. Being close to Easton always made that happen.

He gently massaged the sides of my belly like the instructor told him to do, his cheek right next to mine.

I breathed in deeply, telling myself to just enjoy this moment with him and not worry about what the future held for us.

As I listened to the sound of Easton's breathing and felt his heart beating strongly against my shoulders, I had a hard time remembering why we were fighting in the first place.

The baby kicked a second later and Easton gasped. "Did he just kick?"

I nodded. "Yeah. I think he likes this, too."

Easton's hands stilled for a moment as he waited for the baby to kick again. And he didn't have to wait long.

"He's getting strong, huh?" Easton said in a soft voice.

I opened my eyes for a moment to take in his expression. He was smiling down at my stomach. "He's probably five or six pounds now," I said.

"Does he ever kick you really hard in the kidneys or anything like that?" Easton asked with an amused tone.

"I don't know about the kidneys, but he really enjoys banging his head on my bladder these days. I think that's his favorite thing to do, actually."

Easton smiled. "Really?"

I nodded. "Yep. Pretty sure he'll be all about torturing his future sister's best friend, kind of like you."

Easton nodded, but he didn't smile like I'd expected. Instead, he got a far-off look like he was thinking about something else.

He broke from his trance a second later and said, "Hopefully, he'll be nicer than me."

We were quiet again as the baby continued to move around. Easton gently rubbed his fingers along my stomach with just the right amount of pressure.

I looked at the clock on the wall. Our class was about to end and then we'd have to go back to being two people who couldn't agree on what to do with their baby.

I wanted time to just stand still.

Easton slid his hands up my arms and massaged my shoulders and neck.

"How does this feel?" he asked softly, his words caressing my ear.

"Really nice," I said, resisting the urge to moan because I didn't realize how tight my shoulders were until that moment.

"Good." He pressed his thumbs into my tight muscles before placing a light kiss at the base of my neck.

Heat flashed across my skin at his unexpected touch, my breath caught in my throat. Did he do that on purpose?

Maybe he was just taking to heart the instructor's speech on how holding, cuddling, and kissing could release the powerful hormone of oxytocin.

Maybe.

But when he did it again, I had the feeling that it was more than just the instructor's words behind the action.

# CHAPTER TWENTY-FIVE

"CAN I walk you to your car?" Easton asked when the class was over.

"I was actually planning to walk the path around the hospital before going home, since I didn't get my evening walk in yet."

The hospital had created a really nice path a couple of years ago, landscaped with trees and bushes, and even a small waterfall around the back, with benches along the way for patients to rest on when needed. It was one of my favorite walking paths in town.

"Mind if I join you?" he asked.

"Sure," I said. I thought about adding the requirement that he wasn't allowed to kill my peaceful feeling by talking about our plans for the baby...but decided against it. He didn't look like he was in an arguing mood, either.

I pulled on my soft pink jacket when we got outside, and Easton put his dark blue one on.

I kept my gaze down as we walked. "Thanks again for coming tonight. I was about to leave before you came."

He shoved his hands in his pockets. "Sorry I was late. I

remembered what we'd be doing and thought it would probably be better if I didn't stink like the locker room when I came."

"You knew about the cuddling stuff?" I didn't remember the instructor talking about this last week. She had only mentioned breathing exercises.

"Well, when Maddie was coming to these classes, I would sometimes show up in case Jaxon didn't make it. So I got to learn about this stuff just watching Maddie and Jaxon go through it."

"I always admired how willing you were to be there for Maddie during that time."

He looked at me carefully. "I watch out for the people I care about."

I nodded and looked away. "And you care about the baby." I said it so he wouldn't have to clarify that he had come for the baby and not me.

"Not just the baby."

I looked back to him with a furrowed brow. "Really?"

He got an uncomfortable look on his face before he shrugged and said, "You know how I feel about you."

"Do I?" I asked. "Because the way we left things on Friday convinced me otherwise."

"My feelings didn't just disappear over the weekend. I still care about you."

"Of course you do." I couldn't keep myself from sounding sarcastic.

He stopped in the middle of the sidewalk. "Why do I get the sense that you don't believe me?"

I crossed my arms. "Because I don't."

He moved closer, and I backed up automatically, my foot on the grass. He said, "Just because we don't agree on everything doesn't mean I don't like you anymore."

He'd said *love* on Friday. *Like* was different from love, so that had changed.

"But having strong opposing views makes it harder for the feelings to survive," I said.

I'd seen enough of my friends' parents get divorced through the years to know that sometimes, love wasn't everything people chalked it up to be.

He stepped closer, and I took another step back. "I don't want to play this game where you tell me how I feel. I know where my feelings are. I don't need to prove anything."

"But what if I want you to prove it?" The words were out before I could stop them.

What the heck did I mean by that, anyway? How could he even *prove* his feelings for me? By giving in and signing away his parental rights just because I wanted him to?

That wasn't fair.

That wasn't love.

But he seemed to have something else in mind entirely because he cornered me until I had nowhere else to go—my back bumped against the trunk of a big tree.

But I wouldn't want to go anywhere, even if I could. I didn't want to fight with him anymore.

He leaned in so close that his hot breath was on my cheek. "I want to be yours, Juliette. And I want you to be mine."

His eyes were hungry now. Deeper. Desperate. He was searching me like he was trying to find the answers to all our problems. Like if we just cared enough about each other everything would work out.

And maybe it would.

He lifted his fingers to trace their way along my lips, across my chin, and then down my neck. The only thing left for me to do was close my eyes and sigh.

"I'm still in love with you, Juliette." His warm minty breath was on my mouth, his lips hovering only a couple of centimeters away. "I want to find a way to make things work with you."

I could feel the heat radiating off his body, feel the strength in his chest as his heart beat wildly with hope, and I couldn't take it anymore. I had to kiss him.

So I arched my back and tilted my chin up to press my lips against his. He went still, like he hadn't expected me to actually kiss him, but his lips moved with mine in the next instant, like they'd been ready just in case.

As our lips moved and our breath mingled, every rational thought I had about the future disappeared. We would figure out the logistics later. We'd think later. Right now, we would just *feel*.

He slid his left hand behind the back of my head, his right hand tightening around my waist as he pressed his chest against mine. And I remembered why we'd gone too far last time. Our chemistry was something that was hard to keep a handle on. It made it hard to breathe. Made me forget why I even needed oxygen because all there was that existed was Easton. This moment.

And nothing else mattered.

I knew I'd probably regret kissing him tomorrow when reality came back to me, but I didn't care. I wanted to be loved. I wanted to remember how it had felt to be loved by Easton. How his arms around me made me feel strong and safe, like I could take on the world with him by my side.

We could do anything together.

I would keep things in check this time. I wouldn't push things too far.

But I would let myself live and love. I wanted that, and he seemed to want it, too.

I let my hands slide up his stomach and explore the contours of his chest. He was stronger than he'd been the last time I'd touched him like this. He'd grown up just a little bit more, and I reveled in the feel of his muscles beneath my palms as his heart raced so fast it was probably keeping pace with mine.

His lips left my mouth to explore my throat, and my head fell back because his lips on my skin felt amazing. I let my hands explore the lines of his body, the tightly corded muscles just beneath the sleeves of his jacket.

"How is it possible I went so long without kissing you?" he said, his voice husky and his breathing heavy like he'd just run a race. "Why haven't I been kissing you every single moment since you got back from Paris?"

"I don't know," I said as I pushed my fingers in his hair and tilted his head up to bring his mouth back to mine. He didn't hesitate to close the distance between our lips again, but this time, instead of a fast and hungry kiss, he slowed it down and deepened it.

My stomach muscles tightened, electricity shooting through my veins as his kisses took me back in time. But my feet were hurting, and I could feel them swelling up from the pressure of having me and the baby's weight on them for so long.

"I need to sit down." I gasped as I pulled away, my chest rising and falling with my labored breathing.

Easton's eyes looked dazed for a moment before focusing again. He scanned the area before spotting a bench about fifteen feet away. "You want to sit there."

I nodded, and then he was pulling me behind him like he couldn't get to the bench fast enough. He sat down, and I was about to take the spot next to him when he tugged on my arm and pulled me sideways on his lap. And before I knew what was happening, he was reaching his hand behind my neck and we were kissing again.

This was crazy. We couldn't just make out on a bench like this. Sure it was dark, but people sometimes walked this path at night. What would they think when they came across a pregnant girl making out with a guy on a park bench?

But when his arms encircled me, and his fingers accidentally grazed along the skin at the base of my shirt, I didn't really care anymore because I didn't want this to stop. I wanted to kiss him all night if he'd let me.

His hands didn't remain at my waist for long. They slowly slid up my side and down again, ran along my stomach before finding their way to my back once more.

Easton sparked every molecule in my body to life as he kissed me over and over again. I dug my fingers into his scalp and he reacted by making a deep and masculine sound at the back of his throat, which made my fingers tremble at the thought that I could make him moan.

He stared into my eyes for a moment, his pupils blown wide as he looked me over, scanning over every inch of my face—and I couldn't help but feel so vulnerable. As if he could see all my flaws. But instead of turning away and telling me I didn't match up to what he wanted, he murmured next to my lips, "You're so beautiful, Juliette." And then we were kissing again.

The intense, crackling heat continued to turn my brain into liquid as the kiss deepened, and all I could think of was that I wanted more of this. I needed to touch more of him. So I let my hands smooth their way along his shoulders and under his jacket. They traced their way down his chest, finding a path along the thin fabric of his shirt. They rubbed along his sides, but that still wasn't enough. I wanted to feel his skin on my fingertips.

So I let them push their way across his back, lifting the bottom of his shirt so I could feel his hot skin under my fingertips.

He felt like summer. Like the day we'd snuck to the lake and kissed for hours on a blanket on the shore. What I wouldn't give to be back there right now. Tangled up with the edges of his body pressed against the contours of mine.

Too bad my huge stomach kept us from getting too close.

It was almost as if my thought about my stomach triggered

some sort of warning in Easton because he suddenly took my arms by the wrist and pulled them away from his back.

"H-hold on, Juliette. We can't kiss like that anymore." He sounded out of breath.

"Why?" I asked. Stopping our kiss was about the last thing I wanted to do.

He took in another deep breath and set one hand on my stomach. "Because of this. I don't want to play with fire anymore."

"I wasn't trying to have sex with you, Easton."

He rubbed his hand across the top of my stomach. "I know. But we didn't exactly plan on that the last time, either, and look what happened."

I slid off his lap and folded my arms like a sullen child who'd been caught stealing cash from her mom's wallet.

Easton cupped my chin and turned my head to face him. "I'm just stating my boundaries. I'm not trying to get after you."

"Okay, I got it." I held my hands up before looking away, still feeling like he thought I was some sort of tramp who was always trying to take his clothes off.

"Juliette..."

When I ignored him, he scooted closer and put his hand on my leg. "I just want to take things slow."

"I was just touching your back."

"I think you forget how much I like that." He gave me a wicked grin. "I just don't want to push the limits anymore. Kissing and having you touch me like that makes me lose my clarity and I'm much more likely to do things I wouldn't normally do." He looked at me carefully, his eyes darting back and forth between my own. "Can you at least understand that?"

I sighed. "Of course I understand. I'll try not to do it again."

He leaned forward and gave me a hug then he whispered in my ear. "Just let us grow up a little more. We can definitely revisit this topic in the future."

Chills raced down my spine, and I couldn't keep a grin off my face. So he really did want me like I wanted him. He was just better at remembering the reasons why we needed to keep things in check.

He pulled away from the hug and stood, holding his hand out for me.

We continued on the trail to finish the walk back to our cars, holding hands the whole way.

I glanced down at my stomach as I waddled down the path next to Easton. "You'd think this belly would help me remember why people wait until after they're married to have sex."

Easton looked over and grinned. "You would think so. But don't be too hard on yourself. I'm kind of an amazing kisser and I haven't been contacted by modeling agencies for nothing."

"Yeah, yeah." I rolled my eyes but couldn't keep from smiling.

"Are you saying I'm not that hot?" he asked. His tone was light, but I could tell there was insecurity beneath the surface.

Instead of making him sweat, I said, "Do you think I'd have this if I didn't think you were drop-dead gorgeous? I mean, I don't want to make ugly babies."

He laughed. "It sounds like our baby won the genetic jackpot, since his mom is smokin' hot, too."

I tried to smile at his compliment, but I couldn't ignore the fact that he'd said *our baby* and *his mom and dad*. It just brought me right back to the reality that even though we obviously cared a lot about each other, and even though we were insanely attracted to one another, we still had a huge issue between us.

He wanted to keep the baby, but I didn't. And if he kept the baby, I knew I wouldn't be able to be around him anymore. It would just be too hard for me to see him be a great dad to our child—to be reminded of all the ways I wasn't good enough. If Easton and I were to try to date, I would be like a step-mom to my biological son—and how confusing would that be to him if things ended up not working out between Easton and me in the end?

And if things did work out, it wouldn't be fair to Easton to make him do all the hard work for the first few years only to have me jump in later and say, *yeah, we should totally get married now and I'll be happy to start taking care of our kid.*

We made it to the parking lot and Easton walked me to my car.

"Is something wrong?" he asked.

"I was just thinking about how everything would work out after the baby is born."

He nodded. "Do you want to talk about it?"

I shook my head and pulled my keys from my pocket. "Not really. I want to just pretend like everything is easy tonight. We can go back to reality tomorrow."

A pained look crossed Easton's face before he pulled me in for a hug. "We'll figure things out." He spoke into my hair before kissing the top of my head. "We'll make the right decision."

I buried my face into his chest and tried to force the doubts out of my mind. "I hope so."

# CHAPTER TWENTY-SIX

TWO WEEKS LATER, while we were watching a movie in the basement with Lexi and Noah, Easton asked me out of the blue, "How would you feel about going to prom with me?"

Easton and I were tentatively dating, and he had told me he'd look into adoption more and talk to my social worker to understand our different options more fully. But he still hadn't told me his decision yet. And I didn't want to push him because I knew he needed to make the choice he felt the most comfortable with, just like I needed to make the best choice for me.

But oh how I hoped we both came to the same decision. Because I loved him. That was just a fact that wasn't going away anytime soon. And since I loved him so much, I wanted to do whatever we did *together*. No more ultimatums.

Which was also why I had volunteered to babysit the Vincenzo twins down the street with Lexi and was learning all I could about taking care of a newborn...just in case.

"The baby is due like three days before prom. I doubt I'll feel like dancing...or trying to find a prom dress," I told Easton. I'd bet none of the stores in Ridgewater carried maternity prom dresses

—not ones I'd want to wear, anyway. If I wanted to be a fashion designer one day, I couldn't have prospective clients discovering old photos of me in a hideous gown.

"It's your Junior Prom. You should go."

"I'll think about it."

He put his arm around my shoulder and pulled me closer to his side. I leaned my head against his chest and let myself relax against him. I'm sure prom would be fun. But I'd take cuddling up with him on the couch over dancing around in high heels that my swollen feet barely fit in any day.

We continued to watch the movie like that for a while until Easton whispered in my ear. "I think I've decided what I want to do about the baby."

I lifted my head and looked at him, feeling anxious for his answer. "You have?"

He nodded. "I've been talking a lot with our social worker and..."

But I didn't hear the rest of what he was saying because I suddenly felt a popping feeling between my legs. It only took a second for my brain to figure out what that popping sensation might have been. And before I could make a huge mess on the Stevens's sectional, I dashed toward the basement bathroom and sat down on the toilet.

Easton knocked on the door a second later. "Is everything okay, Juliette?"

I drew in some deep breaths as I felt an uncontrollable gush of water came out of me.

"Juliette?" His voice sounded more anxious this time.

"I think my water just broke." I blinked my eyes shut and breathed in a few breaths as I realized what this meant exactly.

The baby was coming.

Tonight.

# CHAPTER TWENTY-SEVEN

"ARE YOU SURE?" Easton's voice sounded more frantic now.

"Pretty sure." I might pee my pants a little every time I sneezed these days, but this was different.

"Do you need me to call an ambulance?" Easton asked.

"Um, I think you can just get me a couple of towels or something. I don't think he's coming out this exact minute."

But we definitely needed to get to the hospital because I had no idea how fast the baby would come, and there was no way I wanted to have him without an epidural.

"Are you okay?" Lexi said from the other side of the door. "Do you need me to come in there and help you with anything?"

The amniotic fluid seemed to have stopped trickling out. "If you could just call the hospital and tell them I'm coming, that would be great. Oh, and call my mom, too."

What was I supposed to do? The baby wasn't supposed to be here for two more weeks. The doctor had said that the baby's lungs would be developed enough to work well on their own at this point, but what if they weren't? Was the baby going to be okay?

Easton came back with towels a second later, and when I opened the door, he looked white as a ghost. "Are you okay? Is the baby okay? I really can call the ambulance, if you need me to."

"I'm okay. I just want to get to the hospital and make sure the baby's fine. I didn't think he'd come early."

Easton's eyes were wide. "Me neither."

I took one of the towels from his shaking hand and did something I would never dream of doing in front of the guy I liked in my prior life. I bunched up that towel and put it between my legs lengthwise, like a diaper that didn't have any Velcro tabs.

I knew I should have bought old-people diapers to carry around everywhere I went.

"Do you want me to drive you guys?" Noah was standing at the bottom of the stairs.

I glanced at Easton. He didn't look like he should drive right now.

"Yeah, that would be great."

Noah went up the stairs first to turn on his car.

"I'll go to your house and pack a bag for you, so your mom can just meet you at the hospital," Lexi offered.

"Thank you."

Easton helped me up the stairs and led me outside, helping me into the passenger seat of Noah's white sedan. Then he climbed in the seat behind me.

It was only eight o'clock in the evening, so there was too much traffic for Noah to speed or run any stoplights, which made me thankful that Noah was the one driving and not Easton. I was pretty sure Easton would have attempted it and that could have ended badly.

As we drove, all I could think about was how I just wasn't ready for this. I didn't have a car seat. I didn't have baby clothes. And I didn't have adoptive parents, either.

Why had I let myself put everything off until the last minute? I was so irresponsible.

Noah pulled into the drop-off spot by the hospital entrance and Easton opened my door. He linked his arm through mine to escort me to the labor and delivery wing.

The nurses had a room ready for me when we got there and they had me change into a hospital gown right away. I was grateful that the judgmental nurse from last time wasn't on duty. I probably would have requested someone else if she was.

When I came out of the bathroom after changing, my mom was in the room with Easton and they were both talking to my nurse.

When Mom saw me, she rushed over and gave me a hug. "Are you okay? Have the contractions started?"

"I've had a few, but nothing too painful yet."

She nodded, but there was a huge amount of anxiety in her eyes. I realized that while I'd been so worried about what I was supposed to do with my baby, my mom had been worried about me. Because I was *her* baby.

The nurse said, "If you'll sit on the bed, we can get these monitors attached and see how the contractions are coming and how they're affecting the baby's heartbeat."

I climbed onto the bed with the help of the nurse and my mom, pulled the thin blanket over my legs, and lifted my hospital gown so the nurse could place thick stretchy bands around my stomach.

Easton was sitting on the small couch in the corner, his leg bouncing up and down as he anxiously waited to see what the monitors would tell us.

The nurse finished adjusting the monitors, and soon lines appeared on the screen beside me. She smiled. "The baby's heartbeat is good. We'll watch the monitor for a contraction to see how he does during one."

A moment later, the line on the screen went up as my stomach tightened. It didn't hurt me too badly, but it felt more painful than the practice contractions I'd been having the past few weeks.

The nurse waited for the line to go down on the screen, completing the rolling hill before patting my leg. "Everything looks good. I'll check to see how far dilated you are, and then we'll just wait and see how things progress."

"Thanks," I said, grateful that she seemed to think things were going well. If she thought everything was okay, then I could relax.

I noticed Easton had seemed to relax at the nurse's reassurance, too. I gave him a soft smile.

All that was left to do now was wait.

And get that epidural when the nurse said I could have it.

I was not going to do this thing without one.

# CHAPTER TWENTY-EIGHT

"DR. GUNTHRIE just called to say that she'll be here in a few minutes," my nurse said.

I'd been at the hospital for eight hours and had only gotten a few hours of sleep. The contractions hadn't gotten super painful until about one in the morning, and that was when the nurse finally said I could get the epidural.

It had worked like a charm, and I'd finally fallen asleep for a couple of hours, but when the nurse checked me an hour ago, she said I was almost complete and that it was time to prepare to push.

"Where do you want me?" Easton asked, coming to stand at my side. He looked as exhausted as I felt, having not gotten much sleep in the chair by my side.

My mom was already on my other side, holding my hand.

"You can stay there," I said.

He nodded and took my other hand in his, giving it a reassuring squeeze.

Doctor Gunthrie came in a few minutes later and immediately got to work washing her hands and getting properly suited up.

"Are you ready for this?" she asked, beaming at me.

I swallowed, not sure how she could be so bright and cheery this early in the morning. "I guess."

*Ready or not, here he comes.*

I just hoped I could survive this.

"You're going to do great." She touched my leg. I couldn't feel it since it was numb, but it was a nice sentiment.

The nurse had Easton help her move my legs into the birthing position, which was kind of awkward. But in a situation like this, awkwardness was the least of my concerns.

Once I was in position, the doctor said, "Okay, let's do a few pushes and see if we can get this baby out and into your arms."

"Okay," I said, feeling nervous. This was really happening. It was time.

# CHAPTER TWENTY-NINE

"YOU'RE DOING GREAT, JULIETTE." Easton massaged my shoulders between contractions. I'd been pushing for over an hour, and it seemed like the pushing would never stop.

I wondered if maybe the fact that I had an epidural and couldn't feel anything from the waist down may have contributed to this. How was I supposed to know if I was pushing right if I couldn't feel anything?

Maybe I shouldn't have pushed the epidural button so many times. I'd just been so afraid it would wear off.

"I don't know if I can do any more," I complained. I was exhausted.

"You're doing great. Just a few more pushes and his shoulders will be out," the doctor said.

The nurse watching the screen spoke. "A contraction's coming. Deep breath in. And push for ten."

I clenched my jaw and pushed as long and as hard as I could as she counted down from ten all the way to one.

"Good," the nurse said, her voice way more positive than I had energy for. "His head's out. Just one more push and his shoulders will be out."

My mom rubbed my hand. "You're almost done. You can do this."

I leaned my head back and looked up at the ceiling as I tried to catch my breath.

One more.

I could do one more.

I drew in a deep breath. When the nurse counted down from ten again, I gave it everything that I had.

And as I pushed, everyone else went quiet in the room.

"There he is," Mom said in a soft voice.

Then I heard him. My baby.

He was crying.

I looked down—though I was completely exhausted—and watched the doctor and nurse as they quickly suctioned out the baby's mouth and nose. When they were done, Dr. Gunthrie smiled as she lifted the baby up.

"Do you want to hold him?"

I hadn't really decided if I wanted to hold the baby. Easton hadn't told me what he'd decided to do. But I suddenly felt an overwhelming urge to hold him. I had carried him inside me for almost nine months. I wanted to hold him in my arms. I needed it.

So I held out my arms to the doctor. "Yes. I want to hold him."

She smiled, and an instant later, my baby was on my chest. And all I could do was look at the warm little guy who was purplish pink with white creamy stuff all over him. I put one hand on his firm little body, the other running over his dark hair, and an overwhelming sense of love for him came crashing over me.

He was perfect.

I looked up to find Easton with tears in his eyes.

He smiled and bent close to my ear. "You did it, Juliette. You made a miracle happen." He kissed my cheek and rested his hand on our baby who was slowly opening his eyes now that his crying had stopped. He looked like he was taking in this new world of his.

And I couldn't keep from crying because I had done it. I'd made it through the hardest experience that I'd ever had to go through. And I got to hold this sweet baby in my arms. As I looked at him, I couldn't help but feel like all the tears, all the fights, all the frustration, and all the pain had been worth it. Because this baby was here. And he was beautiful.

# CHAPTER THIRTY

MY LEGS WERE numb for the next four hours because apparently, I really had pushed the epidural button too many times. But that was okay, because it meant that I got to sleep and cuddle with the baby for a little longer before we switched rooms.

Easton had been so cute with the baby. It completely melted my heart to watch him hold and rock the baby in the chair next to me.

"Will you be okay if I leave for a little while?" Easton asked after they moved me to a different room.

"Where are you going?" I asked. His eyes looked so tired that I wouldn't be surprised if he was going home to take a nap.

He gave me a soft smile. "My dad's here. He's going to help me take care of a few things. I'll be back in a couple of hours."

I nodded, feeling nervous about what they needed to do now that couldn't wait. I wanted to ask him what they were doing, but I got the feeling he didn't want me to ask.

"We'll be fine here," Mom said. "In fact, I think I'll take the baby to the nursery, so Juliette can get some rest."

Easton rubbed my shoulder. "Okay. I'll be back soon."

"What do you think he's doing?" I asked my mom once he was gone.

She took the baby from my arms and cradled him in hers. "I'm not sure." She smiled and cooed at the baby—*doting grandmother* was a good look for her. "Maybe he just needs to be with his dad right now. It's been a big day for him."

I nodded. I kept forgetting how this day was as life-changing for Easton as it had been for me. We had both become parents today.

I closed my eyes as the word "parents" stuck in my mind.

Was that what we were now?

I opened my eyes again to focus on my mom. If I just stayed in this moment, maybe everything wouldn't be so overwhelming. "Are you sure you're okay to take him for a few hours?" I asked, noting how peaceful the baby looked as he just stared at my mom.

She smiled. "We'll be great. You get some rest."

She grabbed her purse off her chair and walked slowly out of the room with the baby, shutting the door behind her.

And I must have been really exhausted because I was asleep in no time.

---

I DIDN'T KNOW how long I slept, but when I woke up, Easton was sitting on the chair beside me. He wore different clothes—a black t-shirt and light jeans—and he was freshly showered. He looked amazing, and if I didn't look so horrible right now, I probably would have begged him to kiss me.

He also had a manila folder on his lap with papers poking out.

My heart stuttered in my chest. What were they?

Were they from the hospital? Or had he brought them with him?

He smiled at me when he saw I was awake.

"How did you sleep?" he asked, leaning closer.

"Okay, I guess."

"Good."

"How long have you been sitting there?" I asked.

"Just a few minutes. I hope I didn't wake you."

I shook my head. "I don't think so."

He swallowed and quickly glanced down at the papers on his lap. He was nervous. But he wasn't saying anything about them.

"Is the baby still in the nursery with my mom?" I asked.

He shifted in his seat to get more comfortable. "Yeah, I took my dad in there to see him. They let me feed him a bottle. He ate really well."

"Good."

I eyed the papers again. I had to ask. "What are those for?"

He looked down hesitantly at the folder before putting them on the ground. "We can talk about these later. How are you feeling?"

"I just pushed out a six-and-a-half pound baby, so not super great at the moment." I looked down at the papers again. "But what are those papers for?" I was suddenly super irritable. Was it my hormones talking, or just the annoying pain in the middle of my back from the epidural?

Easton sighed and picked up the folder. "These are from our social worker. I signed them."

I sat up from my reclined position. "You what?"

He nodded and held the folder out for me. "I signed away my parental rights. We just need your signature, and then someone can adopt our baby."

I sat there in shock, unable to take the folder from him because I couldn't believe what I was hearing.

"You're signing away your rights?"

He looked at me with sad eyes. "It's not that I don't want him." He sighed. "It's just that I finally *heard* what you've been saying all along. I've been talking to the social worker a lot. She gave me a few adoptive parent profiles to go over these past few weeks, and I agree with you now. I don't think he was meant to be ours. I think he had to come through us to get to his home."

My mouth opened but no words came out. Easton was really okay with letting someone else raise our baby?

"How long...? What...?" I tried to speak, but my brain was still having a hard time groping onto the idea that for the first time in months, we actually agreed. "What finally convinced you?"

He pulled his phone out, typed in something, and then handed it to me. On the screen was an image of Nadia, the woman I'd met at the doctor's office way back in December, and her husband.

"I was looking through profiles, and when I came across this one I felt like I knew these people. It was so strange, but as I read about them it felt like my heart knew these people and that they were the right ones for our baby."

I just kept looking at the picture of the couple, unable to peel my eyes away. "I know this lady," I finally said.

"You do?"

I nodded. "I met her at the doctor's office one time. They were at the hospital the night I passed out."

"They were?" Easton frowned, like he was trying to remember.

"Yeah. They *just* had a baby."

"Yeah, that's what their story said on their blog."

"Why would they want to adopt?" I knew she'd said it had taken eight years for her to get pregnant. Maybe they wanted to adopt just in case she could never get pregnant again?

Easton got a cautious look on his face. "Their baby died shortly after he was born."

"What?" I felt the blood drain from my face. "No. That can't be right. That wouldn't be fair." I shook my head. "That couldn't happen to them."

But I remembered she'd said she was only thirty-two weeks when she was talking to the nurse. Had their baby been born too early? Was there some complication that had made her go into labor?

I looked at Easton's phone again and scrolled through their story. It talked about who they were. What they did for their jobs. Where they grew up. What they liked to do for fun. They seemed like a great couple. They were fun and witty, and I could tell that they really loved each other and wanted a baby so badly.

From everything I could see, they would make great parents. A baby would be lucky to have them.

When I finished reading, I handed the phone back to Easton. "Are you sure you want to do this?"

He nodded. "I think I am. I realized that a huge reason I was so insistent on raising the baby myself was because of my own feelings toward my mom. But I know now that doing this would be much different than just up and leaving my child. It would give him a loving home, with two loving people who are ready to be parents. They can provide the kind of environment I always wanted." He looked at me sadly. "The kind of home I hope to have someday but know I'm not ready for right now."

"Is your dad okay with this?" I asked. Though I'd been afraid of what Easton would choose all along, I'd also worried about the influence his dad might have on him.

"He'll support me either way. He wants me to be happy." He opened the folder and showed me the spot where he'd signed it in black ink. "I've already made my decision. Now it's time for you to make yours."

My heart pounded in my temples, and suddenly I wasn't so sure anymore. I remembered what it had felt like to finally hold the baby in my arms. How I had felt so much love for him when he looked up at me.

"I think I'm going to need a little while."

"Take your time." He glanced at his watch. "Lexi and Maddie should be here soon. I'm going to take them to see the baby before we tell him goodbye."

Tears sprung to my eyes at his mention of saying goodbye to our baby.

I just met him.

Easton handed me the folder. "I'll be back soon." He kissed me on the head before leaving the room.

I stared at the folder in my hand for the longest time.

My mom came into the room a few minutes later. "I figured I'd give Easton and his family some time alone with the baby." She shut the door behind her. "He told me you might need me."

I looked up, tears in my eyes.

"Am I making the right decision, Mom?" My voice broke in a sob. "What if I've been wrong this whole time?"

She rushed to my side and climbed onto the bed beside me, pulling me into her arms. "You'll be a great mom someday, Juliette." She smoothed my hair down with her hand. "And I won't force you to choose either way, because this is your decision. One that only you know the answer to. But I think you do know what that right answer is already."

I sniffled. "But what if I miss him? Won't it always hurt to remember that he could have been mine?"

"It probably will always be hard. But I think you know what is right for you and Easton and the baby."

I nodded and wiped my tears before opening the folder. I picked up the pen Easton had put inside and sifted through the papers until I came to the document my social worker had shown me months ago.

I put my pen on the paper for a moment, taking in a deep breath before moving it. And then I signed my name.

# CHAPTER THIRTY-ONE

LATER THAT AFTERNOON, my social worker poked her head into my room. "Mr. and Mrs. Williams are in their room just down the hall. We'll plan on five o'clock for the transfer like you said." She and Mr. Stevens had been doing a lot of work behind the scenes today to make this all come together.

Five o'clock seemed like it was coming so fast. But I knew I needed to stick to that time or it would only get harder and harder. So I drew in a deep breath and said, "Okay. We'll be ready." I had thirty more minutes to hold and cuddle with this baby.

Easton was sitting on the bed beside me. We requested for everyone to leave us alone for these last minutes, so we could just be together as we took turns snuggling with our son.

The baby made a small cooing noise, which made me grin. He was so calm—nothing like the screaming infant I'd imagined all these months.

"I knew he would have your blue eyes," I whispered to Easton when the baby slowly opened his eyes and peered up at us.

Easton put his arm around my shoulder and gently caressed

the baby's cheek with his other hand. "I think all baby's eyes are that color when they're born, but I guess time will tell."

I nodded. There was still a lot of paperwork left to be done for the adoption to be finalized, but Easton and I had spoken on the phone with Nadia and her husband Cameron this afternoon, and we all agreed that an open adoption was something we wanted.

Which meant that while we may say goodbye to our little guy today, it wasn't a permanent goodbye. It was more like our family was just expanding, and we would be involved in each other's lives from here on out.

Not that I expected to be around him all the time, but it was nice to know they'd send us videos and pictures and keep us up to date on everything he was doing. And then we would be invited to big family events, like his first birthday party and his high school graduation.

It was crazy to think about where I'd be at that time, since I still had to wait a year for my own high school graduation.

"I think he has your eyebrows," Easton said, running a fingertip gently across our little guy's brow.

"They look good on him." I smiled and looked closer, trying to memorize every detail about him. The way he looked. The way he smelled. The cute little sounds he made as he slept.

I pushed my finger into his perfect little hand and loved how he reflexively curled his fingers around mine. Like he trusted me completely to make sure he was taken care of.

"It'll be really hard to hand him to the Williams," Easton said, and I felt his body sigh beside mine.

I nodded. "I'm trying not to think about that part."

But I knew it was coming.

Ten minutes later, the social worker opened the door again. My mom and Mr. Stevens were standing behind her, each wearing a wary expression on their faces. They were worried about us.

"It's five o'clock," the social worker said.

An ache formed in my chest. Our time was up. In just a few moments, I would hand my baby to another woman and she would take care of him for the rest of his life.

Easton climbed off the bed first and took the baby from my arms so I could stand up. We'd decided that we would go to them, instead of them coming to us.

Easton held the baby as we walked the few doors down the hall. My heart pounded harder with each step we took.

We stopped in front of the closed door to room one-sixteen.

"I love you, baby," Easton whispered before kissing our boy and hugging him to his chest. "Just remember that. I'm always going to love you."

My heart broke. Easton would have been a great dad.

He *would* be a great dad.

Someday.

He handed the baby to me next, so I could say my goodbyes. I held him against my chest and nuzzled my face on his soft, warm cheeks and whispered, "I love you, baby. I hope you know that."

I hugged on him for just a moment longer, committing everything about him and everything about this day with him to my memory. I knew I would think back on this moment for the rest of my life.

The social worker knocked on the door, and a moment later, it opened to reveal Nadia and Cameron Williams on the other side. They had cautious looks on their faces, like they were too scared to be excited. They'd been this close to having a baby before, only to have it taken away from them at the last minute.

I drew in a deep breath, hoping it would make me brave enough to do what I had to do next.

After hesitating for just a few seconds more, I held out my son to his new mommy. "Here he is."

Nadia quickly glanced to the social worker as if to make sure it was really okay for her to take him from me.

The social worker nodded, and then Nadia reached out, her whole body trembling. She took him from my outstretched arms. We both started crying.

"Thank you," Nadia said, looking at me and Easton with tears in her eyes. "Thank you so much for giving us such an amazing gift."

I nodded. "Thank you for taking him into your home. He's a pretty special guy."

And then because I knew this moment was so special for her and her husband, I knew we needed to leave them to bond with their baby who wasn't mine anymore.

But before I could go, I had to say something else. "Just tell him I love him, okay?" My lips trembled as I spoke. "Tell him we loved him so much that we wanted to give him his best chance."

"We will," Cameron said. "We'll make sure he knows he is loved by so many people who just want him to grow up and be happy."

I glanced at Easton and saw he had tears in his eyes, too. He looked down at me with a sad smile, and I knew it was time for us to really go.

So we said one last goodbye and looked longingly at the baby one last time before turning to walk away.

Once the social worker had shut the door between us, I searched for my mom. I needed her.

She was right there behind me, and so I threw my arms around her as a sob escaped my throat. And she held me as I cried.

I could see from the corner of my eye that Easton's dad was doing the same thing for him, too.

"Let's get you back to your room," my mom said after a while.

I nodded and let her lead me back to my room a few doors down. I climbed into my bed, feeling so heavy with grief I wondered if I could ever be fully happy again. I hadn't expected to feel this sad. I'd known all along that I wanted to do this. I'd felt so strongly that the baby was supposed to be raised by someone else.

How could I feel so much fear and regret right now?

"Is it okay if I come in here, too?" At the door was Easton. His eyes were red, and he looked like he was just barely standing, like the lightest of touches would make him drop to the floor.

I waved him in, and either he didn't realize that my mom was still in the room or he just didn't care, but instead of sitting on one of the chairs, he climbed into the bed and spooned his body next to mine, wrapping one of his arms around me like if he held me tight enough, maybe it would make it so it didn't hurt so bad.

# EPILOGUE
## ONE YEAR LATER

"ARE YOU READY?" Easton took my hand in his as we walked up the path to the Williams's house.

"I think so." I was nervous but also excited to see Cody again. We'd been able to visit him when Easton came home for winter break from NYU this December, and I couldn't wait to see how much he had grown. Nadia had sent us a video of Cody taking his first steps just two weeks ago, and I was eager to see it in person at his birthday party.

"I still think it's crazy they named him Cody," Easton said, his eyes shining bright in the late afternoon sunlight.

"I think it's just a sign that we really did make the right choice. How else could we explain the coincidence of them picking the only name we'd ever remotely agreed on?"

He squeezed my hand. "I still think he would have made a great Titan or Brody. But I guess I'll have to save those for the future."

I laughed. "I still hate those names, by the way."

He grinned. "Well, lucky for me I still have a few years to convince you to come to my side."

I smiled, liking the thought of discussing names for future children with him someday. Someday when we were ready to be parents.

Easton was finally, officially, my boyfriend, and we'd been doing the long-distance thing since he left for Manhattan last September. It would be great to have him home for the summer after his finals, which were coming up next week. And in just a few months, I would join him in New York so I could go to the New York School of Design.

The future looked bright, and I was excited for what was coming next. The past year had been difficult, and we had taken the time to grieve over not being able to raise Cody ourselves. But we got frequent updates from his parents, and eventually, things got easier as time passed—we adjusted and resumed our regular lives of going to school and hanging out with our friends, like regular teens our age.

And going through that experience with Easton had bonded us together even more. It had been healing just to have someone else by my side who was going through the exact same thing I was. We were able to be there for each other in a way that no one else could.

We made it to the Williams's porch and Easton rang the doorbell. I gripped the gift bag in my hand. Nadia had told me that Cody really liked trucks these days, so I hoped he'd like the dump truck we got him. And I couldn't resist throwing a few outfits in the bag. That way, every time she sent me a photo of him wearing them, I could feel like I was next to him somehow.

Cameron opened the door a moment later. "Come on in." He smiled as he waved us inside. "Cody was just about to show off his new walking skills."

I gripped tighter onto Easton's hand as he led the way into a living room full of Cody's grandparents, aunts and uncles, and way more toys and presents than one child could ever need. And in the middle of all the people who loved him was Cody. Nadia sat cross-legged on the ground and held him in her lap—a look of pride and love on her face.

"Is everyone ready for this?" she asked, looking around the room. And when her gaze landed on Easton and me, she gave us a special smile.

"We're ready. Show us what you can do, buddy," Cody's grandpa, Nadia's dad, called to him.

Cody giggled, and when Nadia lifted him from her lap and put his feet on the ground, he immediately started walking to his grandpa who had his arms outstretched.

My heart swelled in my chest as I watched Cody toddle across the room. When my eyes met Easton's, I could tell he was thinking the same thing I was. We had made the right choice. Cody was surrounded by so many people who loved him, and he was happy and thriving.

And he was also adorable, too. He had dark hair like me, but his eyes were big and blue, and he looked so much like Easton's baby pictures.

I was just thankful that I would be able to watch him grow up and see what kind of man he'd become. Because if he was anything like his biological father, all those girls better watch out because they might just get their heart stolen by him, too.

---

"SO HOW DO you think that went?" Easton asked as we drove back to my house after the birthday party.

"It's always bittersweet to see him, but it was really good, too," I said. "I can see how much he adores his parents, and it's comforting to see how the rest of their family loves him, too. I'm pretty sure his grandpa is the same way with Cody as your dad is with Grant."

Easton smiled. "Yeah, looks like he's his little buddy."

He pulled up to my house a few minutes later and followed me inside.

"What time does the party start?" he asked as he followed me up the stairs to my bedroom.

"Eight." I glanced at my watch. We had a little over forty minutes to be there, if we wanted to be on time.

Easton was already ready for the party, since he was a guy and could get away with wearing anything.

But I wanted to change out of my jeans and into something dressier—the dress I had started sewing before I went to Paris and had finally finished sewing last week, to be exact. I'd worried it might not fit me after having a baby, but thankfully, basketball season had helped with that.

I grabbed the red dress out of my closet, keeping it out of Easton's view before I did the big reveal. I closed the bathroom door and quickly changed my clothes. Then I put on a pair of dangly earrings and opened the door again so I could talk to Easton.

"You sure you don't mind hanging out with a bunch of high school students tonight?" I asked, peeking through the doorway to watch him. He was lying down, with his head on my pillows, tossing my basketball into the air and catching it.

"It's not like I'll be the only college freshman there. Noah's coming with Lexi." Then he noticed me looking at him, and he did a double take before saying, "Whoa." And his eyes took in my dress.

"Do you like it?" I asked, doing a slow twirl so he could see it from all angles.

He sat up and set his feet on the carpet. "Like it?" He stood and walked toward me, never taking his eyes off me. "I think it's illegal in all fifty states to look that good."

I pushed on his chest, unable to keep myself from blushing. "You're just saying that."

He grinned and leaned his forehead against mine. "I think I recall having a conversation like this with you before. And I still have freedom of speech, so, no, I'm not just saying that."

"So it's okay then?"

I turned to look at myself again. I may have been sketching clothes for years, but this was the first thing I'd actually brought to life. It was nerve-racking to think about going out in public wearing my own design.

Easton stepped up behind me and slid his arms around my waist to pull me against him. "It's more than okay. You look stunning."

I studied his reflection in the mirror, taking in how he looked in his light blue button-up shirt that really brought out his eyes. Then I turned to face him. "You don't look so bad yourself." I smoothed his collar and gave him a quick kiss on the cheek.

His expression softened. "It's amazing that you're able to create a design on paper and then put it all together. That takes true talent."

I looked up at him through my lashes, feeling suddenly shy. "I just hope the people at the New York School of Design agree."

He took my chin gently in his hand. "They will. You have big dreams, and I know you'll stop at nothing to make them come true."

I smiled, feeling a little emotional at the sacrifices that had been made to get us to this point. "Thanks for believing in me. I'm so lucky to have you."

"I'm the lucky one." He bent his face closer and pressed his lips to mine. "Because I'm the guy who got a second chance with you."

Read the next book in the series!
Raven and Logan's story.

**She was supposed to kiss her crush under the mistletoe. She didn't expect to kiss his bad-boy twin.**

## WANT A FREE BOOK? SIGN UP!

I hope you enjoyed MY SECOND CHANCE! If you haven't already, please sign up for my newsletter so you can stay up to date on my latest book news. Plus, you'll get two FREE books by me, just for signing up! https://subscribepage.com/judycorry

Join the Corry Crew on Facebook: https://www.facebook.com/groups/judycorrycrew/

Follow me on Instagram: @judycorry

Don't miss the first book in the Eden Falls Academy series.

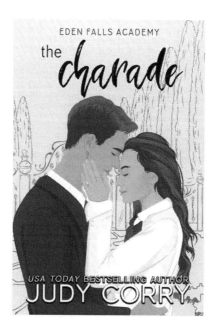

**When my math tutor made me sign a contract
promising I wouldn't fall in love with him, I thought
he was joking.
He wasn't.**

Grab your copy!

Also By Judy Corry

**Ridgewater High Series:**

When We Began (Cassie and Liam)

Meet Me There (Ashlyn and Luke)

Don't Forget Me (Eliana and Jess)

It Was Always You (Lexi and Noah)

My Second Chance (Juliette and Easton)

My Mistletoe Mix-Up (Raven and Logan)

Forever Yours (Alyssa and Jace)

**Eden Falls Academy Series:**

The Charade (Ava and Carter)

The Facade (Cambrielle and Mack)

The Ruse (Elyse and Asher)

The Confidant (Scarlett and Hunter)

The Confession (Kiara and Nash) — Coming 2023

**Standalone YA**

Protect My Heart (Emma and Arie)

Kissing The Boy Next Door (Lauren and Wes)

**Rich and Famous Series:**

Assisting My Brother's Best Friend (Kate and Drew)

Hollywood and Ivy (Ivy and Justin)

Her Football Star Ex (Emerson and Vincent)

Friend Zone to End Zone (Arianna and Cole)

Stolen Kisses from a Rock Star (Maya and Landon)

# EXCERPT FROM MY MISTLETOE
## MIX-UP

"Sorry Noah turned you down at the game," my best friend, Alyssa, said as she parked her Honda a few houses down from her boyfriend Trey's house. "Do you still think you'll be able to get a date before the Christmas Ball?"

I sighed and unbuckled my seat belt. "I have no idea. I wouldn't know who to ask." I'd stuck all my eggs in the Noah-Taylor basket and now I was running out of time to find a date.

Why had I been so stupid to think that just because we'd made out at one party meant he might actually like me?

"Don't worry, Raven. I bet there'll be plenty of guys at the party tonight willing to go with you."

*Willing to go.* That wasn't romantic. I wanted this to be the year I finally had a boyfriend to take to the annual Cheerleader Christmas Ball. A guy who I was excited to go with and who was excited to go with me.

Call me a hopeless romantic, but I dreamed of the day a tall, dark, and handsome guy would want me for more than just a night of non-committal kissing. I wanted a boyfriend. I wanted what Alyssa had with Trey. One of those relationships that everyone envied.

Yes, I knew I didn't *need* a guy. But I wanted one.

I sighed and climbed out of Alyssa's car. She joined me on the sidewalk a second later, and we walked up the hill past the houses lit with colorful Christmas lights. Trey's house, also known as "Party Central," was at the end of the cul-de-sac.

"I think I saw that trumpet player, Harrison, checking you out during the game," Alyssa said, her breath visible in the cold December night air. "I heard he just broke up with his girlfriend, too."

I made a face. Harrison was a band nerd. Sure, I liked music as much as the next girl...but he just wasn't my type. I wanted the type of guy that walked into a room and stole everyone's attention. A guy that you couldn't help but take a second look at and stare at for a few seconds.

There had to be a guy like that somewhere, right?

"We need new guys at our school," I finally said. That was the only option left.

Alyssa laughed. "Or maybe you need to stop being so picky."

I rolled my eyes. "Says the girl who already has the perfect boyfriend."

Alyssa just shrugged. "I'll tell Trey you wish he had a twin."

I smiled. "Yeah, you go tell him to make that happen." Trey wasn't exactly what I'd call a hottie, but he was cute in a boyish sort of way. And him and Alyssa looked good together.

When we were one house away, Alyssa pulled her phone out of her back pocket. "I'll text Trey, so he knows we're here. It's probably a madhouse in there."

"As usual."

Trey was on the basketball team, and since they'd just won tonight's game they were bound to be in a celebrating mood.

We climbed up the front steps and were about to knock

when the door opened wide and Trey filled it. "Welcome to the party." Trey pushed his strawberry-blond hair out of his blue eyes.

Alyssa gave Trey a quick hug and a kiss before walking in.

Once the door was shut behind us, Trey looked at Alyssa with excitement in his eyes. "I have a surprise for you out back."

She furrowed her brow. "You do?"

He nodded. "Yeah. But we need to hurry before he gets too cold."

"He?" Alyssa and I both said at the same time.

Trey grinned. "Yes, *he.*" Then he took Alyssa's hand in his and tugged. "Come on. You're going to be shocked."

Alyssa turned back to me with her eyebrows raised. "I guess I'll be back in a while. Will you be okay on your own?"

I scanned the room. It was full of cheerleaders and jocks. "Pretty sure I'll be fine." These were my people.

I weaved my way through the living room until I found my other friends from the cheer squad, Megan and Rachel.

"Hey, Raven." Megan gave me a quick side hug. "I didn't know if you were coming tonight."

I tucked some of my long, black hair behind my ear. "Uh, yeah. I had a last-minute change of plans."

"Oh yeah, I kind of saw that," Megan said.

Of course, pretty much the whole school saw me get shut down...again.

I turned to Rachel, hoping she'd have something interesting to say so we wouldn't have to keep talking about my guy failures.

"Did you hear the Carmichael twins moved back to Ridgewater?" Rachel asked, her eyes bright with excitement.

"What?" My jaw dropped. Jace and Logan were back? In Ridgewater? "Who told you they're back?" I quickly glanced around the room to see if they were here.

"I totally saw Jace in the kitchen a few minutes ago."

My heart raced at the prospect of Jace being here at the party. Would he remember me?

He'd better remember me. We'd been next-door neighbors all growing up.

Megan looked at us both with a confused expression. "Am I supposed to know who the Carmichael twins are?"

How could she not know who the Carmichael twins were? They were legendary around here.

"They're only the hottest guys to ever walk the earth," Rachel said, matter-of-factly. "It's like God knew he'd made a masterpiece, and so he couldn't help but make two of them."

"So they're hot?" she asked.

"Do you really not remember them?" Rachel furrowed her brow, confused.

"No," Megan said.

It was then I realized why Megan wouldn't know who they were.

"Of course she doesn't remember them," I said to Rachel. "They moved away right before Megan moved here."

Understanding washed over Rachel's face. "Oh. That's right."

Rachel launched into an explanation about how the Carmichael twins had moved away to North Carolina the summer after our freshman year. As she spoke, I scanned the crowd for their familiar faces. If they were really back, that would be amazing.

Memories of all the times I'd watched Jace and Logan play basketball in their driveway next door popped into my head. I'd been ridiculously in love with Jace all through middle school and freshman year. He and Logan were identical twins. The only reason people had been able to tell them apart was because Jace actually combed his hair, whereas Logan seemed like he just ran a hand through his and called it good—and despite my preference for the put-together look, there were many girls who had fallen for Logan's more tousled, bad-boy style.

But not me and Alyssa. We'd been obsessed with Jace all through middle school, always trying to get a peek at him through his bedroom window, which was across from mine, whenever we had sleepovers.

Which was why I'd never gotten the courage to tell him that I liked him. Alyssa and I had both agreed that he would have to be the one to pick between us without us making the first move. That was the only way things would be fair.

But now she was dating Trey, so...

Maybe this was the universe's way of telling me it was time to take a chance. Maybe Noah had to totally turn me down at the basketball game tonight, so I could be open to something with Jace.

"Do you think Jace is still in the kitchen?" I asked Rachel once she'd finished giving Megan the details about the twins.

Rachel shrugged. "He could be."

My hands felt sweaty at the thought.

"Is Logan here, too?" I asked.

Rachel shrugged. "When I asked Jace, he said Logan had decided to stay home to read a book."

"Logan wanted to read a book?"

Rachel gave me a look that told me she was just as surprised as I was. "That's just what Jace said."

Weird.

"I'm going to go grab a drink from the kitchen," I said.

Rachel gave me a knowing grin. "I bet you are."

So it was totally obvious that I was going looking for Jace. Oh well.

I walked into the kitchen but didn't see Jace, just a few basketball players with big red cups, laughing about something in a corner.

That was the one bad thing about partying with the basketball team. They were all about getting drunk on the weekends and didn't realize that some of us wanted to actually remember what we did at parties.

I settled for water from the tap then went to the dimly lit dining room in the back to see if I could spot Alyssa and Trey in the backyard. He had to have shown her his surprise by now.

I peeked through the blinds in the door but didn't see anyone.

I blew out a long breath and turned around. I almost dropped my cup when I saw that I wasn't alone in the dining room. Just a couple of feet away was a guy who looked familiar, but also different. He was a few inches taller than he'd been the last time I'd seen him. His hair was cut in the new trendy way, which looked amazing on him. His shoulders were broader. His jaw more defined.

I'd thought he was drop-dead gorgeous when we were fifteen, but time had definitely been good to him. Jace Carmichael was possibly the most beautiful guy I'd ever seen.

I cleared my throat to get his attention. And when he slowly pulled his gaze away from the window to look at me, my blood completely froze up. Wow. Just, wow. His eyes were as steel-blue as ever.

"Hi," I managed to gasp out as my pulse skyrocketed.

Jace's lips curled up into an easy smile. "Hi."

I sucked in a deep breath through my nose, hoping it would calm me so I wouldn't act like a total fangirl.

"Rachel said she ran into you here. When did you guys get back?" I asked. *Act cool. Don't go all gaga over him.*

But who was I kidding?

He was real.

He was here.

Hopefully he was single, too.

He took a sip from his water bottle. If I'd had any doubt about who I was talking to before, aside from the fact that his hair was actually combed, that water bottle was my clue. Logan had always been the first to suggest raiding his parents' wine cabinet. Jace had been the one with the water bottle to make it clear that he wasn't drinking.

Jace screwed the cap back on his bottle. "We just got here today."

"And you guys are back for good? Not just visiting your grandma for Christmas?"

"Yep, we're back for good."

I bit my lip to try to keep from grinning at the thought of having Jace at school with us again.

"Did you miss me, Raven?" Jace asked, a teasing grin on his face.

Wow, I was being so obvious.

But I couldn't help it. I'd had such a crappy time at the game tonight and seeing Jace again after all this time was too good.

"I guess I sort of missed you."

"Yeah?" He raised his eyebrow and inched closer. "But do you even know which twin you're talking to right now?"

"Yes..." I said it slowly, not quite as confident as I'd been a moment before.

"So which one am I then? Logan or Jace?"

"You're Jace, of course."

His grin stretched broader. "And what makes you think that?"

Well, honestly, it was because Rachel had told me that Jace was at the party and Logan was at home reading a book.

But I wouldn't tell him that. This was my chance to let Jace know just how much I had noticed about him. I knew that the twins had always wanted to be set apart from each other—wanted their own identity. Which was why they had created their own looks. Jace was the clean-cut twin who you could depend on. Logan was the goof-off who was always getting into trouble.

"I know you're Jace, because firstly, you're holding that water bottle instead of a cup filled with beer. Secondly, I haven't heard of anyone getting into a fight yet tonight, and we all know how Logan could never resist starting one. And third, your hair is a dead giveaway. You actually took time to comb it instead of running your hand through it and calling it good like Logan does."

His grin broadened as I finished my list. "I had no idea you were so perceptive, Raven."

I shrugged. "It's a gift. I like to call it my sixth sense."

He stepped closer. "Did your sixth sense clue you in to what we're standing under right now?"

What?

I tipped my head back to see what he was talking about. And to my surprise, I was standing right beneath a sprig of mistletoe. The evergreen shrub with white berries was practically mocking me with how close it was to the door.

My cheeks flushed. "I promise I didn't know that was there."

He gave me a knowing smile. "You sure you weren't planning to give me a special welcome back to Ridgewater?"

My cheeks burned hotter. "I—"

He stepped closer. "Because it seems awfully wasteful not to use this moment. I think the universe might be trying to tell us something." He winked.

"It is?" I managed to say. Was this actually happening?

He stepped even closer until we were only inches apart. He reached his hand forward and twisted some of my hair around his finger. "I've always wanted to do this." The low tone of his voice turned my insides to mush.

Jace Carmichael was touching my hair! "Y-you have?"

He nodded, and his steel-blue eyes bore into mine. "You have to know that I've always had a crush on you, right?"

My heart stuttered in my chest. Was I dreaming? Was Jace

Carmichael, the guy I'd crushed on for years, actually telling me that he had secretly crushed on me, too?

I was speechless. I pinched myself to see if I was really awake.

Jace's gaze dipped down to where I'd just pinched myself. "This isn't a dream, Raven."

Gah. What was I supposed to do?

Usually, I was so much better with guys. I had always prided myself on how easily I flirted. I could go up to a random guy at a party and know for sure that he'd happily make out with me. I'd gotten the nickname "Rebound Raven" for a reason.

But this was different. Because this was Jace. This was the guy who had moved away, who I thought I'd never see again.

He let my hair untwist from his finger and looked up at the mistletoe above our heads again. "So, what do you say, Raven? Want to give it a chance?"

Okay, I needed to get my crap together. I could *not* miss this once-in-a-lifetime opportunity.

And I needed to do it with dignity, too. If I was too scared to kiss him, there was no way the kiss would be any good. I needed to be there for it. I needed to be confident.

I needed Jace to think he was lucky to have a chance to kiss me.

"Do you think you can handle a kiss from me?" I asked, forcing as much confidence into my voice as I could.

"Oh, I think I can." He raised his eyebrows in a challenge.

"You sure? Because I know you haven't been here for a while, but my kissing skills are pretty much legendary."

"Legendary? That's a big word."

My mind was telling me to back off. That I was pushing things too far.

But I wanted him to expect to be amazed, because if he had that expectation, it was more likely to happen.

So I moved even closer until there was no space left between us. I tilted my head up to look at his handsome face. "If it seems like it's the wrong word for this moment, maybe you should help me figure out a better one," I whispered. And when our eyes met, I saw something spark in his.

He really did want to kiss me.

"I'm pretty good with big words." He bent his head close to mine, and his fingers slipped across my neck until he was cradling my head.

My eyes fluttered shut as I became overwhelmed with being so close to Jace. A second later, his warm, minty breath caressed my lips, causing chills to race across my skin. And then his mouth was on mine. I went still, not actually expecting him to follow through with the kiss, but then we fell into an easy rhythm.

I let my hand slip up his chest and neck until it rested against his jaw. His jaw was strong. I'd always wondered what he'd look like once he hit his growth spurt, but my imagination hadn't done him justice. He was a work of art.

I slowly ran my thumb across his jawline as heat swirled in my veins. I had always loved kissing—loved the feeling of being close to a guy I was attracted to. I loved to forget about all the pressures of life. Loved to just live in the moment with someone else, exchanging something we both enjoyed.

But none of those kisses had been like this. Kissing had always been my favorite distraction, but as our lips got to know each other, I couldn't help but think kissing Jace might just be the best distraction of all. I never thought a tiny sprig of mistletoe could change a person's life. But this small moment with Jace just might have the chance to alter mine forever.

The kiss lasted for less than a minute, but when we pulled away from each other, I couldn't keep a huge grin from my face.

I licked my lips, committing his peppermint Chapstick to memory. He tasted like a candy cane. "I think I need to thank

Trey's mom for hanging the mistletoe right here," I said, letting my bravery stay a moment longer.

"I should thank her, too." He pressed his lips together as if he was trying to savor the taste of my lips on his for a moment longer as well.

Had I really just kissed Jace Carmichael?

I was about to suggest that we test the mistletoe again when the door beside us suddenly opened, making me jump.

Jace and I stepped away from the door to allow who ever had opened it to come inside. A second later, Alyssa and Trey walked in holding hands, and behind them was a guy who looked exactly like Jace.

Had Logan started combing his hair?

And why would Logan be with Alyssa and Trey? *Jace* had been Trey's best friend before they moved. Not Logan.

"Oh, hi, guys," Alyssa said when she saw me and Jace.

"Hi," I said, my voice sounding confused.

"We were just coming to show you my surprise," Trey said. "But it looks like you already figured it out."

"Yeah, Jace and I were just reacquainting ourselves with one another," I managed to say, hoping they couldn't read on my face that we'd just been kissing.

I really hoped Alyssa wouldn't be mad at me. We'd always said we'd let Jace decide. He'd been the one to point out the mistletoe...so I had kind of stayed with the plan.

Plus, she was dating Trey, so she shouldn't care, anyway. But when Alyssa furrowed her brow at me, I worried that maybe she was upset.

She pointed to the twin who had come in with them. "But this is Jace."

"Hi, Raven." The Carmichael twin who just came inside waved to me. "Long time, no see."

"Hi...?" I turned back to the guy I'd just been kissing. "Logan?"

A smirk spread across his face, and he took my hand in his and shook it. "It was a pleasure to run into you again, Raven."

I just stood there, completely dumbfounded. Had I just kissed Logan?

His smirk got bigger when he saw the confusion on my face and he leaned in close to whisper in my ear. "You might want to get that sixth sense of yours checked. It was way off." Then he stepped back and spoke loud enough for everyone to hear, "It was great to see you all again. But if you'll excuse me, I have somewhere else to be."

And before my brain could wrap around everything that had just happened, that jerk raked his fingers through his hair a few times to loosen his locks until they looked tousled. Then he opened the back door and left the party.

Read more from My Mistletoe Mix-Up here.

# ABOUT THE AUTHOR

Judy Corry is the USA Today Bestselling Author of YA and Contemporary Romance. She writes romance because she can't get enough of the feeling of falling in love. She's known for writing heart-pounding kisses, endearing characters, and hard-won happily ever afters.

She lives in Southern Utah with the boy who took her to Prom, their four rambunctious children and a dog. She's addicted to love stories, dark chocolate and notebooks.

Made in the USA
Columbia, SC
13 June 2024

37159581R00174